10TH ANNIVERSARY

Special thanks to our well-wishers, who have contributed their congratulations and support.

"The best historicals, the best romances. Simply the best!"
—Dallas Schulze

"Bronwyn Williams was born and raised at Harlequin Historicals. We couldn't have asked for a better home or a more supportive family."
—Dixie Browning and Mary Williams,
w/a Bronwyn Williams

"I can't believe it's been ten years since *Private Treaty*, my first historical novel, helped launch the Harlequin Historicals line. What a thrill that was! And the beat goes on...with timeless stories about men and women in love."
—Kathleen Eagle

"Nothing satisfies me as much as writing or reading a Harlequin Historical novel. For me, Harlequin Historicals are the ultimate escape from the problems of everyday life."
—Ruth Ryan Langan

"As a writer and reader, I feel that the Harlequin Historicals line always celebrates a perfect blend of history and romance, adventure and passion, humor and sheer magic."
—Theresa Michaels

CHERYL ST. JOHN

THE MISTAKEN WIDOW

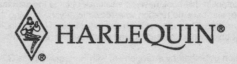 **HARLEQUIN®**

TORONTO • NEW YORK • LONDON
AMSTERDAM • PARIS • SYDNEY • HAMBURG
STOCKHOLM • ATHENS • TOKYO • MILAN • MADRID
PRAGUE • WARSAW • BUDAPEST • AUCKLAND

This book is lovingly dedicated to:
Dad, for being the best PR man a gal could want,
and to Jay,
for telling me I'm beautiful—even as deadline
grows near....

ISBN 0-373-29029-2

THE MISTAKEN WIDOW

Copyright © 1998 by Cheryl Ludwigs

Printed in U.S.A.

I know what I have done is unforgivable…

All I ask is that you do not hate me. I planned to tell you the truth from the very minute I awoke in the hospital. But when I saw your grief, Nicholas, and when you offered protection and shelter for my son, I could not bring myself to speak the words.

I am not Claire Halliday. I was never married to your brother Stephen. I only met him that night of the train wreck. He took me in out of the rain, and he and Claire gave me food and dry clothing and shared their berth with me.

If they had been in that compartment that night, they might still be alive. So you see, I am responsible for their deaths. That is something I will live with for the rest of my life….

Also available from Harlequin Historicals and
CHERYL ST.JOHN

Rain Shadow (#212)
Heaven Can Wait (#240)
Land of Dreams (#265)
Saint or Sinner (#288)
Badlands Bride (#327)

Other works include Silhouette Intimate Moments:

A Husband by Any Other Name (#756)
The Truth About Toby (#810)

Prologue

Lower New York State
April 1869

Wet and weary travelers, eager to return to their seats in the passenger cars, crowded together in the moonlight on the small wooden platform beside the station. Each time the train stopped for coal and water, Sarah Thornton feared she wouldn't have time to find the primitive facilities, wait in a line and return before the train left without her. She hadn't eaten since the day before.

Cold rain drizzled beneath the red-fox collar of her double-breasted wool coat that had been the height of Boston fashion just last winter. Right now the fur looked and smelled more like a drowned animal slung around her neck than the most stunning feature of the coat, which had kept her warm on outings in the Boston Common, trips to the theater and the most exclusive social events of the season. Now the garment wouldn't close over the girth of her burgeoning belly.

She gritted her teeth against the pulsing pain in her lower back and bent to retrieve the bulging leather satchel she'd toted at each stopover for fear of losing her last few precious belongings. Her hand met nothing, and she glanced down at her feet where the bag had been only minutes before.

"My bag!" Panic raced through her shivering body, and she stared at the wet boards, unable to see more than the dark cluster of feet and trouser legs.

"All abo-oard!" The conductor began admitting passengers, and the crowd thinned. She searched the platform in desperation, seeing only a few soggy papers and the sizzling stub of a cigar.

It had to be here! It had to! A sob lodged in her throat. A few straggling passengers clambered past and boarded the train.

"Comin', ma'am?"

Sarah ran awkwardly toward the black-uniformed conductor, who wore his billed cap pulled low against the rain. "My bag is gone!"

"Sorry, ma'am. You'll have to report it to the stationmaster."

Up ahead the whistle screamed and Sarah wanted to echo the broken cry. "I won't have time! The train's leaving."

"Make up your mind. Get on or stay."

Torn, she considered her last few pieces of jewelry, her journal and personal items. She still had a trunk of clothing in the baggage car and a silver and emerald bracelet sewn into the lining of the reticule she held. She stepped onto the platform.

"Ticket, please," the conductor intoned.

Sarah stared at him blankly, her mind whirling. The ticket had been in her bag. "I don't have it."

"Then I'm sorry, you can't come aboard."

"But—"

"Sorry, ma'am."

"I have to get on this train! My other luggage is on it, and I have nowhere else to go!"

"Rules is rules. You got a ticket, you get on. You got no ticket, you don't."

"But, sir, you don't understand—"

"Lady, I've heard 'em all. How many freeloaders you think we get a day, trying to hitch a ride?"

"I am no freeloader." Her Boston accent came across sharply as she straightened her aching back and squinted at him through her dripping hair and the falling rain. "I have a ticket!"

"Off," he said, taking her firmly by the shoulder and urging her toward the portable steps.

She caught her balance by grabbing the cold metal rail. "Wait—!"

"Off, lady."

"Is there a problem here?" a masculine voice asked from behind Sarah.

She turned and looked up into the handsome face of a tall stranger.

"This lady don't have a ticket, and she's holding the train up." The rude man tried once again to move Sarah from the metal platform.

"I do so—"

The stranger wrapped his hand around her coat sleeve, helping her keep her balance, and in surprise she blinked up into his warm brown eyes. "Honey, you've forgotten," he said kindly. "I have the ticket." He reached into his pocket while she stared at him. "My wife will catch her death of cold standing out here. You shouldn't have detained her in this weather. She's just a little forgetful lately." He showed the conductor a ticket that must have satisfied him, for he moved aside, a contrite expression on his rain-streaked face.

"My apologies, ma'am," he said, with a brief touch to his cap.

Shivering, Sarah allowed the gallant man to escort her into the car and along the aisles, until they'd passed through into another car. This stranger had saved her from the rain and from being stranded, but she didn't know him from Adam, and she would not accompany him into one the compartments defined by rows of narrow doors, which he led her toward. She stopped abruptly and pulled back from his steady hold on her wet coat sleeve.

He gave Sarah a conspiratorial grin and raised his hand to rap on a door. It opened immediately.

A tall red-haired woman appeared in the opening, her look of pleasure at seeing the man turning to a question, and then concern when she saw Sarah. "Who's this?"

"She was having a bit of a problem with the conductor."

"Come in, darling," the young woman said kindly, and Sarah realized the endearment was meant for her, not the man. Immediately, the woman helped Sarah out of her wet coat.

The compartment was tiny. Two narrow berths folded down from the walls for sitting or sleeping.

"I'm Claire."

Sarah noticed the woman was younger than she'd first thought. It wasn't her coppery hair or the rouge and lip color on her freckled face that made her appear older, but something more, something indefinable about her eyes and mouth. And as she moved around the tiny cubicle, Sarah noticed she was every bit as pregnant as she herself.

"I'm Sarah," she said, relaxing a bit.

"Well, Sarah," the man said with a warm smile. "I'm Stephen Halliday and this is my wife, Claire."

"I don't know how to repay you…for helping me out

back there. Someone must have stolen my satchel with my ticket.''

"No need to repay me. We all need a little help once in a while. Just do a good turn for someone else in a fix," he replied.

"Well…thank you."

"You're most welcome. Claire, love, why don't you find our guest some dry clothing and make her comfortable? I'll go order us a late dinner and come back for you. We'll eat in the dining car and Sarah can rest here alone for a while."

Claire nodded and cast her husband a loving smile. The adoring looks on their faces touched an aching spot within Sarah's heart. They were in love. Claire's baby would have a loving father and a stable life. She blinked away the sting of tears and stiffened her back against another gnawing spasm.

Stephen Halliday left them alone in the compartment, and Claire chattered to Sarah as she found her a long satin gown and wrapper. "Isn't he a dear? Some days I wake up and marvel that being his wife isn't just a dream. He's a playwright, a talented one, too." She pulled a pair of man's socks from a valise and dangled them in the air. "Sorry, my slippers are all packed. These will have to do. We've just returned from a honeymoon in Europe, and I had no idea how to plan for the trip."

"These are fine." Sarah took the socks.

Claire helped Sarah out of her dress and shoes, then turned her back when Sarah hesitated to remove her damp underclothing. Quickly, Sarah changed into the nightclothes and struggled with pulling the wool socks on her cold feet.

"Isn't he somethin'? I met him in New York when I was designing costumes for a play he wrote. He's taking me to meet his family in Ohio. I doubt they're going to like me, though.'' Claire turned back and took Sarah's wet clothing.

"Why wouldn't they like you?"

"Let's just say I'm not cut from the same cloth as the Hallidays. They're rich. Stephen's father started an iron foundry years ago, and now they send stoves and such all over the country—even to Europe."

Halliday Iron? Sarah remembered seeing that imprint on the cast-iron stove the cook used in her father's Boston home.

"My daddy was a factory worker in New York before he died when I was little. My mama and I hung on any old way we could. Not exactly blue bloods, you know."

"I'm sure they'll like you anyway," Sarah said, placing more hope than certitude into the thought. She knew exactly what the upper crust thought of those they considered lower class. She knew how important social strictures and appearances were to well-to-do men and women like her father. Stephen, however, didn't seem like Morris Thornton or his snobbish acquaintances.

Claire rambled on, and Sarah fought to keep her eyelids from drooping. Finally Stephen returned, bringing Sarah a tray of steaming meat and vegetables and a cold glass of milk. Her stomach rumbled at the smell, and she was so grateful she could have cried.

"We'll be in the dining car," he said. "You eat and rest. I'll bring Claire back later, then I'll find a game of cards to keep me occupied the rest of the night."

His generosity at giving up his berth for the night warmed Sarah more than Claire's wrapper and his wool socks. Her thanks were inadequate, but all she had to give. She ate the delicious food, better than anything she'd tasted since leaving home several months ago and, ruminating her stroke of luck, made herself as comfortable as possible on the narrow bunk.

Thankfully, neither Stephen nor Claire had mentioned

the fact that Sarah was quite obviously pregnant, nor had they asked any prying questions or expected an explanation. That was why she'd begun this dreadful journey in the first place. Rumor said people were less strict the farther west one traveled. In the newly developing country of cattle ranches and mines and railroads, people weren't asked nosy questions about their backgrounds.

She had no idea how far she would have to travel before she found work and a place to stay, but she had no choice.

Every week the *Boston Daily* printed dozens of announcements for women wanted. Western men needed wives; Sarah knew how to plan a dinner party and set a formal table, but her experiences with men hadn't given her a great desire to marry one and suffer his temperament.

Establishments needed cooks and waitresses, but her skill involved planning a menu and instructing servants. Teachers were in short supply, though, and she'd been to school. She prayed she'd find a place where she and her baby would fit in. Perhaps Indiana or Illinois would be far enough. Sarah squeezed her eyes closed and tried not to cry over the pain in her back and the fear of being alone and solely responsible for another life.

Sarah placed her hand over her extended abdomen and fought tears. Yes, she was a foolish girl, just as her father had accused. Yes, she'd been rebellious and gone against his wishes, ignoring the young men he'd chosen for her, and accepting an offer from one less appropriate.

Gaylen Carlisle, without intentions of marriage or fidelity, had seduced her, then abruptly left for the Continent when she'd voiced her fear of pregnancy.

Sarah had waited until she could no longer hide her condition before she confessed her transgression to her father. Outraged, he had immediately tossed her out of his home before she could cause him further embarrassment.

She'd found a room over a butcher's shop until last week, when her funds ran frighteningly low. Due to her father's intervention, no one in Boston had been willing to give her a job or take her in. She'd sold a necklace, one of the pieces of her mother's jewelry that she'd inherited, and tried to make her way toward a new life. One thing after another had waylaid her, until this last, and worst, predicament.

The nagging pain in Sarah's back snaked around to her abdomen, and she nearly groaned aloud. But the rhythmic rocking of the train as it chugged its way westward combined with the soothing warmth of the dry clothing and bedcovers as well as the contentment of having food in her stomach. Exhaustion overcame discomfort, and she drifted into a sound sleep.

A sudden jarring movement and the deafening sound of scraping metal woke her. Disoriented, Sarah had no way of knowing how much time had passed, but the compartment remained dark. A sense of vertigo overtook her, and the motion of the railcar was all wrong. She clamped her teeth together, and with a scream, she was flung from the bunk toward the opposite wall.

The last coherent thought that crossed her mind was fear for her baby.

Chapter One

Sarah's leg throbbed with an intensity that overrode the pain in her back and told her she was still alive. The coppery smell of blood was strong, and overhead, incessant rain pounded against metal. Her pulse throbbed violently in her head and leg. She wanted to cry, but she wouldn't. She wanted to pray, but she couldn't. Gratefully, she succumbed to the pain and blackness.

Sometime later the stringent smells of antiseptic and starch burned her nostrils. Her leg still hurt, but it wasn't the same torment as before. Now she could feel her head, too, and it pounded with every beat of her heart. She cracked open an eye and peered at the painfully bright sunlight streaming through the small window into the drab green room. She opened her mouth, and a dry croak came out.

"Lie still, dear. You've taken a nasty bump. Doctor says you mustn't move."

"Whe-where am—"

"Shush now. Don't fret yourself. Rest your eyes."

Sarah closed her eyes as the woman instructed. A nurse. She was in a hospital. A crisp sheet covered her; cool fabric draped her skin. Her leg wouldn't move. She tested her hands, opening and closing, and lifted one arm at a time, barely off the mattress.

She opened her eyes again, and her right hand moved instinctively, protectively, to her belly.

Her flat belly!

"Oh, my—." Sarah tried to raise her head from the pillow.

"No, no, lie back," the nurse soothed.

"My baby! Where's my baby?" The motion and those words sucked all her energy and, dizzy, she collapsed back against the hard bed.

"Your baby's just fine," the woman said.

The woman's face swam in a flesh-toned blur that blended into the ceiling. Fine? Her baby was fine?

"Whe-ere?" she managed.

"We're taking good care of him until you feel better. Rest now, so you'll heal and can take care of him yourself."

Sarah closed her eyes against the acute pain throbbing in her head. He? She had a baby boy? A single tear slipped from beneath her lashes and trickled across her temple.

The next time Sarah wakened, it took her a few minutes to remember where she was and what had happened. She'd been on a train. Something awful had happened, and now she lay in the hospital. She had a son.

She struggled to a sitting position, and pulled the covers away to reveal her swollen and bandaged left leg. Grimacing, she ran her fingertips over the bandage on her head.

"What are you doing? You shouldn't be sitting up!" The admonishment came from the doorway, and a uniformed nurse rushed in to press her back against the pillows.

"I want to see my baby," she demanded.

"I'll get the doctor." She shook her finger under Sarah's

nose, punctuating her next words. "Don't you move again."

A few minutes later, a short, wiry doctor appeared, two starched nurses flanking him. One held a tiny bundle of flannel.

"Oh!" Sarah pressed her palm to her chest and waited as the woman carried the baby forward. "Can I hold him?"

The nurse looked to the doctor who nodded his permission, then placed the infant in Sarah's arms.

The red-faced baby blinked at his surroundings, much as she had upon awakening. He had fair hair and a ruddy complexion. The eyes he tried to focus were a deep, deep blue, with a look of wisdom more fitting an old man than a baby. He frowned and when he did, he looked just like Sarah's father.

"He's a handsome one," the nurse said. "He's the biggest, sturdiest boy we've had in a long time."

Sarah sighed her relief. Her baby really was fine. Better than fine. Big and sturdy.

"We'd better take him back to the nursery now, so you can rest, Mrs. Halliday."

Reluctant to let him go, the woman's words didn't register for a moment. When they did, she blinked at the nurse. "What?"

The doctor came forward then, and the nurse took the baby from her arms. "I'm afraid we have some disturbing news for you."

Sarah blinked. Wasn't all this disturbing enough?

"Your husband was killed in the accident."

Sarah tried to sit forward again.

The doctor urged her back.

"But, I—" Sarah began.

"You've taken quite a blow to the head, Mrs. Halliday. You shouldn't move around any more than necessary for a

few more days.'' The other nurse had moved up beside
Sarah with a glass of water.

Sarah drank obediently and lay back. She needed to
straighten something out with these people. The room tilted
crazily and she lost consciousness.

This time she would get some answers. She ran her
tongue over her teeth, grimaced at the horrible taste in her
mouth, and struggled to remember. *"Your husband was
killed in the accident...Mrs. Halliday."* Sarah thought of
the kind, red-haired woman and her handsome husband
who had so generously taken her in and shared their room
and brought her food.

They thought she was Claire Halliday.

How on earth could she explain what had happened?
Every time she tried to talk to the doctor or nurses, they
treated her as though she were feeble in the head and dosed
her with laudanum.

They allowed her to sit up and eat some bland oatmeal
and drink a cup of tea. Later, a nurse she hadn't seen before
brought the baby and instructed her to nurse him. Sarah did
the best she could, naively, painfully, and watched in wonder as her tiny son instinctively knew what to do when she
didn't. She touched his downy soft head, his tiny fingers,
and opened the flannel wrapping to look at his wrinkled
pink skin and marvel at his toes.

He was so tiny...so helpless...and—tears welled in her
throat and stung her eyes—so completely and totally de-
pendent on her. *Her!* How on earth was she going to care
for this child all by herself? She had no money, no place
to live and no prospects. The realization terrified her. Never
in all her life had anyone ever needed Sarah before. And
now that someone did, she was unprepared for the responsibility. She couldn't bear to let him down.

The nurse returned for the baby later, and Sarah napped briefly. When she woke, the doctor stood beside her bed.

"Good afternoon, Mrs. Halliday. You've made great progress today." He removed the bandage and examined her forehead. "It's safe to move you now, I believe. You still can't walk on that leg for some time. Not if you want it to knit so you can use it like you used to. It was a nice clean break, however, and you're young and healthy. It will heal quickly."

Where was he planning to move her to? she wondered.

"Mr. Halliday, your husband's brother, that is, arrived yesterday. He's waiting for my approval to take you home. I think it's safe, as long as you follow my directions. You may leave with him in the morning. I will give him instructions for your care."

Sarah bit her lip. She was afraid to object for fear they would sedate her again. She pretended calm, nodded and laid her head back against the pillow. The doctor left.

She could find her baby and leave on her own before morning. Sarah glanced at the bulky outline of her leg beneath the covers. And what? Become a cripple? She really doubted she could put any weight on it, anyway. And what would she do if she ran off? Where would she go? She would be unable to work for weeks—months maybe, let alone care for herself or her baby.

She thought of her father and her comfortable childhood home, and squeezed her eyes shut. It hurt unbearably to know she hadn't meant enough to him for him to forgive her. He hated her now. She had to wonder if he'd ever really loved her, or if she'd merely been a convenience as long as she kept the house running and entertained his clients. Going back was out of the question.

When this Halliday fellow showed up, she would explain

to him what had happened. He would be easier to reason with than the doctors and nurses had been.

Sarah spent a fitful night, waking often, dreaming of twisting metal, cold dark alleyways and crying, hungry babies. Finally, morning arrived, and with it, nurses to assist her. One washed her hair and helped her bathe while the other laid out unfamiliar black clothing.

"I tried to find something—appropriate—for your trip, Mrs. Halliday," the nurse said hesitantly. "Your trunks were sent ahead, and Mr. Halliday asked us to shop for you." Not *her* trunks, Sarah thought. She'd only had one. Apparently Claire's trunks had been sent ahead. Obviously, the Halliday name carried much weight, and they were treating Sarah as though she were one of them.

She looked at the black wool skirt, handkerchief linen blouse and short velvet jacket with eyelet embroidery, all purchased with Mr. Halliday's money.

The nurse gave her a hesitant look. "Don't you like the suit? Buying it ready-made, I didn't have much to choose from."

"It's lovely—it's not that, it's just that..."

"What, dear?"

She could hardly leave in the cotton hospital robe she had been wearing. She would have to accept this traveling suit and somehow repay Mr. Halliday. "Nothing. Thank you."

The nurses helped her dress, then situated her awkwardly in a wooden chair with wheels and brought the baby to her. He'd been outfitted as well, and was accompanied by an enormous valise. Sarah stared at the flannels and changes of clothing with a growing sense of unease. "Where did all this come from?"

"Mr. Halliday had them sent for the baby, ma'am." The nurse opened a round box and presented Sarah with a smart hat made of the same velvet as the skirt and jacket. One side of the brim curled upward, trimmed with black silk ribbon and ostrich feathers. "Do you like it?"

Sarah stared at the hat, apprehension roiling in her stomach. Where was the man? He'd gone to all this expense without even laying eyes on her, without giving her a chance to explain!

"You don't like it." The nurse's voice held disappointment.

"I've never worn anything so—mature." She was, in their opinion, a married woman with a child, she remembered, and she wished she hadn't said anything.

"You are in mourning," the nurse reminded her.

"Of course." She accepted the hat and turned to the mirror the nurse held. She would throw herself on the man's mercy when he arrived.

Sarah sensed the atmosphere in the room change. Slowly, she turned and found a tall, elegantly dressed man just inside the doorway. Eyes as dark as black coffee, full of questions and uncertainty, swept the length of her skirt and jacket, touched on her fair hair beneath the hat she held in place with one hand, and then met her gaze. She recognized his pain at once. Grief had etched lines beside his firm mouth and shadows beneath his unsmiling eyes.

"I'm Stephen's brother, Nicholas." His voice was low and resonant, a rumbling sound a woman heard in her soul as well as with her ears. He was darkly handsome, like Stephen, with the same chin and hairline, but there the resemblance ended. Where Stephen's face had been open and candid, with just a touch of laughter behind his eyes, this man's was closed and unfriendly, without a sign of humor.

But then, he'd been handling painful details. He'd undoubtedly had to identify his brother's body. Had he buried him? Sent his body home? Stephen had been a charming and generous man, cut down in the prime of his life. Grief wedged its way into Sarah's chest.

And Claire. The lovely young woman had not deserved her fate. She'd had her entire life ahead of her, a life with her husband and baby. Sarah blinked back stinging tears.

And what of Claire's body? If they thought Sarah was Claire, what had happened to the real Claire? Dread pooled in her queasy stomach. Guilt swept over her in a torrent: She'd been spared and his family had died! She couldn't manage to voice a coherent thought. The words she needed to say lodged in her throat.

His intent gaze slid to her baby on the bed, and he moved to stand over him. A protective instinct rose in her chest, and then abated when he turned back.

"Mother wants me to tell you she's eagerly anticipating the arrival of you and your son, and to assure you that you will have a home with us for as long as you want to stay."

Sarah tried to coax words from her throat.

"I've taken care of the debt and purchased this chair for you."

"The debt?"

"The hospital and doctor's fees. Are you prepared?"

He'd paid her bill already? Of course. The man was efficient, as well as decisive. She should have looked into it herself. "H-how much?"

"You needn't worry over that. It's taken care of."

A panicky little sob rose in her throat, and she clenched her teeth against the desire to rail at her heartless father. If only she could have wired him, could have had someone to come to her aid. *Alone.* She'd never been so alone.

"I asked, are you prepared? I have a driver waiting. It will take a couple of days to get there, and I've business waiting for me."

There was no talking to this man. Sarah realized that with

a cold, hard certainty. He would never understand. What would happen to her son if Nicholas Halliday demanded she repay him then and there or be thrown in jail?

"Yes. I'm ready." She turned back to the mirror and stabbed the long pin through fabric and hair until the hat was secured. She would have to take her chances with him until she could talk to his mother. Surely a woman would be more understanding and responsive. She would understand and let Sarah settle up with them when she was able.

The nurse moved Sarah's chair closer to the man.

"I claimed your things," he said. "They've been sent ahead." He paused, and with no small amount of dismay Sarah discovered she'd been watching his mobile lips as he spoke.

She raised her attention to his dark eyes.

"I didn't want to go through your personal belongings without your permission," he said, by way of explanation. "I asked the nurses to shop for enough clothing and personal items to get you home."

"Thank you," she replied simply. How did he plan to travel, and—she swallowed hard—where were they going? She raised a questioning gaze.

As though reading her trepidation, he said, "I've brought my carriage and driver. I thought you'd prefer that."

Thank God he hadn't chosen a train! She sighed in silent relief.

The nurse placed the baby in her arms, and moved behind her to wheel the chair. Nicholas Halliday stepped around Sarah's extended leg, picked up her bags and followed. The chair rolled her down a corridor, toward a door that led to the outdoors and an uncertain journey.

Heart hammering, Sarah carried her son close. Whatever the future held, her own welfare was not the concern. Her baby was all that mattered now. And she would do what she had to do to take care of him. Unlike her father, she meant to take her responsibility seriously and love her child, no matter what.

Even if that meant pretending to go along with this man for a little while longer. His mother had to be easier to talk to than he was. Had to be! After all, Stephen had been a kind, warm individual.

Sarah prayed he'd taken after his mother.

Chapter Two

Nicholas experienced a measure of guilt for thinking that Claire wasn't predictably like Stephen's previous acquaintances. The girl was obviously under a great deal of stress and physical discomfort and could hardly be expected to keep up a steady flow of chatter. Her withdrawn manner and silence since they'd left the hospital that morning didn't necessarily reflect her personality. Or...perhaps she wanted him to believe she was grieving over Stephen's death.

He cast her another sidelong glance. After the noon meal they'd settled themselves in for the long ride, and she'd removed the hat. Good Lord. Her hair, precariously gathered up and invisibly secured on her head, caught his attention immediately. The tresses radiated a fascinating blend of wheat tones, some dark like honey, some as light as corn silk, some nearly white, with brassy threads of gold woven into the springy curls. One coil hung against the translucent skin of her temple, and another graced the column of her neck. The spirals looked as though he could tug them and watch them spring back.

He decided immediately that it was not a wise idea to look at her hair and have such absurd notions, so he watched the spring countryside blend into the freshly plowed farmlands of Pennsylvania. From time to time, as she closed her eyelids and rested, he studied the sweep of her golden lashes against her fair cheek, the interesting fullness of her upper lip and the tiny lines beside her mouth that showed she *had* smiled. He wondered at whom. Stephen?

Even her ears appeared delicate, with a single pearl dangling from each lobe. Her eyebrows were the same color as the dark undertones in her hair, narrow slashes above eyes that he'd noticed right off were a pale, somber shade of blue. Everything about her was somber, from her expressions, to her voice, to the way she focused her vigilant attention on the infant in the basket beside her.

He just couldn't ignore the gnawing fact that she didn't fit the picture of the woman Stephen had written them about. Stephen hadn't gone into any detail, except about her wit and charm and vivacious personality. The material facts had come after Nicholas had investigated her background.

Her gaze lifted and she caught him studying her.

"Are you feeling all right?" he asked.

She nodded and her earbobs swayed.

"You're getting tired. We'll stop for dinner and the night. He'll be waking again soon, no doubt."

A blush tinged her neck and pale cheeks. He hadn't imagined her a woman easily embarrassed by feeding her child or the calls of nature. If he didn't know better, he'd think her a gently bred young lady. Each time the baby woke, he'd had the driver halt the carriage, and he'd waited outside. Once they had stopped to use the facilities at a way station, and he'd been glad he'd purchased a pair of crutches, because she had insisted on being left alone.

The baby made tiny mewling sounds, and she leaned over the basket.

"There's a town just ahead." He unlatched the leather shade and called instructions to his driver, Gruver.

Claire once again placed her hat over her hair, worked the pin through and picked up her gloves.

"Where's your wedding ring?" he asked, noting the absence of that particular piece of jewelry.

Her clear blue gaze rose to his face, and quickly, she averted her eyes. "My fingers were swollen," she said softly, and pulled the gloves over her slender fingers. The perfect lady.

Or a hell of a good actress. Time would tell.

The carriage slowed and stopped before a two-story wooden structure with Hotel painted in black letters on a weathered sign that swung in the breeze. He raised the shade and studied the building. "Doesn't look like much. We can go on."

Her earnest gaze dismissed the building and turned back to him. "I'm sure the accommodations will do fine, Mr. Halliday."

"Call me Nicholas. After all, we're family."

Immediately, her gaze dropped to her gloved hands.

The door opened and Gruver, his dark-haired driver, a man in his early thirties, lowered the step. Nicholas stepped out of the carriage and strode to the rear where he unstrapped the wooden wheelchair, wiped the road dust from it himself and rolled it to the bottom of the steps. As she had when they'd stopped earlier, Claire accepted his hand hesitantly and lowered herself into the chair.

He placed the basket containing the now fussing baby on her lap and pushed her forward. It took both him and Gruver to lift the chair up several wooden stairs to the broad boardwalk, and the driver went back for their luggage.

Nicholas signed the register and received room keys. "Up the stairs and to the right for twenty-four," the desk clerk said. "Twenty-seven's a little farther and to the left and twenty-eight's across from it."

"Don't you have something on this floor? Mrs. Halliday can't walk."

"Nope. Kitchen, dining room, and private quarters only on this floor." The man scratched his pencil-thin nose and blinked at them.

Nicholas turned to Claire. Her complexion had grown paler and dark smudges had appeared under her eyes. He couldn't ask her to go any farther tonight. This would have to do. "Very well, then. I'll be right back."

He took the baby, basket and all, from her lap, climbed the stairs and located the first room. He left the now wailing infant on the bed and thundered back down the stairs.

Claire wore a wide-eyed look of surprise as he approached her. Gruver had entered the tiny lobby with their luggage. Nicholas motioned him over and handed him a key. "Carry Mrs. Halliday's chair, please."

Nicholas bent toward her. "Lean forward."

Her eyes widened, but she did as he asked. He slid one arm behind her back, the other beneath her knees, somehow managing her voluminous skirts in the process, and raised her effortlessly, being careful of her injured leg. She didn't weigh much, but she was an armful, nonetheless. His head bumped her hat, sending it askew, and she caught it before it fell. Her hair tumbled, the soft springy curls grazing his neck and chin, the sweet fragrance touching him somewhere more elemental.

She grasped him around the neck, her hat bouncing off his back, her full breasts pressed against his jacket. He cursed his immediate and unexpected physical reaction, but reined in his distressing response and concentrated on the stairs, one at a time, until they reached the top.

The baby's cries carried down the corridor, and Claire sucked in a breath, which Nicholas felt to the tips of his toes.

Sarah's heart beat so swiftly, he must have felt it through their layers of clothing. Against her breast his chest was broad and hard, as hard as the arms banding her back and secured behind her knees. She could smell the starch in his shirt, and the faint smell of shaving soap that lingered about his chin and jaw, masculine features that were close enough to scrape her cheek should she be foolish enough to turn her head.

Her son's plaintive wails had released a tingling in her breasts, accompanied by a seeping wetness she feared would soak through her clothing to Nicholas's.

He carried her into the room and paused. Her heart raced as his driver maneuvered her chair through the doorway. The man placed her hat on the seat of a rocker and excused himself.

Gently, Nicholas lowered her into the chair. "May I help you with your jacket?" he asked above the baby's cries.

"No!" She glanced down, relieved to see her jacket still dry and covering her. "I mean, no thank you. I can see to myself now."

He straightened and cast a helpless look at the basket. "Can I send a servant to help you?"

She nodded gratefully. "Thank you."

He backed up a step, then turned and left, pulling the door shut. Sarah struggled with the jacket, an awkward situation because of the chair arms, but she finally removed it and unbuttoned her blouse.

The baby rooted for a mere second before latching on to her breast and suckling noisily. She had to laugh softly. "You don't care where we are or what's happening, do you?"

He'd finished eating by the time a young girl with a dark coronet of braids wrapped around her head brought water and towels. "The gentleman paid me handsomely to help you with the baby, ma'am. I have five brothers and sisters, and I've taken care of all of them. Can I bathe him for you? Rock him maybe, so you can rest?"

Nicholas's thoughtfulness touched Sarah. Gratefully, she

allowed the girl, who told her her name was Minna, to change and wash the baby while she raised her throbbing leg on a pillow and leaned back into the mattress.

"He's a pretty one, Miz Halliday. What's his name?"

Sarah had been dozing, her thoughts drifting from the stern-faced Nicholas to their mysterious destination, and she opened her eyes, an odd feeling of shame curling in her chest. How could she have overlooked something as basic as giving her baby a name? "Why, I—I haven't thought of a name for him yet."

Minna looked at her curiously, but turned back to her task.

"I was in an accident and just came around a few days ago," she said, by way of explaining her lack of thought.

"Oh. That's what happened to your leg?"

Sarah nodded.

"Your husband takes fine care of you. I'm sure you'll be better in no time."

"Mr. Halliday is not my husband."

The girl didn't turn around, but Sarah knew what she must be thinking, and cursed herself for opening her mouth on the subject. "He's—my brother-in-law," she said, using the first and easiest explanation that had come to mind. She cringed inwardly and waited for a lightning bolt or the rumble of an earthquake, but the only sound was the gentle lapping of water as Minna rinsed the baby.

A knock sounded at the door. Minna glanced toward it, but her hands were occupied.

"Who's there?" Sarah called.

"Nicholas."

"Come in."

He appeared in the doorway, wearing a fresh shirt beneath his dark jacket. He glanced from Sarah to the girl and back. "Would you care to join me downstairs for dinner, or shall I have something sent up?"

"I'll stay here with the baby," Minna offered immediately.

Sarah imagined him carrying her down those stairs and back up again, and thought it would be a whole lot safer to eat in her room. "My head hurts terribly," she said in excuse. "May I just stay here?"

"Of course. I'll see that you get a powder for your headache."

"You're very kind."

He gave her a brief nod and closed the door.

"Is Mr. Halliday married?" Minna asked.

Sarah stared at the door, a speculative question forming in her own mind now that the girl had brought it up. She knew nothing of this man or his family. "I don't know."

Minna placed the towel-wrapped infant on the bed and dried his flailing arms and legs.

Sarah captured her son's tiny hand in hers, and watched as the girl skillfully diapered and dressed him. Her own attempts at changing him had been slow and clumsy. Surely she would gain more confidence soon. Thank goodness Nicholas had provided help immediately.

I will learn, little one, she intoned silently. *I will be the best mother a little boy ever had.*

"He's a nice man," the girl went on. "Handsome, too."

Nicholas Halliday did seem like an admirable man. A man who deserved better than deceit. She hadn't asked for luxuries, however, hadn't expected the man to provide elegant new clothing and servants to help her. She looked at the new luggage beside the door, at all the items it took to care for the baby, even at the clothes she wore, and knew at this rate it would take a long while to repay him.

She had no more means to make it on her own today than she had the day her father had turned her out. By leaving with Nicholas, she'd made a decision. Now she had to be Claire Halliday until they reached their destination.

The morning dawned as clear and crisp as winter, though it was early April. The scent of spring floated on the air: freshly turned earth and garden flowers. Nicholas admonished himself to enjoy the scenery and not to regret the working hours he'd lost by not taking the train. He could count on Milos Switzer to handle anything that came up in his absence. The work would be there when he returned.

Relief surged through him that Claire looked a little better today, her face not as pale or as drawn. The long stopover the night before must have done her good. She wore a freshly pressed blouse beneath her traveling suit. And her hat—he noticed when a stiff breeze caught them as they'd stopped for the noon meal—had been safely secured.

He'd paid the proprietor of the eatery to allow Claire to use their private quarters to see to her and the baby's needs.

They would need to stop one more night before they reached Mahoning Valley. The stamina of the horses was no concern, and Gruver had driven nonstop day and night many a time. No, Claire was the one giving him concern. She was far more delicate than he'd imagined, more refined, and obviously not accustomed to long travel or hardship. She said nothing, neither in complaint nor observation, and he wished he had access to the thoughts in her curly blond head.

"Stephen said you met last fall," he said at last.

Sarah's heart leaped, and her mind raced, searching for a way to avoid any questions she would be forced to answer with lies.

"Where is Stephen's body?" she asked.

His expression became even more grim. "I had it sent ahead. He's buried in the family cemetery. We will have a memorial service when you're well enough."

What about his beloved Claire? she wanted to ask. They would have wanted to be together. If there had been a way to tell him…an opportunity…she would have. Certainly, she would have. She studied him warily. If he was as strict and unyielding as her father, he would cast her to the side of the road. She couldn't take that chance; she'd have to wait.

He stretched his long legs to the side, one knee cracking. Claire wondered how old he was. More than thirty probably. She wanted to ask him the question that Minna had lodged in her mind the night before. She studied the landscape for a few minutes, her thoughts streaking forward with uncertainty.

"Where are we going?" she dared to ask finally.

He looked at her as if she'd asked what color the sky was. "You don't know?" he replied, that resonant voice a low rumble.

Sarah cringed inwardly, regretting her haste. Claire would have known where she and Stephen had been headed. "I only knew his mother lived in Ohio," she said quickly.

"Mahoning Valley," he said. "Our forges, factory and home are near Youngstown."

"Who lives there?" she asked a minute later. "In the house?"

"Mother and I. A few servants."

He didn't mention a wife. Why did she care?

"It's a big house," he went on. "There's plenty of room for the two of you."

She hadn't been concerned about that. She'd only wondered how many people would be expecting Claire to show up. The fewer she had to face, the better.

They made another afternoon rest stop, then rode as far as St. Petersburg, near the Allegheny River. They could have made it the rest of the way that night, Sarah overheard Nicholas say to the driver, but he didn't want to push too hard. Meaning her, she knew. The rest of them were holding up beautifully. Even the baby. He ate and slept, oblivious to what was going on around him.

The St. Petersburg Hotel had a cable elevator, sparing

them a repeat of the previous night's encounter. Sarah wondered if Nicholas had known about the elevator and chosen their stop accordingly.

He settled her in her room. "Dinner sent up again?" he asked.

"Please."

"We'll arrive at the house tomorrow. I'm wiring ahead to have the local doctor call in the afternoon. The doctor in New York said you have bandages on that leg that will need to be changed, and we haven't tended to that." He started to close the door.

"Mr. Halliday?"

"Nicholas," he corrected, pausing.

"Nicholas," she managed. "You've been very considerate. Thank you."

His dark gaze flickered momentarily, but his expression didn't change. "What else would I do for my brother's *wife?*"

She didn't reply. The inflection in his tone was almost...acerbic. Her heart skipped a tiny beat.

But then he wished her a polite good evening, pulled the door closed, and she wondered if she'd really heard it.

Something told her he was skeptical. He treated her politely and provided more than she could ask for, but it was there, lurking behind his eyes and beneath his words. Doubt.

And tomorrow, she would have to face Stephen's mother and tell her the truth.

Again and again, while picking at her dinner, while feeding the baby and settling him down for the night, she went over her pitiful options. And each time, she came to the conclusion that she had no choice. She would plead her case with Stephen Halliday's mother and hope for the best.

What was the worst thing that could happen?

Mahoning Valley, Ohio

Leda Halliday, garbed in black, her eyelids swollen, greeted Sarah with welcoming arms. And Sarah knew, in some deep recess of her heart as she pulled herself to stand on her good leg and let the sobbing woman embrace her, that this was the worst thing that could have happened.

The small-statured woman smelled of violets and faintly of camphor. Her ample bosom shook against Sarah's waist as she cried openly. To her surprise, responding tears came to Sarah's eyes, and she accepted the violet-scented hankie the maid pressed into her fingers.

Leda pulled away, dabbing at her nose, and let Sarah sit back down but didn't release her hand. "You are just as beautiful as Stephen wrote us," she said on a sob. Her fleshy face crumpled, and Nicholas was there to take her in his arms and hold her against his broad chest. When he raised his face from his mother's silver-streaked dark hair, there were tears on his dark lashes.

Sarah's heart ached for them both. A pang of guilt shot through her chest like a sword of cold steel. She couldn't meet Nicholas's eyes. How was she going to say the words? If only Nicholas would leave them alone.

Finally Leda pulled away from her towering son and glanced toward the door. The driver stood in the opening, the basket firmly in his grasp. "Well, bring him here, Gruver, bring him here," she said, motioning the man forward.

Her expression held anticipation, as well as curiosity. When she caught sight of the baby, she covered her trembling lips with her fingers for several long seconds. Sarah saw how badly she wanted to see her son in this tiny child, and regret yawned in her chest.

"He's just beautiful," she said at last, her voice thick with emotion. "What's his name?"

Embarrassed, Sarah edged her gaze away from Nicholas and looked directly into Leda's gray eyes. "I haven't named him yet," she said, knowing the older woman would think that as strange as Minna had.

Instead Leda glowed as though she'd been gifted with a king's ransom. "We can do it together."

Nicholas's eyes narrowed, but Sarah wouldn't lock gazes.

"Your rooms are ready," Leda announced. "I think you'll find everything in order, but you need only ask."

Sarah glanced at the grand curving marble staircase that led to an open hallway above. She met Nicholas's dark eyes.

"They're upstairs," Leda said, and then as if just now realizing, turned back. "Oh dear."

"Not to worry, Mother," Nicholas said. "Claire and I have perfected this transportation problem. Gruver, if you'll just carry the little fellow up, you'll be dismissed for the rest of the day. Take tomorrow off, too. I'm sure you've missed your family."

"Thank you, sir."

Nicholas swooped forward and waited for Sarah to reach for his neck. She did so, and he slid his arm beneath her legs, brought her against his chest, and turned to his mother. "See, Mother? All those peas and carrots paid off in the long run."

"I told you so." The woman chuckled and followed them up, her skirts rustling. Her small laugh eased some of Sarah's discomfort, and Sarah was strangely grateful to Nicholas for making his mother smile.

This time Sarah didn't fight the sensations his nearness created. His interaction with his mother and his treatment of his driver said more than a million words could have. He was a good man. A sincere man. A respected, decent man.

And she was still taking advantage of him.

She rested in the security of his arms for just these few minutes. Enjoyed his strength, the masculine scent of his hair and the crisp, fresh smell of his clothing. And wondered just how long she had before she was truly, deeply, impossibly past the point of turning back.

Leda had hired a nursemaid to care for the baby. The woman, a tallish, gray-haired widow who called herself Mrs. Trent, took him while Nicholas and Leda made Sarah comfortable. Sarah sighed in relief when Nicholas finally excused himself and left the room.

"Mrs. Halliday…" Sarah began.

"Leda, dear. Please." The older woman patted the counterpane into place over Sarah's good right leg and made sure the other one was settled on a pillow.

"Leda. I've been waiting for a chance to talk to you."

"I know, darling. We're going to have plenty of time together. You're going to be the daughter I never had. And this little man…"

Leda took Sarah's son from Mrs. Trent and held him to her cushioned breast. Tears ran down her cheeks openly. "This little man is going to keep me from dying of a broken heart."

At the woman's anguish, a great suffocating weight burgeoned in Sarah's chest. "I'm not who you think I am," she choked out.

"I don't care who you are," Leda said on a half sob. "If I hadn't had you and the baby to look forward to these past few days, I couldn't have borne the sorrow. A mother should never have to lose her child. Never," she said fiercely. "You're what I need to go on living now. You and him." She nuzzled the infant's downy head, and Sarah choked on the confession that welled in her soul.

But she didn't have the courage to say the words that would destroy the woman who'd already lost her son. All her good intentions fled like dry leaves before a storm, and the secret cowered in a shadowy corner of her heart.

Not now. Not just now. She could wait. Until Leda had a chance to get over Stephen. By then Sarah's leg would be better, and she'd be able to leave. Until then…how much harm would it cause to let the woman think they were her family for just a little longer?

Sarah prayed she wouldn't have to know the answer to that.

The spectacled Mrs. Trent did as she was bidden, taking care of the baby's laundry, bathing and changing him with efficiency, but never getting in the way when Sarah wanted to perform the tasks herself. In fact, she was more than pleased to share her knowledge, answer Sarah's questions and assist her in learning to do what she could herself.

Leda visited Sarah and the baby often, but Sarah didn't see Nicholas for the next few days. The portly middle-aged doctor called twice, proclaiming her leg better, but still not well enough to put her weight on. He checked her head, asked about the baby's eating habits, looked him over and wished her a good day.

Sarah and her son slept and ate and grew stronger. At times, beneath Leda's doting concern, Sarah didn't feel so alone—until she remembered the gracious woman believed she was someone else. Her identity was a secret she bore alone. A burden she carried each day and each night, its weight squeezing her heart and her conscience.

Late one afternoon Leda came to her suite, and soon after tea was served. "I thought we might decide today," the woman said, a note of hopefulness in her voice.

"On what, Mrs. Halliday?"

"*Leda*, please. On the baby's name, of course."

"Oh, yes, of course."

"Tell me, did you and Stephen have any names you particularly wanted to use? Your father's perhaps?"

Sarah didn't know Claire's father's name, so she shied away from that idea. Her own father's name would only remind her of his hurtful rejection. She shook her head. "I like Thomas. Or Victor. Peter is nice, too. Did you have any you particularly like?'' Sarah asked, knowing full well she must.

"Well." She settled her cup in its saucer and patted her lip with a linen napkin. "My father's name was Horatio. Stephen's father's name was Templeton."

Sarah hoped the woman had some relatives with acceptable names. Sarah had, after all, suggested she needed help choosing.

"My grandfather was William—"

"William is quite nice," Sarah cut in quickly.

"Do you like it?"

"I do. I like it a lot."

"He needs a middle name," Leda commented.

Sarah nodded, grudgingly.

"How about Stephen?"

Sarah thought about the kind young man who had taken her in out of the rain and given her his bed for the night. If he'd been in that bunk, he would probably be alive right now. Naming her son after him wouldn't make up for the debt, but it would be appropriate. "I think Stephen is more than suitable."

Leda clapped her hands together in almost childlike excitement. "William Stephen Halliday! Isn't it a grand name?"

Guilt fell on Sarah like a cold Boston fog and dampened her spirits. But seeing Leda this happy made her unwilling to change anything that she'd said or done. "It is indeed. It's a wonderful name."

"Nicholas will come and get you for dinner tonight," Leda said, rising. "We'll tell him then." She bustled from the room.

Sarah wheeled her chair over to the alcove where the ornate iron crib Leda had purchased nestled beneath a brightly painted, sloping ceiling. She touched her son's downy hair and patted his flannel-wrapped bottom lovingly. "William," she whispered. "Sweet William."

A trapped sensation gripped Sarah. What had she done? Doubt and shame clawed their way to the surface, and she was forced to admit to her part in this deception. She hadn't told Nicholas the truth. She hadn't told his mother the truth. Too much time had passed for them to understand now.

And she had just let Nicholas's mother name the baby after her grandfather. A Halliday!

Sarah bit her lip, hating the self-reproach lying on her heart like a lead weight, and knew she had just passed the point of no return.

Sarah met with a problem in choosing a dress for dinner. Claire's trunks had been delivered, and Leda's personal maid told her she'd pressed the dresses and hung them in the armoires.

She opened the double-doored cabinet and stared at the collection of clothing. Satins and silks, vivid colors with plunging necklines and daringly visible underskirts lined the rod. What outlandish taste Claire had! Sarah rifled through her belongings, finding nothing suitable for mourning. Nothing suitable, period! Finally, she discovered a black silk gown with a lace insert from the bodice to a collar piece, and asked Mrs. Trent to help her with it. Thank goodness the bust was roomy enough for Sarah's new full figure.

She was supposed to be a widow, after all, so black was an appropriate choice. The color washed her out, however, so she pinched her cheeks and applied a dab of lip rouge she found in her dressing table drawer. Claire had possessed an astonishing assortment of face tints and decanters. Sarah sniffed one of the perfumes and replaced the stopper with a grimace, feeling funny about using Claire's personal items.

Nicholas appeared on schedule. Mrs. Trent stayed with William while Nicholas scooped up Sarah and carried her downstairs.

"My chair," she questioned, looking back over his shoulder.

"You won't have need for it," he replied, his voice vibrating against her breast. He wore a linen shirt and lightweight jacket, and Sarah felt every sinewy muscle pressed against her body. "You won't need to go anywhere that I can't take you."

His words and his voice spawned a quavery shiver along her spine, and her reaction to his nearness abashed her.

She concentrated on the house he carried her through. The furnishings and decor were as lovely as—no, lovelier than—her Boston home had been, more costly, yet more understated. The dining room they arrived in was paneled in rich walnut, with two sideboards and built-in china cabinets. Gilt-framed paintings of hunting scenes and meandering rivers lined the walls.

Leda waited impatiently for them. "Good evening, darlings!"

Nicholas placed Sarah in a chair at the corner of the table, across from Leda, and seated himself at the head. The older woman's glance took in the dress.

"I have nothing appropriate for mourning," Sarah said softly.

"Of course you don't, and we didn't think of it, did we, Nicholas?"

He shook his head and paused with a raised brow as he poured wine. "Claire?"

"None for me, thank you."

He placed a stemmed crystal glass in front of his mother. "I'll send for the dressmaker tomorrow," she said.

"Oh, that won't be necessary," Sarah objected.

"Of course it's necessary. You're a widow, after all. And a Halliday. You mustn't be seen in public without proper dress."

It was true, she couldn't possibly wear any of those dresses that had been Claire's. Whatever had the woman been thinking of to buy them? What kind of person had Claire been?

Nicholas had been looking at her oddly for several minutes. "Your accent sounds more like Boston than New York," he said finally.

"Does it?" She took a sip from her water glass and tried to appear unconcerned. "I think we tend to imitate the people we're around, and many of my friends are from Boston."

"Are they now?"

She nodded.

He appeared unconvinced, and she knew she'd have to be more careful of her speech. She was getting in deep now.

"You had an announcement?" Nicholas queried his mother over the top of his wineglass.

"Yes," Leda replied with a broad smile. "We wanted to surprise you tonight, darling. Claire has chosen a name for the baby."

His expression revealed neither surprise nor curiosity. Calmly, he took a sip.

"William Stephen Halliday," Leda declared proudly. "Isn't that a fine name?"

Nicholas's knuckles tensed on the glass. "William was—"

"My grandfather's name," his mother finished for him.

Looking as if he knew he was expected to say something, he cleared his throat. "It's fine."

"And he'll carry on Stephen's name," Leda added softly.

A maid came through the doorway, platter in hand, and served dinner. Nicholas watched Sarah select her portions and pick up her fork. They ate in silence for a few minutes.

"Did Stephen have any plans for work?" he asked.

Sarah's bite of braised beef paused on its way to her mouth. "Work?"

"Taking a position here? Going back to the coast? All

his wire said was that he was bringing you home to meet us. He failed to mention whether or not he intended to stay this time. Perhaps he only meant to leave you off to have the baby while he continued his pursuit of folly in the East.''

"Nicholas!" his mother admonished.

"Well, it's true he never took any interest in our family's business affairs. And very little interest in our family, for that matter.''

"Nicholas, please," his mother scolded. "Your brother is dead. Can't you let this rest? You've spoiled Claire's dinner.''

"No," Sarah denied. He was testing her. And Lord, save her from herself, she resented it. That was crazy. "He hasn't spoiled my dinner," she said to Leda, then turned her gaze on Nicholas. "I'm quite aware that you and Stephen differed on many subjects. I don't know if he had any plans for involving himself in the business. I do know he wouldn't have left his wife here to have the baby and have gone on his own way.''

"How can you be so sure?" Nicholas asked. "You only knew him a few months.''

Sarah remembered the loving way Stephen spoke to Claire, the way he touched her as though he needed that contact for his very sustenance. "I may not have known him a long time, but I recognize love when I see it.''

"Of course you do, darling. My son is just too old and stuffy for his years, and he thinks everyone should be just like him. Don't you dare upset our Claire, Nicholas. I'll not accept your rude behavior.''

"I'm sorry, Mother. I'm sorry, Claire," he included her in the apology with a curt nod. "Why don't you tell us all about your whirlwind courtship with my brother? So we'll better understand, of course.''

A sarcastic undercurrent ran close to the surface, but Leda seemed not to notice.

Sarah placed her fork on the edge of her plate and nervously wrapped her fingers in her napkin. "I will tell you this. Your brother was one of the kindest, most generous people I've ever met in my life. He was accepting and caring and considerate. He laughed out loud and he loved deeply. And I can tell you he probably has a lot fewer regrets now than most people will when their lives are over."

Nicholas chewed slowly and swallowed before meeting her unyielding gaze. "Have you finished putting me properly in my place?" he asked.

Her heart hammered. She didn't know what to make of him, of his questions. Was it his brother he resented, or just her?

"Come now, children, we have important things to discuss," Leda said. "We have plans to make."

"What plans are those?" Nicholas turned his attention to his mother, and Sarah breathed a sigh of relief.

"Stephen's memorial service. Now that our Claire's feeling better, we can get things settled."

A dark expression clouded Nicholas's face. His lips flattened into a hard line.

"We can see to it, darling," his mother said, reaching over and placing her age-spotted hand over his large hair-dusted one. "You've done quite enough already, handling the affairs in New York."

He turned over his hand and encased hers. "I didn't mind, Mother. And I won't mind helping with the service."

"I think *we* need to do this," his mother said, and looked to Sarah for verification.

Sarah recognized Leda's desire to do this thing for Stephen on her own, and to spare her remaining son another unpleasant task in the process. "Yes," she agreed softly. "I'd like to do it."

"Of course." Nicholas gave in, and studied Sarah with a guarded expression, as if gauging her reaction.

She hadn't tasted most of the meal, and her stomach rebelled against placing any more food in it. She sipped her water, and tried to calm her fluttering nerves. A memorial service! How would she ever manage to play the part of Stephen's wife in this scenario? What would be expected of her? How many people would she have to see?

"A Saturday afternoon would be most appropriate, don't you think?" Leda asked.

A Saturday afternoon. Only one afternoon. She could get through that. She nodded and gave Leda what she hoped was an encouraging smile.

Nicholas folded his napkin and stood abruptly. "If you ladies will excuse me, I have business to attend to."

"There's dessert," his mother called after him, but he was gone. "We'll eat his share," Leda said with a brave smile.

Sarah wished she could bolt from the room as Nicholas had. But she'd gotten herself into this situation. Now she'd have to see it through. She observed Leda's determined expression and resigned herself. The least she could do was assist the woman and be as much help and support as she could. She owed them that much. And more.

After all, how long could a memorial service take?

Chapter Three

The memorial service would be interminable, if the arrangements were any indication. Leda arrived at Sarah's door early the following morning. Together they came up with the appropriate wording for the invitations, and Leda had Gruver deliver the text to the printer.

The following day Virginia Weaver, a plump seamstress, arrived to measure Sarah for dresses and undergarments. She brought catalogues from which she and Leda selected a double-spring elliptic skirt to shape the full bell skirts, as well as six corsets. Sarah watched with growing trepidation.

"I'll need to make you at least a dozen petticoats," Virginia claimed. The women gathered in the enormous dressing room that was a part of Sarah's suite.

The idea of Halliday money buying her clothing made her increasingly nervous.

"I'm not usually this...full-figured," she argued, hoping they'd see what a waste so many new garments would be after her figure returned to normal.

"Of course not, darling. But you will be for the next year, and by then, the styles will change again."

Uncomfortable going along with this plan, Sarah glanced at Leda, who said, "Virginia is right. You know..." She stepped forward with her palms pressed together. "I think

Claire should have one of those bustles, don't you? Perhaps I will, too. And a few dresses to fit it.''

"It's the latest fashion," Virginia agreed.

Sarah thought of all her own clothes that had been in her trunk on the train, and wondered what had happened to them.

All she had was the emerald bracelet she'd sewn into the lining of her reticule, and that had somehow miraculously been delivered to the hospital with her. She prayed it's sale would bring enough money to get her started on her own when she left here.

Virginia opened a valise of fabric samples. The new dresses would all be black, of course. Muslin, bombazine and corded cotton for day wear; silks, grosgrain taffetas and shiny sateen for evenings and outings.

"How can you keep these on your feet?" Virginia asked, now kneeling before Sarah and noting Claire's slippers. She poked one finger between her heel and the soft leather. "They don't fit you!"

"Well, I—I don't have to walk, just yet," Sarah stammered.

"Your slippers are too large?" Leda asked, peering at Sarah's feet with curiosity.

"My feet were terribly swollen before William's birth," Sarah tried to explain, her cheeks growing uncomfortably warm.

"You poor dear," Leda said, and her gray eyes misted. "And our sweet, sweet Stephen bought you all new slippers."

"Yes." The word came out as little more than a whisper. It did sound like something Stephen would have done for the woman he so obviously adored. That wasn't so hard to believe.

"Her dress for the service must be extraordinary," Leda said firmly. "Stephen would have wanted it so. Elegant and fashionable, even though it's for mourning."

"A bustle, then," Virginia determined. "And I have some black French lace I've been saving for something special."

"But no one will even see it with me in this chair," she said, wanting them to see reason.

"It doesn't matter," Leda said. "You're a Halliday. Hallidays have a position in this community. Measure her feet. She'll need slippers."

William's cry alerted them to his feeding time. Mrs. Trent appeared in the doorway holding him.

Glad to escape the escalating dressmaking plans, and always eager to spend time with her son, Sarah opened her arms for the infant. "Will you wheel us into the other room, please?"

Mrs. Trent did as Sarah asked. "I'll have his bedding laundered now, and take my noon meal, if that's all right with you, Mrs. Halliday."

"Certainly." Appreciative of the woman's time away, Sarah sat near the lace-curtained balcony windows, nursing William and humming softly. Soon she'd be able to do more to care for him herself, and then she would feel more like a mother. Leda and Mrs. Trent pampered her so, their constant attention and sometimes smothering concern had started to annoy her.

Each day drew her further into indebtedness to the Hallidays, both financially and emotionally. But there was no backing out now, no way to loosen the comfortable but certain ties that were binding her to this home and these people.

She brushed her fingertips over William's silky pale hair and inhaled his milky, sun-dried cotton smell. Where would they be now if not for Stephen's kindness and Leda's misplaced loyalty and trust? If not for Nicholas's tolerance?

The possibilities were more than she wanted to consider.

She would have to honor her benefactors and the Halliday name. She would make a proper appearance before their friends and associates. Leda and Nicholas were the only ones who ever had to know the truth. Later, she would spare them the humiliation of a public discovery by simply letting others think Claire had chosen to return to her own family.

But for now, she'd narrowed her own choices and had none left but to play this charade to its inevitable conclusion.

Nicholas sat beside his mother in the church pew. In the aisle at his right, his sister-in-law sat in her wheelchair. He fixed his gaze on the brightly colored stained-glass windows forming an arch above the clergyman's head. The minister's softly spoken words floated on the air along with the scents of candle wax and Leda's flowery violet toilet water. Nicholas took her hand with the tear-soaked hankie between both of his and absorbed her tremors.

Anger at the pointlessness of his brother's death coursed through his own limbs. Why that train? Why that particular night? If only Stephen had stayed at the university. If only he'd been more sensible. If only he'd listened to Nicholas's counsel on finishing his studies and then coming into the foundry business.

If not for Claire, they could have had Stephen with them the last few months. Unfairly, Nicholas wished Stephen hadn't linked their family to this girl with questionable motives, and he resented sharing their grief with her.

Against his will, his gaze moved from her leg, jutting straight out beneath layers of black fabric, to her black-gloved hands clenched in her lap. If his mother hadn't been determined to bring her safely to Mahoning Valley, Nicholas would have paid her off and sent her back to her New York tenement where she belonged, posthaste.

She'd had the last weeks with Stephen. The last moments.

The realization that he would never see his brother again

hit him squarely between the eyes. Stephen had been a handful, even as a boy, and Nicholas, older and bearing the responsibilities for the business and his mother and brother, had done his best to bring Stephen up as he'd believed their father would have done.

Stephen had resented his intrusive concern. And he'd deliberately done all he could to get under Nicholas's skin. Claire happened to be one of those deliberate and rebellious stands against what was expected of him. Their marriage would have turned into a farce.

Now Nicholas was left to deal with her.

"Nicholas?" his mother whispered. "It's time for you to speak."

He stood and walked the few feet to the pulpit the minister had vacated. The first person he looked at was the last one he wanted to focus on, but he couldn't help himself.

Claire sat with her head lowered and her hands in her lap, presenting the top of her hat. She raised her head. The black veil prevented him from seeing her eyes, but it left her delicate chin and deceptively vulnerable mouth visible. Her lips had a puffy look, as though she'd cried recently. Convincing—to everyone else. She'd sewn for actresses, he reminded himself. She would know how to make herself up.

Nicholas drew on his years of steadfast responsibility and dependability, and in a calm voice spoke of Stephen as a child, as a growing boy, and as a young adult. He said all the things that his mother wanted and needed to hear. All the things that their family and friends expected of him. All the things that he'd deliberately avoided thinking of until now. And then he took his seat.

And screamed silently on the inside.

Stephen. Stephen. His free-spirited brother with the unflappable zest for life and laughter. With so much yet to do and discover, his life had ended...leaving so many things between them unsettled. Would this gaping void of pain and loss ever heal?

The time had arrived for the mourners to get into their carriages and ride to the cemetery. Fearing she would crumple if he didn't support her, Nicholas helped his mother stand. Milos Switzer appeared at his side, and Nicholas directed him to push Claire's chair.

It didn't matter who pushed her chair, Sarah's thoughts were consumed with the actuality of what was taking place and what she'd done. Someone helped her into the carriage, where she sat with her foot on a padded crate and stared idly out the window, grateful for the cloaking anonymity of the veil covering most of her face.

Now his grave. She would have to see Stephen's grave. And come to terms with the fact that he might have been alive had he been riding in his own compartment that evening.

They stopped and moved away from the carriage again. Nothing mattered but the sight of the canopy ahead. Her heart raced and panic rose in her chest. Somewhere in her peripheral hearing, a bird sang its sweet morning song.

Spring rain had turned the grass a bright green; scattered headstones and mourners dotted its perfection. Beribboned flower rings and colorful bouquets couldn't hide the crude mound of freshly turned earth that covered Stephen Halliday's body.

The overpowering floral scent struck the indisputable fact of Stephen's death into Sarah's heart with all the force of a bullet. She stared at the distressing sight, the ghastly horror of what she'd done hitting her squarely between the eyes.

She'd thought about Claire's body before, but had banished the morbid thoughts from her mind. Now she had to deal with them.

Where was Claire? Where was Stephen's real wife? She should be lying here beside him throughout eternity, but because of Sarah's treachery, no one even knew enough to locate her body.

The thought physically weakened her and brought a sob to her throat. Leda reached a hand over to pat hers, multiplying Sarah's feelings of hypocrisy.

And the baby Claire had been carrying! That tiny life deserved a burial place with both parents. There was no one to mourn for Stephen and Claire's baby.

No one but her.

That burden crushed the air from her lungs and brought quick tears. Where were Claire and her baby? If they were separated from Stephen here on earth, would they be separated in the hereafter, too?

Sarah fumbled in her reticule for a handkerchief and covered her trembling lips.

The minister went through his prepared speech, but it was lost on Sarah. God had spared her and William for reasons unknown to her, and in thanks she'd lied to Stephen's grieving family.

One of Leda's friends sang, and the clergyman prayed again. Sarah waited for lightning to come down and strike her where she sat. At that moment she'd have welcomed the escape. Lost in her own private guilt and misery, the only thing she could pray for was for this day to end.

"It's time to go." Milos Switzer stood beside her chair, and she realized Nicholas's right-hand man had been silently waiting there for some time. The others had dispersed, and she sat alone on the grassy slope beneath the awning.

He pushed her chair over the uneven ground to where the carriage waited on the road, then lifted her in and assisted Mrs. Trent, who carried William. Once the women were situated, Milos seated himself at Sarah's side, and the carriage pulled away.

"Stephen had so many friends," Leda said, her voice hoarse with tears. "Just look at how many came."

Nicholas rubbed his mother's hand.

"He's resting in a lovely spot, isn't he, Claire darling?" she asked. "At his father's left."

Sarah was sure more blood drained from her face, if that were possible. She pressed the handkerchief to her lips to keep from sobbing aloud. Once Leda knew the truth she would hate Sarah for keeping Claire and her real grandson from their rightful resting place with Stephen.

William chose that moment to let out a wail. Mrs. Trent jostled him, and finally Leda took him and gave him her finger to suckle until they arrived home.

Claire sat with the handkerchief pressed to her lips. Observing, Nicholas wondered if she was ill.

"I'll assist Mrs. Halliday," he said to Milos once the carriage pulled to a stop in front of the house. "Help Mother, please."

Milos tossed him an odd look, but said only, "My pleasure."

Nicholas reached for Claire and she flinched, but composed herself. He lifted her against his chest and backed from the carriage.

In his arms, he discovered her trembling as fearsomely as his mother had. "Are you ill?"

"No," she replied weakly, and steadied herself with a gloved hand against his shirtfront.

Yes, she smelled as exotic and erotic as he remembered, and he now regretted that Milos knew the pleasure of her soft feminine curves against his body. She was a Halliday.

Nicholas didn't approve of her or trust her but he was responsible for protecting her and seeing to her well-being and that of her son. Like it or not, Stephen's obligations were now his. His chest constricted at the reminder that this woman's welfare belonged to him.

He didn't want the responsibility of meeting her needs.

He didn't trust her.

Or was it himself he didn't trust?

He had no choice.

Aware of the slick cool fabric of her dress on his wrists, the mysterious rustle of petticoats beneath, and the jolting beat of his heart against her breast, he climbed the stairs.

He entered her suite and started for a chair.

"The bed, please," she said with a fatigued wave.

"You *are* ill." He leaned forward and deposited her against the bolster of pillows.

"No. Just tired."

Nicholas reached for her hat, remembered it would be anchored somewhere, and instead flicked the veil back revealing her colorless face. Those solemn blue eyes met his gaze in surprise and...embarrassment? Or was it shame?

"This day was difficult," she said softly.

He moved to stand at the end of the bed.

A dark smudge beneath each eye proved either her words or her skill with cosmetics. He fought against viewing her the way she wanted him to: fragile and painfully in need of care and guardianship. The vulnerable person he saw here contrasted vividly with the hard-edged women who had been his brother's preference.

But he wasn't about to be fooled. He had his mother and the business his father had built from the ground up to protect.

William's cries carried up the stairs and along the corridor. Claire peeled off her gloves.

"I'll go for your chair," he said.

"Just leave it in the hall, please. I think I'll rest here for a while."

He nodded in consent.

Mrs. Trent bustled through the doorway with the squalling baby. Claire unpinned her hat, and a long strand of her hair caught and fell to her shoulder. She tossed the hat aside and watched the older woman. The governess carried him to his crib.

Nicholas followed and observed as she changed the

baby's wet clothing. William was a sturdy little fellow with fair hair that looked as though it would be feather-soft to touch. He had smooth pink cheeks that invited Nicholas's fingertips to test the softness, but he kept his hand firmly at his side.

The baby's flailing chubby legs testified to his health and appetite. He was a child anyone would be proud of. A little fellow who would be hard to resist if Nicholas didn't know better. Yet he still wasn't convinced this was really Stephen's son. He studied the child, seeking something to significantly identify him as a Halliday.

The reports he'd received on Claire testified that Stephen had not been the first man with whom she'd kept company. She'd worked as a seamstress, but spent her evenings among the theater crowd. That was where, after brief relationships with at least three other men, she'd met Stephen.

A baby looked like a baby, Nicholas concluded. How could one compare those tiny features to an adult's? It was impossible. His mother would be devastated if this were not Stephen's child.

Mrs. Trent finished her task perfunctorily, rewrapped William and gave Nicholas a questioning glance.

"Give him to his mother," he said.

She carried the child to Claire. Claire looked up at Nicholas, and embarrassment gave her cheeks the first color he'd seen on her face that day.

Feeling very much like an intruder, he excused himself and quit the room. For a woman who'd known her share of men, she certainly played the demure and modest young mother to her fullest advantage. And why shouldn't she? As Stephen's widow, she would never have to work another day in her life...or play another man's mistress.

Mrs. Claire Halliday had it made.

Realizing he'd left his gloves behind, he stepped back to the partially open door, paused with his hand on the knob and peered around the mahogany panel.

Claire reclined against the stark white pillows, the baby suckling her full, ivory breast. The expression on her face was a lifetime away from Mrs. Trent's when she held the baby. Claire studied her son, tenderness and adoration reflected on her lovely face. Nicholas wasn't imagining the love shining from her eyes.

Okay, she loved the boy. She was his mother, so that didn't prove anything. In fact she may have been so desperate to give him a father that she'd used Stephen to that end.

Nicholas had gone through the box of Stephen's papers that had been forwarded, and if he remembered the date of their wedding correctly, it had been only about seven months ago.

William's birth could have been brought on prematurely by the accident, however. He would probably never know for certain.

Nicholas observed mother and son a few minutes longer, coming to a conclusion. He wouldn't know for sure if this were Stephen's child—unless he got Claire to tell him. She was the one with the knowledge. His job was to wrest it from her.

By any means possible.

Chapter Four

Throughout dinner that evening, Nicholas sullenly speculated on the men Claire had consorted with. Was it something she enjoyed? Or simply a means to snare a fortune?

She wore another of her new black dresses, this one for evening wear, yet still properly modest. Against his will, he wondered what she looked like in russet or teal, or a shade of green. Even pastels would complement her multicolored gold- and wheat-toned hair and pink cream skin.

It was no secret why Stephen had fallen for her. Her seeming grace and delicate beauty had snared him. Stephen had appreciated her soft and flawless skin, the full ripe plushness of her lips, just as any man would. Perhaps those springy curls against her neck had captured his attention from the moment he'd met her and he'd yearned to place his lips there.

Beneath his scrutiny, a blush touched her cheekbones. Did her skin beneath the black dress pinken, too?

A highly inappropriate image of his brother touching her, kissing her, making love to her, burned an indelible impression in Nicholas's mind and seared his body with unwelcome awareness.

Shocked at his presumptive and reproachful thoughts, he dropped his fork on his plate and excused himself.

Sarah glanced at Leda, who appeared too exhausted to notice her son's odd behavior. "You really must get some rest," she said to the woman. "This was an exhausting day for all of us."

"Yes." Leda leaned back and gestured for the maid to remove her plate. "I'm grateful it's over now. I'm also grateful that I had you to help me through it."

"It was my pleasure," Sarah said honestly. Doing anything she could to lessen Leda's pain assuaged her conscience.

"I believe I'll go to my room," Leda said after a few minutes of companionable silence. "Will you ask Mrs. Pratt to bring me wine later? That will help me sleep."

"Certainly. Sleep well."

Leda left her alone in the dining room.

"Anything else I can get for you, Mrs. Halliday?" the servant asked from her side.

Sarah instructed her on Leda's request and rolled herself from the room. She'd never been abandoned downstairs before. Nicholas usually carried her back to her rooms after dinner. If he didn't come for her, she could ask one of the servants for help. Sarah wasn't worried. When William grew insistent, Mrs. Trent would come looking for her.

She took her time perusing the lower level of the Halliday home, admiring the handsome decor and elegant furnishings. Wood and brass and a minimum of glassware affirmed the masculine influences. Eventually, she came across a closed set of walnut doors and leaned forward to rap on the wood.

"Enter."

Sarah rolled one of the doors back and edged her chair into the impressive but livable room, lit by a flickering fire and the golden glow of a hanging oil lamp.

Nicholas, sitting in a wing chair near the fireplace, turned his head at her approach. "Claire?"

"Pardon the interruption," she said.

Swirling the golden liquid in his stemmed glass, he gestured to the decanter at his elbow. "Brandy?"

"No, thank you."

"You don't drink?"

"Whatever I eat and drink affects William."

"It seems we both have responsibilities where William is concerned."

"Are you feeling burdened?" she asked.

"Not at all. William's care is of the utmost importance."

She studied him curiously.

"He is the Halliday heir, after all."

Guilt surged anew and Sarah turned and studied the surroundings with feigned interest. Bookshelves lined one wall, paintings adorned another. An enormous desk occupied an entire corner, papers and ledgers in orderly stacks on its surface. How much longer would she have to play this risky game?

A portrait hung over the fireplace.

"Your father?" she asked, changing the subject.

Nicholas nodded, the dancing flames highlighting his hair.

She noted the similarities between the darkly handsome gentleman and his sons.

"Stephen had your mother's smile," she observed aloud. The man in the painting appeared as somber as Nicholas.

She perceived his gaze and met it.

"Did you want something?" he asked.

"Actually, I did."

He waited, his expression disclosing nothing. Few of his emotions were ever revealed on his face, and she wondered about the man inside the stoic mask.

"I wanted to tell you how very sorry I am for your loss," she began. "I know how deeply you loved Stephen. All this must be difficult for you. You are wonderfully supportive of your mother."

He said nothing, but she went on. "You've dealt with

Stephen's death since it happened, making the arrangements, coming for me, seeing to the things that had to be done.''

She smoothed her skirt over her knees, thinking of the many ways he'd made this horrible time easier for both her and Leda. If Sarah really were Claire Halliday, he would still have been as much of a godsend to her as he was to Sarah Thornton. "I guess what I want to say is thank you. And to tell you that if there's any way I can help you, I'd like you to ask me."

A muscle twitched in his cheek. He appeared decidedly uncomfortable with the subject. Or perhaps it was just her presence. Perhaps he resented her forwardness. After all, even though he recognized an obligation, he merely tolerated her in his home.

It had been a bad idea to come to his office.

She turned her attention to the fire.

Nicholas watched her expressions with equal amounts of rancor, frustration and desire burning hotter than the brandy in his belly. The things she'd said drew on emotions he didn't know how to deal with. "I have no use for your pity," he said finally.

She turned those somber blue eyes on him. "I'm not offering you pity."

"Beware of what you do offer. I'm not the same fool my brother was."

Her eyes widened with surprise. A moment later, her gaze hardened and she looked away. She moved her hands to the wheels of her chair, but he stopped her from leaving with an outstretched foot in the spokes. "You need help up the stairs," he said.

"I will find someone." She tried to roll away.

That was what he was afraid of. He'd been angry with himself at dinner, and in his haste to get her out of his mind, he'd fallen back in his duties. But he wouldn't allow anyone else to assist her. Even though the only male besides himself in the house was Gruver, a happily married man, Claire was a temptress, and he couldn't expose his people to her.

He downed the last of his brandy and set the snifter aside, then rose and gladly wheeled her from his private domain. At the bottom of the stairs he paused, lifted her into his arms and started the climb.

Her arms came around his neck, her rounded breast flattening against his shirt. Her soft hair touched his ear, his cheek. He resisted the insane impulse to turn and bury his lips in the curls. He hated himself for having these intense reactions to his brother's wife. Falling for her charms made him feel like a callow boy.

Perhaps she'd planned it. Perhaps she'd deliberately aimed for a vulnerable spot by offering sympathy. He was the stable one. He was the one who took care of others and did the comforting and handled what was unpleasant. No one else had comforted him. No one else had offered their concern and assistance. Even if there wasn't a damned thing she could really do for or to him, she'd effectively searched out a weak spot in his armor.

He reached the top of the stairs and proceeded to her room. "A chair or the bed?" he asked.

"A chair," she replied quickly. "Will you ring for Mrs. Trent, please?"

He propped her foot on a stool and pulled one of the bell cords connected to the servants' quarters and the kitchen. When he turned back, she was attempting to remove her slipper by using her other foot.

"May I?"

She blushed to the roots of her hair. "I'm sure Mrs. Trent will be along shortly. It's just that my foot seems to have swollen, and the shoe is quite painfully snug."

He knelt before her extended leg and gently removed the shoe, noting her wince. It was ridiculous to allow her to suffer, so he reached beneath her skirts, found the stocking held up by her cast and gently rolled it down her ankle and from her foot, deliberating ignoring the rustle of petticoats and the feel of cool silk.

Her delicate toes were several shades of green and another shade almost yellow. Mrs. Trent came through the doorway just then, and a look of disapproval immediately puckered her face. She placed the sleeping William in his crib and hurried to Claire's side.

"Fetch us some ice," Nicholas ordered before she could take over the task of caring for Claire.

"Sir, I—"

"Now."

Hastily gathering her skirts, she did as he instructed and returned with the ice.

"I'm going for her chair. After you've helped her with her nightclothes, prepare us some tea."

"You'll be taking tea *here?*" she asked in a deprecating tone.

"This is my home, Mrs. Trent. I'll take tea wherever I see fit. And you'll do well to keep your moral judgments to yourself."

The woman pursed her lips and remained silent.

He returned with the chair to find Claire on the side of the bed and the nursemaid gone.

"Let me help." Nicholas turned Claire to get both of her feet on the bed. He propped a pillow beneath her left leg and placed an ice pack on her swollen toes.

He noted her other foot, small and dainty, her ankle slim. The white nightdress exposed a curvaceous length of her calf.

"Cover me, please," she asked in a strained voice.

He draped the counterpane over her legs, leaving only the foot he was treating exposed. "Do you have something to take for pain?"

"I don't want to take it. William wakes during the night."

He sat near her feet. "Mrs. Trent sleeps nearby. She can get him."

"Yes, but I must feed him."

"Perhaps we could find William a wet nurse."

"No!"

Surprise brought his head up.

She looked away quickly.

"All right. I was thinking to make things easier for you."

"That's taking him away from me. That would not be easier for me."

"You obviously have strong feelings about this."

"He's my son. I have strong feelings for him, certainly."

"Certainly. He's all you have left of Stephen. Besides a fortune in stock and investments Stephen left you in his will."

She met his eyes, and the anguish he thought he read there almost made him sorry he'd said it.

Mrs. Trent returned with a tray, and placed it on the nightstand with a clatter that rattled the cups in their saucers.

"That will be all," he said to her. "You may retire."

Censure brought her brows together and she pursed her lips in a line.

"Good night," Nicholas said deliberately, then poured. "Cream or sugar?"

"Honey, please," Claire replied softly, with a sideways glance at Mrs. Trent.

The woman slipped into the dressing room where she slept on a narrow bed so she could hear William.

Nicholas stirred a spoonful of sweetener into Claire's tea, handed her the cup and saucer and poured himself one.

"Call me if you need me, Mrs. Halliday."

Mrs. Trent stood in the doorway in her robe, the front clenched tightly in her fist.

"Mrs. Halliday will call if she needs you," he affirmed. Did the senseless woman think he was going to ravish his sister-in-law right here with her son a few feet away and his busybody nursemaid straining to hear?

She disappeared again, and he turned his gaze back to Claire. "You must have learned to favor honey in your tea from Stephen," he said.

"I've always taken my tea with honey." Noncommittal. Safe. Neither admitting or denying she knew of Stephen's preferences.

"What were the qualities you appreciated most about Stephen?" he asked, leaving the side of her bed and carrying his cup to the nearby chair, where he sat and balanced it on the arm. He didn't quite understand his need to press her about her relationship with his brother, but the desire to persist burned in him like a well-stoked fire.

She stared into her tea. "His concern for others. He was a warm, generous man."

"Generous with Halliday money," he agreed.

Her lips flattened into a line of displeasure, and she looked up. "When we met, I had no idea that Stephen had resources."

"No idea, Claire?"

"You didn't have much respect for your brother, did you?" she asked, taking him by surprise.

"Why do you ask?"

"You thought him foolish enough to marry a woman who was out for his fortune."

"Are you?"

"You wouldn't believe me if I denied it."

Nicholas held his cup by the rim, and considered the truth of her words. "Let's just say my brother didn't always make the wisest decisions."

"The decisions you wanted him to make, in other words."

He set the cup down, glanced at the waning fire and got up to add a log that should burn most of the night. He was deliberately inciting her. He was grieving for his brother and her presence irritated him, so he baited her.

"How does this new life compare to the one you had in New York?" he asked.

"My life is nothing like it was before. Nor is it anything like I anticipated it being."

"In what way?"

"In the obvious way. Stephen is gone."

"He took you to Europe before bringing you to meet his family. Didn't you think that was odd?"

"Not at all. If you treated him with as much disdain as you treat me, he wouldn't have had a pleasant start for his honeymoon. Did you?"

"Did I what?"

"Treat him with disdain."

He didn't like anyone turning the tables on him. "Didn't he tell you all about his family?" he asked.

"No. He didn't. I didn't know anything about you until I was almost here."

"So you just fell head over heels in love with my brother and married him without knowing his background or even whether or not he was capable of taking care of you. Didn't you wonder how he earned a living? Or if he did?"

"I knew about his plays. They were successful productions in the East."

"So you thought you were marrying a struggling playwright. Then lo and behold, it turns out his family has made a fortune in the iron industry."

"I never asked for a cent of your money," she said, blue eyes flashing. "You're the one who came for me—who carried me out of that hospital. You're the one who brought me here. Leda insisted I have the clothing. I've accepted everything because she wanted me to have it."

And as Stephen's wife, all that was due her. And more. Being rude to Claire wasn't going to bring Stephen back, and holding her responsible was only a small comfort.

At odds with his resentment was his appreciation of someone to keep his mother's spirits up and to give her days purpose and pleasure. Claire had been nothing but a comfort and companion for Leda. A fact that ate at him.

"You're a Halliday now," he said, turning back to her, "no matter what you were before. No matter why Stephen married you. And that makes you my responsibility. It also gives you responsibilities."

"And what would those responsibilities be?"

"We'll discuss that tomorrow. I have a few papers to go over tonight."

"And a bottle of brandy to finish."

"If I see fit."

"I'm sure you'll see fit."

"Good night." He left and closed the door, admiring her for holding her own while at the same he congratulated himself for being right. At last her true colors were bleeding through. She wasn't the demure little flower she pretended.

Weariness caught up to him. The days had to get easier after this one. He'd thought giving his mother the news of the train crash had been hard. He'd thought identifying Stephen's body and shipping it home had been difficult. He thought finding Claire alive and making the arrangements for her and the baby had been tiring.

Appearing today before friends and family had taken every last ounce of reserve he had left. Nothing could ever be this difficult again.

Unless of course, it was fighting this sordid attraction to his sister-in-law and sorting through the feelings of betrayal that had come to haunt his nights.

He was testing her, purely and simply. And she was failing miserably because of her total unpreparedness. She didn't have a clue who Stephen or Claire Halliday were. And since it appeared her stay with the Hallidays was stretching into infinity, she'd better do something about her lack of information. Soon.

She could learn about Stephen from Leda. The woman loved to talk about him, and it would seem only natural to discuss and share their loss.

Claire, however, was another matter. The more Sarah thought about it, the more she became convinced that Nicholas would have had Claire investigated to protect the family's interests. And if that were so, the results of the investigation were in his office somewhere, probably in that enormous, organized desk. If she could read the report she'd at least have an idea of who she was supposed to be playing. She'd know the same things that Nicholas knew.

She learned from Leda and the servants that he went to the foundry each day, and she formulated a plan.

The next day at supper she invited Leda to come to her room that evening, and when the woman arrived, they sipped tea and played cribbage by the fire.

"Tell me all about Stephen when he was a boy," Sarah begged.

Leda smiled a forlorn smile. "He was as delightful as a boy as he was as a man," she said. "He got into his share of mischief, mind you, but he was sweet and loving."

"What about when he was in school?"

Leda told her story upon story, and as Sarah had hoped, she reflected on something in his adulthood from time to time. Sarah hung on every word, asking questions and joining her laughter and her tears. She felt close to Leda Halliday, closer than she had a right to, and she appreciated the time and the concern that the woman afforded her. Being there for solace and companionship was the least she could do.

She dreaded that one day she would have to tell her the truth and see the anguish her masquerade had wrought.

Once the hour grew late, Leda left for her own quarters, and Sarah prepared for bed.

The doctor arrived early the next morning.

"I think you're well enough to walk on crutches. You haven't had any dizzy spells or imbalance?"

"No," she replied. "I'm feeling well."

"I suggest you seek assistance on the stairs. We wouldn't want you to take a tumble and break anything else."

The following morning Sarah discovered her bottom worked quite well to make her way down the stairs. Sliding her crutches ahead, she slowly, determinedly, made her way to Nicholas's office. She had only William's nap time to use. Someone would come looking for her if she wasn't there when he woke.

Nicholas's filing cabinets were exceedingly neat and organized, but since she had no idea what Claire's maiden name had been, the search proved tedious. The top drawers were especially difficult to reach because of the need to balance on one leg and rest often, but after nearly an hour she'd systematically gone through each file and folder without success.

In frustration, she discovered his desk drawers locked, and searched the top of the desk and every nearby surface for a key. Of course it wouldn't be in plain sight. What would be the point of locking something if the key were readily visible?

William would be awake by now. She would have to discover the whereabouts of the key and return.

Sarah grabbed her crutches and left, sliding the doors closed behind her.

Leda and William took their naps about the same time each afternoon. She would risk less chance of discovery then than in the morning when the maids were cleaning. The following afternoon, Sarah left Mrs. Trent dozing in the rocker beside the crib and made her way along the upstairs hall, checking doors, and investigating rooms.

She recognized Leda's rooms by merely cracking the door. The scent of violets wafted into the hallway. Sarah closed the door silently and continued her search.

The corridor turned into a separate wing. Sarah hobbled along the hallway, listening for servants, but hearing nothing save the steady muffled clump of her crutches on the carpeted floor.

Massive double doors stood at the end of the hall. Leaning on one crutch, she tested one and it opened.

Maneuvering herself as quickly as possible, she entered and closed the door behind her, noting the maid had already been there, for the bed was made and the chamber conspicuously clean.

The enormous room held a heavy grouping of furniture before a fireplace on one side, a writing desk in the corner, and a massive bed with ornately carved headboard and footboard on a platform on the opposite side. A matching armoire stood against the wall, and one door led to a dressing room, another to a small, unfurnished room.

Where to start? This was all a waste of time and a foolish risk, especially if Nicholas carried the key with him, which he probably did. But the papers she wanted might be here.

The desk was the most likely place to begin her search. The drawers were unlocked, and unfruitful, occupied by neat stacks of writing paper, pens and ink and an assortment of letters.

Sarah shuffled through them, finding they were all from Stephen. She opened the first one, dated several years previous, and read an account of his experiences at a production in London. The next one related a tale of an interesting woman he'd met in the East, and another the excitement of an opening night for a play he'd been wanting to see in New York.

She replaced all but a few and slipped them into the deep pocket of her skirt. Nicholas wouldn't miss these, and she would return the remaining missives after she'd learned more about Stephen. The knowledge would be useful when Nicholas tested her again.

The other drawers held nothing of any interest and, disappointed, she headed to the armoire. The scent of freshly starched cotton and linens assailed her. The smell triggered the disturbing memory of being held close against his hard chest, and for a moment the recollection was so strong, she could have sworn he was right there. Guiltily, she looked around, but she was alone.

A unique scent, perhaps something he used on his hair, combined with clean linen and a faint trace of tobacco to represent Nicholas.

Quickly, Sarah went through the drawers, careful not to disturb anything and feeling criminal for going through his private things. The top of the cabinet held a wooden chest. A logical place to keep a key. In one compartment she discovered two roses, one dried, one looking as though he'd placed it there within the past few days. But why? Sarah pulled the dying flower to her nose.

She remembered the flowers heaped upon Stephen's grave, and the answer came to her. Where had the old brittle one come from, then? The portrait over the fireplace in his office came to mind. His father's funeral? The sentimentality of the idea seemed incongruous with the stern, untrusting man she knew.

Perhaps a woman had given them to him. She replaced the flower.

A garnet ring in a heavy gold setting, several diamond stickpins, a pocket watch and some gold coins were all she found in the other compartments.

The stand near the bed came next, followed by the drawers in the tables beside the chairs.

A soft gong sounded, and Sarah jumped and glanced around. A clock on the armoire ticked a vigilant accusation. She took her hand from her thumping heart.

This was hopeless. If he wanted to hide a key it could

be behind a painting or in any of the hundreds of pockets in his clothing. More and more she leaned toward the theory that it was on his person.

It would be inconvenient for him to come up here to use this desk. And he obviously didn't keep any kind of business papers in his sleeping area. If he had, they would have been with Stephen's letters. She would never have access to the key if he carried it with him.

Sarah propped the crutches beneath her arms and prepared to leave. The unmistakable sound of heavy footsteps echoing down the hallway struck terror into her heart.

As quickly as she could, she hobbled in the opposite direction, in a quandary over where to hide. She passed into the unused room just as one of the huge walnut doors flew open behind her, followed by the sound of Nicholas's angry cursing.

Chapter Five

Reaching the privacy of his room, Nicholas swore to his heart's content. He jerked out of his blood-spattered jacket and tossed it over the valet, his shirt following.

The safety of his workers was of supreme importance to him. He'd been working in his office at the foundry when he had heard the emergency bell and run to see what had happened.

Thomas Crane, one of the metal workers, had been injured when a pulley broke loose and struck him. He'd fallen several feet but had been conscious. Nicholas had immediately taken control of the situation, sending for a wagon and stanching the flow of blood from the man's arm with his own hand while the foreman fashioned a tourniquet.

He'd accompanied Thomas to the physician in town, and waited while the wounds were stitched and dressed and his ribs were wrapped.

Gruver entered with the copper tub. "Is Thomas going to be all right?" he asked.

"Dr. Barnes said he'd lost a lot of blood and at least one rib was broken, but he thought Thomas would have adequate care at home. He'll need a couple weeks of rest to get him back on his feet."

The Cranes had several small children. Nicholas had seen

Thomas's family at Halliday Iron's picnic each summer. Even a week's wages would be sorely missed. He would instruct Milos to see that food was provided over the next few weeks.

Gruver placed the tub on the stone hearth. Two of the maids followed with pails of water, shying away, apparently having heard Nicholas's angry entrance.

"I'm not going to bite, Mrs. Pratt. You needn't look like I've lost my good sense."

"Yes, sir. I mean, no, sir."

"Don't bother with more water. This will do. I have a meeting in thirty minutes, and I haven't time. Lay out my gray serge with the vest, please, before you go."

He always took care of his own dress, but he was in a rush just now. She hurriedly did as asked and left.

"Can I help you?" Gruver asked.

"Thank you, Gruver. I would appreciate a hand this once." He stripped off his trousers and stepped into the half-full tub. "Find a shirt and accessories, if you will."

Sarah heard each terse word from her hiding place just inside the next room. Her heart pounded erratically. A quick glimpse revealed a door she prayed led to the hallway. But her clumsy tread with the crutches on the bare floor would surely echo in this empty room.

Water splashed.

Did she dare attempt to transverse the room? How much time did she have, and whom would she run into in the hall?

The keyhole just below the brass doorknob drew her attention, and awkwardly she bent forward at the waist. The afternoon sun lit the room she peered into, and the gleaming copper tub sat directly in her line of vision. And standing in that tub...

Mercy!

Sarah had never seen a man in all of nature's glory before. Nicholas stood facing away from her, scrubbing at his arms and hands, soaping his chest.

The sinewy muscles in his broad back, flexing with each movement, tapered to a narrow waist and the most arresting sight she could ever remember seeing: firm muscled buttocks, strong thighs, proportioned in an incomparable manner that stole her breath.

Mercy, mercy! Her heart hammered so loudly she feared it would give away her hiding place.

He leaned to the side, picked up a pail of water and poured it over his head, the water sluicing down his broad back and strong limbs. Rivulets streamed from his elbows, creating shiny puddles on the stone hearth.

Sarah straightened quickly, heat suffusing her face and neck. She couldn't stay a second longer. She'd escape now while he was bathing, and pray that Gruver was still occupied with selecting clothing. William might be awake by now, and Mrs. Trent might come looking for her.

Painstakingly, she made her way across the bare wood floor, careful to keep her crutches from tapping. Perspiration broke out on her forehead and down her spine. Any minute he could throw open that door and...and...

And, oh Lord, he'd be naked.

And wet.

She reached the door and tested the knob, hand trembling. It opened. She inched her way into the hall and stealthily closed the door, her frantic gaze darting up and down the corridor.

She was blessedly alone.

For the time being.

Grateful for the carpet that muffled her erratic steps, she made her way away from the wing as quickly as possible.

Mrs. Trent was awake, but working on her needlepoint when Sarah entered her room.

"He's just begun to stir," Mrs. Trent said, and if she thought it odd that Sarah had been gone, she said nothing.

For all she knew, Sarah was the young mistress of the house. She had every right to her freedom and to come and go as she pleased.

Sarah patted the letters in her pocket. She would read them when she was alone that evening.

She'd had a baby, but she'd never seen a naked man before. Sarah couldn't look at Nicholas over dinner without picturing his muscled backside and well-molded torso and shoulders. The memory inspired a darting little flame that quivered in her stomach, then spread up through her chest and filtered the heat of embarrassment to her cheeks.

No matter how hard she concentrated on the roast lamb and the conversation about the accident at the foundry, she couldn't shake the image of all that glistening flesh and muscle. How *wondrously* a man was created...and all that hidden beneath his *clothing.* Sarah studied his charcoal-gray serge suit and bright white shirt with new respect. *Mercy!*

Sarah remembered the unfathomable way he looked at her from time to time, and wondered if he had the same thoughts about her! Surely not! He thought she was his sister-in-law!

"Claire?"

At the sound of his low-pitched voice, she glanced up.

"Will you come to my study after dinner?" he requested.

Her throat grew tight. What did he want? Had he discovered she'd been in his room? Had he found the letters missing? "Yes, of course."

"Are you feeling all right, dear?" Leda asked. "You're quiet this evening, and you're flushed."

"I feel fine," Sarah hastened to assure her.

"You'll learn to live with the loneliness," the older woman said. "You will find other things to occupy your days and your thoughts as time passes. And there is quite a let-down feeling after the birth of a baby that has nothing to do with losing Stephen.''

Sarah nodded in agreement and kept her eyes lowered. It was almost unfair how many excuses she had for her moods, her silence, her very presence here. As Claire she had an excuse for everything.

As Sarah Thornton she was responsible for all the lies and deception. Life as Claire was a lot easier.

Mrs. Pratt took away her untouched dessert.

"Are you ready to join me?" Nicholas asked.

Sarah's heart jumped, and she nodded.

"Mother? Care to join us?"

"No, thank you, darling. Gruver is taking me to the Austins' for a cribbage game."

"See that he stays and waits for you." He kissed his mother's cheek and escorted Sarah through the house to his study.

"Will the smoke bother you?"

She looked up to see the narrow cigar between his thumb and forefinger. A gentleman always asked a lady's permission, and Nicholas was above all a gentleman. "No. My father smokes a pipe."

"Smokes? It was my understanding that your father was dead."

She wanted to bite her tongue. "He is. I meant to say he smoked a pipe." And before he could grill her any further or torture her with waiting to know what he'd asked her here for, she asked, "What was it you wanted to discuss with me?"

Kneeling casually before the fire, he lit his cigar with a piece of kindling. The rich aromatic smell of fine tobacco filled the room. He stood and faced the flames.

Sarah's distracted mind carried her back to the shocking vision of him through the keyhole. She would never be able to look at this man the same way again. Once again warmth flooded her chest, but this time it sank to her abdomen and created an unsettling, restless feeling.

He turned to face her. "I want to discuss the responsibilities I touched on last time we spoke."

"All right." She seated herself in the wing chair farthest from the fire. She was warm enough already.

"As Stephen's wife and William's mother, you have obligations to the family."

Sarah waited for him to continue, knowing intuitively he had another test planned.

"Stephen didn't always live up to his responsibilities," he said.

Why did he always find it necessary to tell her of Stephen's shortcomings? "Perhaps it was your expectations he didn't live up to."

"Stephen owned just as much of Halliday Iron as I do," he bit out. "He shirked that responsibility."

The full impact of his words and his resentment resounded like cannon fire, and she felt like an idiot for not realizing it sooner. She hadn't grasped the entire reason why Nicholas didn't trust her. "Exactly how much of Halliday Iron did Stephen own?"

"A third. Mother and I own the other two thirds. Upon her death, her third was to be divided between Stephen and I."

The money. This was all about the money Claire and her child would have inherited. "And now that Stephen is dead? What about his third?"

"As if you didn't know."

"How could I know? I haven't spoken with anyone but you and Leda, and neither one of you have told me."

"And Stephen didn't tell you?"

"Stephen didn't plan to die!" She heard the disgust in her voice, and knew he'd heard it, too. "His married life had just begun."

His dark-eyed gaze traveled her hair and face before he

abruptly turned and flicked an ash into the fireplace. "William inherited Stephen's third. When Mother dies he will inherit half of her third as well. Half of Halliday Iron will be his."

Of course. Stephen planned well for the welfare of his wife and child. One thing she was certain of: Stephen and Claire had loved each other deeply. Why wouldn't Stephen have wanted to make certain Claire and their baby were secure if anything should happen to him? "He wasn't so irresponsible, after all, was he?" she said, unable to prevent the smug little smile that surged to her lips. "He saw to it that his son would be taken care of."

His deep brown eyes shot sparks.

"And—" she stopped herself from saying 'Claire' "—me?" she asked. "Where do I figure in?"

Nicholas gave her a look that could have lacerated even the thickest skin. "You have accounts set up in your name. They're paid into annually from company profits." He blew smoke into the air. "Are you going to tell me you weren't aware of this?"

Anger welled in Sarah's chest on Claire's behalf. How dare this man accuse the kindhearted woman she'd known briefly of the underhanded manipulation he was suggesting! "Would you like to come out and accuse me of staging a train wreck to get at Stephen's money?"

His expression denoted he'd been taken aback by her vehemence.

"Do you think I wanted Stephen dead?" she asked, her voice louder and more shrill than she'd intended. She took a deliberate calming breath.

He tossed the cigar into the flames and moved from the fire.

Sarah's pulse pounded in her veins. She had no business arguing with this man. She had no place angering him, or opposing him, or even challenging his right to his doubts and anger. She was nothing to him. But Stephen and

Claire's kindness and generosity had meant everything to her. They had meant her life.

"No, I don't believe you wanted Stephen dead," he said finally, his voice calm, his tone under control. "But I'm not convinced of the reasons you married him."

Sarah kept silent. She didn't say that it didn't matter what he thought Claire's reasons were. Stephen had married her. The deed was done and obviously the legal ramifications of his financial planning were binding. The way she saw it, if Claire were still alive and here right now, Nicholas's responsibility would have been to carry out his brother's wishes regarding his wife and child.

Sarah believed he knew that, too. "And what of the responsibilities you spoke of?"

"I will honor my brother's will," he said without answering her question.

"What about his marriage? His wife? Will you honor them?" She cringed as soon as the words were out. "I'm sorry. I shouldn't have said that. I don't want to argue with you. Just tell me what you expect of me."

He moved to stand a few feet from her. "I expect, Claire, that you will honor the Halliday name. That you will behave in a manner suiting a Halliday. And that you will start to assume the duties my mother has performed all these years on her own. It wasn't always easy for her. The early days, while the foundry was getting started, were hard. She deserves some rest now."

Sarah had no doubt that was true. Besides, she would feel better if she were earning her keep. She owed more than that to Stephen.

"I have no wife," he continued. "If and when I choose to marry, my wife will share the tasks."

"What exactly is it you want me to do?"

"See to the entertaining, the running of the household. Supervise the servants, shop, plan the menus. Mother will help you learn."

She would be expected to play the part of Claire in front of guests. The idea brought a cold dread to her limbs. "How often do you entertain?"

He met her gaze, and his expression was unreadable. He was probably thinking the idea terrified her, but for different reasons. "Whenever business associates are in town. Once or twice a month. Perhaps more often. Maybe less."

Assuming Leda's responsibilities disturbed her more than anything. What would happen once Sarah left? With any luck, she would only have to entertain a few times. But then she'd be on her way and Leda would be left with all the work again.

This was only getting her in deeper.

If Claire had been here, she'd have gone along with Nicholas's wishes, though, would she not? What else could she have done? She would have owed it to her baby to learn her position and see to his future.

That was the way Sarah would have to play it. Anything else would seem too suspicious. "All right. Will you speak with your mother about this?"

"I'll talk to her in the morning."

She recognized the tension in the set of his shoulders, the way he held his head. "I'll do my best."

His look was one of uncertainty mixed with a dash of surprise. "See that you do."

It wasn't a threat. Not really. But Sarah escaped to her room, feeling as though there would be dire results if she failed this test.

What did she care? She had only a few more weeks at the most to remain and bear the brunt of Nicholas's resentment. After that she'd take William and find a place far from Mahoning Valley. A place where she could start over and build a new life.

A place where no one knew her or expected anything from her.

She would get by until then. She had no choice now.

Chapter Six

Of course. William's christening *had* to be the first event on the schedule. And a reception to follow. Stephen had been buried and mourned; now the Halliday heir must be welcomed.

Sarah cringed at the thought of bringing her imposter heir into the presence of God and asking His blessing. What adverse fate awaited her after this latest in her long line of transgressions?

Somehow, while organ music filled the Youngstown church and the scents of candle wax and expensive perfumes wafted through the air, she made it through the ceremony. Sarah didn't allow herself to think about her child being christened with a false name. And as each time something this monumental had shaken her to her very soul, she thought of her father, silently cursing Morris Thornton for his role in this charade.

She longed for her old home, for the safety and security she'd once foolishly believed were hers. Her misjudgment had changed all that, and she'd been swift to learn that her father had only loved her as long as she'd been an asset to him, as long as she'd never been a burden or an embarrassment.

William would never learn a cruel lesson like that, she

vowed. She would love him no matter what he did. She would be a compassionate and forgiving parent. Sarah made her silent oath before leaving the church and hurrying to the house to oversee the last-minute preparations.

The reception was informal, with a buffet set up in the dining hall. Nicholas observed that after a servant had taken each new guest's coat and added their gifts to the growing pile, Claire greeted each one personally. Everything about her dress and behavior that day was exemplary, from her gentle admonitions when the help didn't attend to the food table quickly enough, to the way she welcomed the guests.

She didn't know these Wick Avenue industrialists and bankers from the man in the moon, yet he passed a small group she stood within and overheard the questions she asked to stimulate conversation.

"If this canal is such a grand idea, why hasn't the project been undertaken?" she asked.

"Far too costly," replied Edward Coughlin, a retired banker. "And the mills are doing more business by train than by barge now."

"The canal idea has been kicked around for a hundred years," Mayor Veys said. "One of these days someone will come up with enough money to underwrite the project."

Mayor Veys seemed taken with Claire. Nicholas noted the way the hawk-nosed widower preened beneath her attention. He observed as she drifted to another group, somehow managing to make her steps with the crutches appear graceful.

"What do you think of my sister-in-law?" Nicholas asked, reminding Phillip Veys that the object of his attention was a Halliday and under Nicholas's protection.

"A striking woman. Damn shame about your brother. They must have been a fetching couple. She's young and beautiful. She'll remarry soon."

Nicholas's stare swung from the mayor to Claire. Remarry? It was perfectly natural for someone to think that.

Yes, she was young. And she was beautiful. And why should she settle for a lonely life as a rich widow when she could be a doubly rich wife?

"You haven't been at the theater for a while," Edward said to Nicholas. They shared a box in the balcony, and Nicholas usually accompanied Leda. "Why don't you bring Claire on Saturday evening? She and the missus can get acquainted—give her a chance to get to know someone."

The Coughlins were the cream of Youngstown society. Once welcomed into their circle, Claire would be an important part of the social structure. Nicholas followed her with his eyes.

Milos Switzer, wearing handsomely creased black trousers and a gray coat, stood off to one side of the drawing room. Claire stepped over to speak with him. He leaned forward, a lock of his sandy hair habitually falling over one temple. His steel gray eyes held a perceptible spark of interest.

"Saturday night then, Nicholas?" Edward asked.

Claire seemed to say something just for Milos's ears, and touched his sleeve. He smiled and responded to her words, and Nicholas couldn't explain the unease their exchange evoked.

"Yes," he replied. "We'll see you then." Moving swiftly across the room, he drew up beside his sister-in-law.

Milos looked up. "Claire has done a marvelous job with the food, hasn't she?" he asked. "Did you try the goose pâté?"

Nicholas tried to reason with his unfounded exasperation. "Yes. Mother is an excellent teacher."

Claire's clear gaze rose to his, and if he hadn't known better, he'd have thought he saw hurt behind her quickly masked expression. She might have everyone else easily fooled, but he wasn't going to fall for her wily charms and her phony New York accent.

"How was Thomas when you stopped by the Cranes'?" Nicholas asked his assistant.

"He's doing well. Just frustrated over the loss of work. Mrs. Crane sent her thanks for the supplies."

"Do you think it was enough?"

"It was half a wagon load, Nicholas." He grinned.

"Your generosity is admirable," Claire commented.

"Don't let this fool you," Milos said. "He's as tight-fisted as they come. Nobody wrests an extra penny from him in business dealings. He'll haggle over the price on a pound of steel until his suppliers give up from exhaustion."

"My father started this business with a loan from Coughlin's Savings and Trust," Nicholas said. "I would be a poor son if I didn't honor his memory by increasing his hard work and investments."

Claire's shadowy blue eyes darkened.

Samuel Breslow, a mill owner, stepped up beside him. "And you've done that twice over, Nicholas. Now you need to make yourself an heir to take the reins, so you can enjoy your old age."

An awkward silence lapsed. Nicholas resisted meeting Claire's gaze. "It will be a good many years before I'll be ready to let go of Halliday Iron," he assured the man.

"I have no doubt of that," the man said with a chuckle. "I've brought you a box of cigars back from Georgetown. What do you say we go sample them?"

Nicholas gave Claire a slight bow. "Excuse us."

Sarah nodded, and the two men made their way through the clusters of visitors.

"I can picture him being a shrewd businessman," she said to Milos. "It's his other side that's hard to accept. The one with compassion."

"He's loyal to his employees," Milos said.

"And his family," she added.

"And his family," he agreed.

"Have you known him a long time?"

"A very long time. We once fell in love with the same girl."

"Oh?"

"We were ten."

Sarah looked up to see the good humor on Milos's handsome face.

"We hated each other for about a month."

"What happened?"

"I made it look like he put ink on the teacher's seat. He gave me a bloody nose. Then Mary Joy moved to Chicago, and we forgot about her."

Sarah smiled.

"He and Stephen were like oil and water," Milos said. "Nicholas did everything just the way he was supposed to, following the rules trying to please Templeton."

"Their father?"

He nodded. "And Stephen went against the grain, broke all the rules, and didn't care what anyone, let alone the old man, thought of him."

"Did their father favor Nicholas, then?"

"Quite the opposite. Oh, he tried not to show it, but Stephen was his favorite. It was apparent in the way Stephen got away with the most outrageous behavior. While Nicholas..."

"Yes?"

"Well, Nicholas just tried harder and harder to earn his respect. Now that I look back, it was like he was trying to make up for the disappointment Stephen caused." His expression changed abruptly. "I'm sorry."

"Whatever for?"

"I shouldn't have said that. You're Stephen's wife."

"No, no. I'm grateful you're frank with me. There's so much I don't know or understand about this family. The more I know the more it helps me deal with my situation."

Nicholas had never let on that Milos was anything more than a valuable employee. But of course, he'd been there with the family through the memorial service, a steadfast and supportive presence. Now she could see more to the relationship between the two men.

A thought came to mind. "Did you find it surprising that Nicholas had me investigated?"

His surprised gaze met hers levelly. "Did he?"

"Didn't you know?"

"No."

"I thought perhaps he'd told you."

"I'm sure it was sound judgment on his part. Someone in his position can't be too careful in protecting his property and investments. Anyone Stephen would have married would have received the same scrutiny. No doubt Nicholas will have his own wife investigated before he says his vows."

He seemed sincere enough. Apparently he'd be little help in gaining information about Claire. But his friendliness and easygoing charm made her more comfortable than she'd been all afternoon. "What did he tell you about me?"

"Just that you would be arriving with a child, and that you'd been injured. He's a fine-looking boy. I'm glad the two of you are all right."

The afternoon grew late. Sarah and Leda opened the assortment of colorfully wrapped gifts and, a few at a time, their guests departed. Leda gave Sarah an enveloping hug, assured her she'd done a wonderful job and headed to her room to rest.

Seeing that the servants were cleaning up, Sarah made her way toward the stairs. Her leg, which had begun to ache hours ago, now pulsed with a dull throb. She'd had her weight on it too much that day. Paused at the bottom of the staircase, she gazed up, steeling herself for the climb and tightening her grip on the banister.

"Why didn't you say something?"

Nicholas's deep, silken voice caught her unaware, startling her. She turned and found him beside her. "About what?" she asked, her heart hammering.

Had he learned something about her? Had one of the businessmen here today recognized her? She hadn't seen anyone familiar. She'd had no reason to fear one of these steel industrialists would have had business with her father's company. But it was possible she had entertained one of them in Boston and forgotten.

"About your leg hurting," he replied. "That is the source of the crease in your brow, is it not?"

Relieved, she leaned against the glossy oak banister. "It's not that bad," she said. *Not compared to other types of pain.*

"No reason to act like it doesn't hurt," he said. "That's foolish." Without preamble, he stepped forward and scooped her into his arms.

He smelled faintly of tobacco, and strongly of that starched linen smell that emanated from his wardrobe, and more disturbingly like his own unique male self. For a moment she held her body stiff in his arms, resistant to his presumptuous action. But by the time he'd climbed a few stairs, she recognized just how grateful she was for someone's concern. Though the man was curt-mannered and duty-bound, his arms were strong, and his care appreciated.

Sarah allowed herself to relax into the unfamiliar measure of security his arms gave her, feeling safe, feeling as though she didn't have to take the whole world on alone just yet.

He reached the top of the stairs and Claire's eyes, huge and round against her pale face, turned up to his. For a moment Nicholas thought his boots were stuck to the floor. After only a second's resistance, her soft body had melted against him, her submission indicative of the extent of her exhaustion.

It had only been a few weeks since she'd been in a terrible accident, as well as given birth. Watching her today, his conscience had nagged at him bitterly, making him question if he'd been too hard on her. No matter who she was, it was wrong of him to overtax her strength or jeopardize her health.

He carried her swiftly to her bed and lowered her to the edge. As he pulled away, she yelped, and it relieved him to find only a loose strand of her hair caught on a button on his vest. Nicholas lowered himself to sit beside her, and studied the wild tangle.

"I'm sorry," she said softly, catching her pink lower lip in her teeth, an action that made her seem girlish, yet touched him in the erotic way only a woman could.

"Let me. Move closer." He said the words before he realized moving her closer would place all that marvelously scented hair beneath his chin.

She leaned forward obligingly, and he reached for the snagged ringlet, untangling it from his button with great care. The ringlet was pure silk against his fingers. Once he'd loosened the tress, he held it, rubbing the satiny texture between his thumb and forefinger.

She raised her head, not pulling away, but bringing her solemn gaze to his, and he read the question in those liquid depths. He made a visual inspection of her creamy-looking ivory skin, her disturbing bow-shaped lips and the riot of her wheat- and gold-toned hair.

And without knowing he was going to do it, without waiting for his sensible mind to dissuade him, he took the strand of hair that hung beside her cheek between his fingers and stroked it, envying the lock its place against that temptingly beautiful face.

In the next minute, he found his fingertips against her jaw, discovered the incredible softness of her skin, and saw her rise of color, but couldn't remember ordering his hand to touch her.

Against his lips, her fluttering breath tasted sweet and inviting, hypnotically drawing him closer. The seductive scent of her hair and skin set his senses aflame. She drew a shaky breath through provocative lips, and his craving desire to taste them melted his good sense like a hot knife through butter.

His fingers sank into the mass of wanton ringlets at her temple. His lips came down over hers. She drew in a quick breath of surprise or pleasure—he wasn't sure which—but he covered her mouth before she could object or move away.

Adrift in the staggering sensations of desire the kiss unlocked, it took Nicholas a few minutes to realize she had pressed her palm against his chest in gentle protest.

The action brought him to his senses, and he took his mouth from hers, pulled his hand from her hair and stood, his heart thudding.

She sat with her gaze lowered, one hand supporting her weight on the bed beside her, the other rising to tuck back the recalcitrant lock of hair, then flutter to her lap.

"I'm sorry," she said on a whisper, and a silvery dot shimmered on her lashes.

"I'll take responsibility," he said quickly. Too quickly. Too sternly, angry with himself.

The dot became a drop that trailed down her exquisite ivory cheek. She dashed it away.

"I'm sorry, Claire," he forced himself to say. "You're vulnerable right now. That was quite dishonorable of me. You have every right to be angry."

She shook her head gently, and only mouthed the word "No."

"I promise to behave with more discretion in the future."

She remained still and silent.

"Look at me, for God's sake, it was just a kiss."

She did. And he wished like hell she hadn't. He wished like hell he hadn't insisted. Because when those glistening eyes rose to his, when he read the overwhelming bewilderment and hurt in their depths, he knew the truth.

Oh, no. No form of denial would be sufficient.

It hadn't been just a kiss.

Sarah prepared for the evening at the theater, wishing instead she were staying at home while Leda and Nicholas went out. That way she'd have hours to replace Stephen's letters and read the remaining ones. So far, they'd availed little, containing mostly stories of his travels and the productions of his plays. The information would serve her well at some time, she was sure, but for now disappointment suffused her. She just wished an opportunity would arise to go through Nicholas's clothing and find the key to his desk. She'd come to realize that the probability of that was nil.

Sarah chose one of her new dresses, an onyx-black silk brocade trimmed with deep flounces of French lace, seed pearls in a cluster on the shoulders and in a triangular design on each side of the bustle as well as at her waist. The blouse cut to a deep V between her breasts and the overdress draped in a V shape from each shoulder to a point at her waist, a slimming design.

She studied herself in the mirror, still unaccustomed to the womanly changes in her body. Her breasts were fuller, her hips more rounded and less girlish. What would her father think if he saw her now?

That thought changed as she remembered the evening Nicholas had carried her to her room. And kissed her. Exactly what did *Nicholas* think of her?

What did it matter? He didn't even know her true identity, she told herself. But she couldn't help wondering if she'd done something to encourage that kiss.

And every time she wondered that, the more probable reason for the kiss came to mind: It had been just another test. A test to find out what kind of woman his brother had married, to prove the caliber of the mother of the only current Halliday heir. And each time she went over her reaction, she wondered if she'd passed or failed.

Having little experience with kissing men, she had only minimal comparison. Nicholas's kiss still kept her awake at night, still gave her pause to reflect over its meaning and its heady effect on her senses. She'd never been kissed like that.

Not with that tenderness or depth of sensitivity, as though she were someone deserving of reverence.

But that was silly. Nicholas hardly thought of her as special or honorable. Just the opposite, so why did that worshipful distinction stay with her above all else? Above the warmth and the genuine sensuality of it? Above the shocking fact that he'd kissed her at all?

She'd failed the test. His brother's widow should have slapped his face and shared her affront with anyone within hearing distance. But she hadn't.

She hadn't.

She'd pressed her palm to his shirtfront, felt the rapid beat of his heart and the heat of his muscular body. She'd remembered the heart-stopping sight of him in his bath, and paralyzing heat had encompassed her. Through the din of blood rushing through her veins, she'd heard the voice of caution reminding her of her obligation to her son, and she'd pushed against the chest she desired to pull closer.

She'd fought falling into a trap, and remembered the last time she'd believed a man's sincerity.

That thought raised her sensibilities into action. Nicholas had a purpose, and it boded no goodwill toward her. Sarah had doubled her effort to push him away, and he'd released her.

She turned away from the mirror, away from the blush of humiliation and desire that even now tinted her skin at the memory.

William was still awake in his crib, having just been fed

before she donned her dress. She cradled him close and carried him to the window. "Mama won't be gone long," she promised, kissing his forehead. "And I will miss you terribly."

He gave her a toothless grin that melted her heart and brought a wide smile to her own face. "You are the most precious boy."

He smiled again, and her heart welled with love.

"William is still awake?" Mrs. Trent asked, coming to stand behind her.

"Yes. He's starting to stay awake for longer periods. See that you pay him attention this evening."

"It's my pleasure, ma'am."

"Thank you." She handed the baby to his governess and retrieved her reticule, placing its contents, along with a fresh handkerchief, in one of Claire's evening bags. Testing the bulky lining of her reticule, she discovered the bracelet where she'd ineptly sewn it, and with a few deft plucks at the thread, released her very last possession.

From their silver settings, the emeralds winked at her as though they shared her secret. She wrapped her fingers around the precious piece of jewelry, the gems cool against her skin. What would her life have been like if her mother had lived? Perhaps a woman's tutelage and direction would have prevented her mistake with Gaylen Carlisle. And if she had still made that mistake, perhaps her mother could have stopped her father from banishing their only daughter—their only child—from their home.

She would never know. She fastened the bracelet to her wrist. She had only two things that rightfully belonged to her: William and the bracelet. She might as well enjoy the jewelry before it too became a part of her past.

Nicholas waited for her in the cathedral-ceilinged foyer. His formal black evening wear and pristine white shirt emphasized his devastating handsomeness.

His unreadable tobacco-dark gaze scanned her hair and clothing, settling on her face. "Ready?" he asked.

"What about your mother?"

"She's dining with friends this evening. Didn't she mention it?"

The two of them were going out together? Alone? For a brief moment, Sarah allowed the thought of him kissing her to steal her breath and start her heart pounding, but she took her errant thoughts captive and banished them to a back corner of her mind.

"No," she replied. "She didn't say anything to me."

"Does it make a difference if she's not going with us?"

It had been months seen she'd been to the theater, since she'd been anywhere, and she planned to enjoy herself. Nicholas Halliday and his tests and his kisses be hanged. She gathered her skirts and stepped past him. "Not in the least."

The production was one she'd seen done with more skill, but that didn't lessen her pleasure over being there.

Edward Coughlin's second wife, Elizabeth, was only a few years older than Sarah, a petite, vivacious brunette with a melodious laugh and her banker husband wrapped around her little finger. When their escorts disappeared during the intermission, Elizabeth seated herself beside Sarah and carried on an entertaining, if one-sided, conversation. The Coughlins had two young children, and Elizabeth was involved in a variety of women's organizations.

"I'm having a charity luncheon for the Ladies' Aid next week, Claire. You must come."

"Thank you," Sarah replied. Nicholas must have arranged this so she'd become involved. Or to gauge her reaction to society functions. "I'd love to."

The men returned, the scent of imported cigars clinging to their clothing, and the theater darkened once again.

A few minutes into the act, Sarah glanced over and noticed Elizabeth cuddled against her husband, his hand lovingly holding hers. The intimate sight gave her a start. Not because she was shocked—she had already seen how much the couple cared for each other in spite of the difference in their ages—but rather because she recognized the grim jolt as longing. As loneliness. Their happiness made her feel all the more alone.

She had planned to have a loving husband one day. Her dreams had included an adoring man in her life, children to raise together.

What would happen to her and William once they left the security of the Halliday residence and name?

She would have to pretend to be a widow, otherwise they would be scorned wherever they settled. More lies. But she couldn't provide a decent environment and education for her son if she lived the truth. No one would rent to them or hire her to work.

William would be her only family. And she was responsible to do the very best for him.

Staring blankly at the performers on stage, Sarah became aware of Nicholas's gaze from beside her. She glanced over to find him watching her, and quickly banished her self-pitying thoughts.

"I should have realized this would be a painful reminder of Stephen," he said softly, and to her astonishment, he took her cold hand and warmed it between his palms.

The sensation raised gooseflesh up her arm and across her shoulders, and she wanted to fold her entire body into his inviting warmth. Oh, but she was a pathetically desperate creature if she drew any measure of comfort from this hard-hearted man. Was she so love-starved that she'd accept attention from just anyone?

Let him think she'd been pining for Stephen. The ruse gave her an advantage she sorely needed.

Halfway through the next act, when he still hadn't released her hand, a surprising question ran across her mind: *Or was he drawing comfort from her?*

Sarah chanced a surreptitious glance at his profile. No. Surely not the great Nicholas Halliday, man of steel. Then again, she'd witnessed his tender moments with his mother, so she knew there had to be more to the man than he'd ever revealed to her.

She drew her gaze from his face and her hand from his. No. Everything he did, each action and word and plan had a motive. She was under his scrutiny and at his mercy at all times. *Do exactly what Claire would do,* she reminded herself with strict caution.

That task would be so much easier if she only knew who Claire was.

They had reservations for dinner, and after the play ended Gruver drove them the short distance to the elegantly furnished restaurant the Coughlins had chosen. Sarah declined the wine, and sipped at a flute of white grape juice. Her full breasts decidedly uncomfortable, she wished she could excuse herself and leave without causing a scene.

Elizabeth entertained them with stories of their trip to Europe a few months before. She looked up with delight as several performers from the play passed their table. "Oh, I so enjoyed your performances this evening!" she said, gesturing to the party.

A willowy redhead came close and replied with a smile. "Thank you." She wasn't nearly as striking offstage with her makeup removed and wearing a camel-colored organdy suit.

The redhead, Patrice Beaumont, introduced the troupe and Elizabeth introduced their small group.

"Halliday?" a well-endowed brunette named Judith Marcelino questioned, moving to the front of the group. "Are you related to *Stephen* Halliday?"

Nicholas appeared decidedly uncomfortable with the association. "Yes," he replied, standing and hesitantly taking the hand she proffered. "I'm his brother."

"I performed in one of Stephen's plays in New York last

winter," she said. "We were all devastated to hear of his death. Please accept my sympathies."

The others added their condolences.

"And *Claire,* of course," she said, stepping closer and leaning down to press her powdered cheek against Sarah's. "Sweet Claire. You must be lost without our dear, dear Stephen. Tell me, what can I do for you?"

"Well, I—I—" Sarah stammered, hating the limelight, and wanting to bolt from the restaurant. "Nothing. Stephen's brother is taking care of us."

"Us?"

"Claire has a baby," Elizabeth offered.

Judith's pale green eyes inspected Sarah's face and hair, then took stock of her dress. She reached for Sarah's hand, and her thumb encountered the emerald bracelet. "What a lovely piece of jewelry," she commented, and her assessing gaze slid to Nicholas.

Sarah pulled her hand away, experiencing sudden nausea. "Thank you."

"Where are you from?" Judith asked, her narrow brows raised.

Sarah's cheeks burned. She'd tried to lose her Boston accent, but the speech undoubtedly gave her away from time to time. "New York, mostly," she replied.

"Ah, I do love New York. You meet the most *interesting* people there."

"Thanks for coming to the production," Patrice said with a wave, and the group departed.

Sarah didn't look up again until certain they were gone. When she did, she met Nicholas's flint-hard stare. "Did Stephen give you that bracelet?" he asked, low enough so the others couldn't hear.

She shook her head and swallowed hard, fighting the nerves in her stomach. "It was my mother's."

His brows rose in surprise, and Sarah bit her tongue. She shouldn't have said that. "Extravagant gift for a mill

worker to give his wife," he commented. "Or for a seamstress to buy herself."

"It—it was in her family for years," she replied quickly.

He lifted one dark brow as though he still didn't believe
her.

"Where do you think I got it?" she asked. "Do you
think I stole it?"

"I don't think you need to steal anything," he replied,
his tone lowered to a smoothly modulated accusation.
"Who you were with before Stephen is your business, isn't
it?"

Slow anger whipped her senses to a barely restrained
froth. "I don't particularly care what you think. The bracelet was my mother's. It's all I have left of her, and it gives
me pleasure to wear it."

"You speak like your mother is dead," Nicholas whispered.

His penetrating stare pinned her to her chair like a
trapped moth. If Claire had a mother, he must wonder why
she hadn't contacted her! Heat careened though her body.
Her stomach lurched. "I need to leave now," she said
abruptly. "I don't feel too well."

"But our food has just arrived."

"I'm sorry, but I'm not hungry. Just send me to the
house and Gruver can come back for you."

"Claire, that would be rude. The Coughlins invited us
as their guests."

She turned to Elizabeth. "Elizabeth, I'm sure you'll understand if I need to leave right away. I'm not used to being
away from William for so long."

"I certainly do understand, darling," Elizabeth said.
"Having two babies of my own, I remember all too well.
Don't give it a second thought. We'll do it again, and I'll
see you Thursday of next week."

Relieved, Sarah gave her hand a grateful squeeze, gathered her crutches and hurried from the restaurant.

Chapter Seven

She studied the street, dimly lit by gas lamps, and took off at a fast clip. Nicholas came up beside her, and surprised her by merely escorting her until they came to his carriage.

Gruver promptly left the two other drivers he'd been playing cards with and hurried over.

"Mrs. Halliday's in a bit of a rush," Nicholas said.

"I'm sorry you have to come back for Mr. Halliday," she apologized.

"No, you won't," Nicholas said to his driver, then turned to her. "It's far too long a drive for him to return at this hour. I've said my good-nights to the Coughlins."

He stowed her crutches and lifted her into the coach, then climbed in to sit across from her. Gruver placed the step inside. The carriage rocked as he climbed onto the driver's seat, and in minutes they were well on their way.

"I'm sorry to spoil your evening," she said.

He sighed and leaned wearily against the rich upholstery. "You haven't spoiled my evening. I only went to please you, and to acquaint you with Edward's wife."

His low-spoken words took her by surprise. He'd raised the leather shade, and moonlight caressed his rigidly cut features as he studied the passing countryside.

Yes, he was as hard and unyielding as the steel from his mill. He was insufferably cautious and suspicious of her.

And he had every right to be.

She was deceiving him and his gracious mother. She was playing a game for her own gain, and he was her pawn as well as her opponent. The absurdity of her getting angry with him struck her with maddening clarity.

"Thank you, Nicholas," she said softly, honestly. "I enjoyed the theater very much. And I'm ever so grateful to meet Elizabeth. I will enjoy knowing a woman my own age."

His head turned, and she sensed his gaze in the semi-darkness. He hadn't bothered to light an interior lamp. After what seemed a lengthy time, he commented, "Stephen's plays were better than that one, weren't they?"

"You've *seen* Stephen's plays?" she asked incredulously, having believed all along that he'd ignored his brother's chosen profession.

"A couple of them."

"Did he know?"

A sadness seemed to come over him and squeeze even more starch from his spine. He shook his head and turned to gaze out the window once again.

He had as many regrets as she. They were both playing a part. But Sarah admitted her role to herself. She knew her audience. Nicholas, on the other hand, worked hard at fooling himself. She remembered Milos's words and knew how deeply Nicholas had loved his brother. Therefore she understood how deep his anguish went.

"I know you didn't approve of Stephen's choices," she said softly. "But I also know you loved him very much."

He turned toward her, and she could only see half his face in the darkness. "How do you know that?"

"I've seen your pain. And I need to remember that your mistrust and defensiveness comes from wanting to protect your family."

He said nothing.

"No matter what went on between you and Stephen you meant well. You wanted the best for him."

He seemed to consider those words. "Meaning well isn't necessarily enough, though, is it?"

"Now you sound as though you may be blaming yourself for some of the problems."

"Lady, you don't know the first thing about me or my relationship with my brother."

"I'm beginning to think I do."

He turned away, and Sarah knew the conversation had ended. He never liked it when the tables were turned.

This was all going to end miserably unless she found some way for her time here to make a difference. Perhaps there was something she could do that would show Nicholas she was more than just a taker. She'd been given two hands—one to receive with and the other to give with. What could she possibly give the Hallidays that they didn't already have?

The question gave her thought during the long night that followed.

Milos had been withdrawn for the past few days. Nicholas had known him enough years to know there was something sticking in his craw. He looked up from the stack of mail he'd been shuffling through and studied Milos at his desk across the room. With his usual precision, his assistant tallied a line of figures and rechecked each one.

"Is there a problem with the numbers?" Nicholas asked.

Milos shook his head.

"We met our production quota?"

"A few thousand pounds over actually."

Nicholas tapped the desktop with the tip of his mother-of-pearl-handled letter opener. "You may as well say what's on your mind, then."

The man ran a hand through his sandy hair, leaned back

in his chair with a creak of leather and springs and contemplated Nicholas. "All right. It's Claire."

Nicholas threw down the letter opener in disgust. "I knew it. What? What has the woman done now?"

Milos studied him over the top of his steepled fingers. "She's done nothing that I know of, except marry your brother and then fall into some unfortunate circumstances. That's why I don't understand your attitude toward her or your suspicions of her."

"What nonsense did she fill your head with?" Nicholas asked with a scowl.

"Did you have her background investigated?"

There was no reason for him to feel guilty about protecting his family's interests. "Of course. I'd have been a fool not to."

"And did your findings influence your feelings toward her in any way?"

"Of course. Her father was a factory worker in New York. He died when she was very young, and her mother took in alterations. The mother's income was somewhat questionable, however."

"And Claire?"

"Claire went to work in a clothing factory when she was thirteen, but she left that job to sew costumes for productions at the theater houses. She had intimate liaisons with at least three men before Stephen, all theater people."

"Don't you think Stephen was an adequate judge of character? Would he have married a woman who was only using him to get to his money? That is what you're thinking, isn't it?"

"Of course it's what I'm thinking. What I'm having trouble seeing here is why *you* can't see through her. She lived in a Slay Street tenement before she moved out on her own!"

Milos closed the ledger on the now-dry ink and stood. He stepped away from his desk and studied Nicholas. "I thought I knew you, but I don't. Where a person comes from does not make them a good person or a bad person.''

A crisp edge that Nicholas had seldom heard had crept into Milos's voice. What in the world had Claire said or done to get Milos on her side? "Of course not, but it defines their character.''

"How so?

"She hasn't contacted her mother one time since she's been here. Now if she was a woman of high character, wouldn't she see that her mother was taken care of? She left that city without a backward glance. And I'm not the mathematician you are, my friend, but even I can calculate that she was not married to my brother when William was conceived.''

"And you would discredit her for loving your brother?''

"Not if William is really my brother's child.''

Milos worked his jaw and stood with his weight on one leg. He sliced the air with the edge of a palm, punctuating his next sentence. "Do you have reason to believe he's *not* William's child?''

"I have reason to question it,'' Nicholas replied sharply. "She was poor. Stephen was rich. By marrying him, she became rich, too. She'd had relationships with other men before Stephen.''

"None of that is damning evidence by itself.''

"Which is why she's here,'' he said, slamming his fist on the desktop. "I can't prove it.''

Milos pierced him with an unyielding gray gaze. "I thought she was here because she's your brother's wife.''

Nicholas swallowed the anger that had risen to a dangerous level. Why was his friend defending the woman! Why had Stephen married her? Damn him! Damn them both.

Milos approached Nicholas's desk. "This case against Claire isn't just about her,'' he said, his penetrating eyes seeking confirmation on his friend's face. "This distrust is more about Stephen, about your disapproval and your lack of respect for him. He could have married an Eastern socialite with a dowry, and you'd have found reason to disapprove."

"That's not so."

"It is so. And if you'd look past Halliday Iron long enough, you'd see it."

"You don't have to tell me the mistakes I made with Stephen," he said, his voice carefully controlled. "I'd like nothing better than to go back and change those things. But I can't do that."

"No. Once we've made our mistakes, there's no taking them back," Milos agreed. "So don't make a bigger one with Claire."

Nicholas absorbed those words, his anger abating. If anyone but Milos had said them he'd have thrown him from his office. Milos knew that. And in order to speak with such candor, he obviously trusted the strength of their friendship.

"Point taken," Nicholas conceded. "And while we're at it, let me give *you* some advice: Don't let yourself make a big mistake with her, either."

Milos seemed to think about that, as if wondering exactly what that mistake would be. He nodded thoughtfully on his way back to his desk.

Nicholas returned to his mail, intent on thinking about work and not Claire for the rest of the day. Milos had made some strong points. But of course his feelings about Stephen influenced his reaction to Claire. Stephen's choices had never been the best ones for Halliday Iron. Nicholas couldn't be expected to overlook all of that and blindly accept this last and most outrageous choice.

Claire had certainly found an ally, though, hadn't she? He hoped his forewarning was enough to keep Milos from championing her cause to the point of interfering with their professional relationship.

The thought set off yet another warning bell. If she was devious enough to use Milos to her advantage, he stood to lose even more. He couldn't let that happen.

Another thought insinuated itself into his conscience. He'd been foolish enough to kiss her, but he'd been wise enough to steel himself against his own reactions and remind himself who she was and what he stood to lose. But kissing her could easily make any man her ally.

Had she kissed Milos like that, too?

The Coughlins' home was every bit as elegantly appointed as the Hallidays'; however, a woman's hand was more visible in the touches of color and grace. The luncheon was held in a sun-splashed music room where lacy ferns in enormous jardinieres and hanging begonias lent a rich-scented outdoor feel.

Elizabeth introduced Sarah to each of the women as they arrived. Each one expressed her sympathy and greeted Sarah warmly. Apparently the Halliday name and the association with the Coughlins were direct links to social acceptance.

She sipped tea, visited and for the first time had an opportunity to speak to other women about nursing babies and raising children. For a few short hours, she forgot her situation and felt like any young mother out for an afternoon's social activities.

Their guest speaker was from the Ladies' Aid Society. She spoke on the many needs in their community, and how each donation of time and money would be put to use. She described a steel worker who had been placed out of work recently, and whose wife was now ill. More than funds, help cooking and caring for their children was desperately needed.

Could this be the same steel worker she'd overheard Nicholas telling Gruver about? The same one Nicholas had sent provisions to? Halliday Iron wasn't the only iron works in the valley.

After the speech, Sarah drew the woman aside. "One of Nicholas's workers was injured," she said. "His name is Crane."

Phoebe Graham nodded. "The very one I spoke of. My maid tells me his wife is now quite ill."

Sarah didn't have funds of her own to donate, but she had time. Especially in the afternoons when William took his longest nap. Immediately she remembered wishing she could repay Stephen's kindness by using his own advice: *Just do a good turn for someone else.*

"Could you give me the address?" she asked. "I'd like to make a trip to the Cranes' myself."

"I'll send a messenger with it this evening," Mrs. Graham promised.

Sarah thanked her. She was sure if Nicholas had known about the Crane woman's illness he would have sent someone. His concern with his workers was one of his best qualities.

That evening at dinner Nicholas related an upcoming event.

"Three of my business associates and their wives will be staying with us for about a week. I expect you to make the arrangements for their stay." He raised a brow at Sarah. "Plan an evening's entertainment, as well. Quinn Kleymann is an important stockbroker. Monty Gallamore and Sherwood McCaul are two of our biggest buyers."

She nodded and glanced at Leda. The woman smiled encouragingly. "You'll like them, dear. And I will help."

Sarah turned back to Nicholas and replied, "I will handle the preparations."

As soon as Nicholas excused himself and left the table, Sarah turned to Leda. "Will we need to hire extra staff for that week?"

Leda confirmed her thoughts.

"I'll handle that, and I'll work with Mrs. Pratt on menus this evening, but I have something I need to do tomorrow afternoon."

"Oh?"

She explained about the Crane woman.

"Claire, darling, please don't take any chances with your own health and safety. Nicholas can send someone over."

"No, no, you have nothing to worry about. I've been trying to figure out some way to help more, and—"

"But you're a tremendous help to me."

"I'm afraid Nicholas doesn't see it that way. This is something I need to do."

Leda gave her an uncertain look, but she nodded. "Do what you feel you must."

Impulsively, Sarah leaned forward and kissed her cheek. "And you leave the evening's entertainment to me. I'll think of something lovely."

"I'm sure you will."

They smiled at one another affectionately.

Gruver came for her at precisely twelve-fifteen, just as she'd asked. He knew the area the Cranes lived in, delivered her to their door and assisted her to the ground. "Mr. Halliday won't be needing me until late. I can wait for you."

She surveyed the row of shacklike cabins with a shiver of unease. The yards were relatively tidy, and the meager structures themselves in good repair, but she'd lived her whole life in luxury and had never seen homes so obviously poor.

"I don't want you to spend your whole afternoon waiting," she said. "Just let me make sure this is the right place."

"It's safe, Mrs. Halliday," Gruver said, assuring her. "I wouldn't leave you off anywhere I thought something would happen to you."

Sarah made her way along the dirt path to the cabin. A window box beneath each of the two front windows held an assortment of spindly red and yellow flowers. She knocked on the weathered door.

A small child appeared in the crack that opened. "Yeah?"

"Hello there. Is this Thomas Crane's house?"

"My pa cain't get 'round just yet," he said.

"I know. That's why I'm here. Is—is your mother here, please?"

"Mama's abed sick. If you got wash, you can take it to the Paulsons'. It's down there a ways. They's a stump in the yard."

"No, I don't have wash. I came to help your mother." She turned to Gruver, who was watching curiously, and called, "Come back at four."

He saluted his understanding, and pulled the carriage away.

Sarah stepped past the little boy guarding the door. He took on a startled expression and ran into the room to stand by a man reclining on a lumpy sofa, his shirt opened enough to reveal the bandages encasing his ribs. His right arm was wrapped and supported by a sling.

The man looked up at her with the same shocked expression the boy had worn.

"Mr. Crane? I'm S—" She caught herself. "I'm Claire Halliday. I've come to do whatever I can to help."

"Halliday?" he asked, his dark eyebrows climbing to the middle of his lined forehead.

"Yes. Nicholas's sister-in-law."

"I'm sorry about your husband, Mrs. Halliday," he said with a nod.

"Thank you. Where's your wife?"

"In the bedroom there. The oldest took her some tea before she left, but Mary wouldn't hear of her missin' any more school, so she sent her off."

Sarah removed her velvet cape and hung it beside a threadbare jacket and a homemade shawl on hooks beside the door. She entered the bedroom.

At her approach Mary Crane opened deep brown eyes wide, and Sarah introduced herself. A baby about a year old pulled himself to stand in an iron crib against one wall, and the strong smell of urine hit Sarah.

An older child, a girl of about three, played on the floor.

"Has Dr. Barnes been here?" she asked the woman.

"Yes. He gave me something to help with my stomach. I just pray David doesn't get it." She glanced toward the wide-eyed baby.

"Can you eat?" Sarah asked.

"Maybe. The tea stayed down this morning."

"I'll fix you some lunch and some fresh tea, and then I'll clean up David and take the children out for some air. What's your name, sweetie?"

The little girl stood, stuck a finger in her mouth and said around it, "Elissa."

Sarah searched the cupboards, finding adequate supplies. Nicholas had indeed seen to it that the Cranes' stores were set by. It appeared that very little had been used, however, since neither Tom nor Mary was up to cooking.

Sarah hadn't had a whole lot of practice herself, but she managed a hot meal for the family. Afterward, she bathed the baby, changed his bedding and sent Alex, the boy who'd answered the door, to the Paulsons' with the soiled sheets.

"You take in laundry?" she asked Mary as she fitted clean sheets on all the beds.

"I haven't been able to for several days," she said from the chair where she waited for Sarah to finish with her bed. "Mr. Halliday sent food, but we still have bills to pay. Our rent comes due the first."

Sarah couldn't imagine how much one paid for rent of

such a pitiful dwelling, but obviously it was a great deal to the Cranes, and it was their home, no matter how humble.

"You just concern yourself with getting well, and don't worry about that right now," she said gently, and helped Mary back into the bed and tucked covers around her. She was almost certain the Ladies' Aid Society planned to do something about that. At least she assumed that was what Phoebe Graham's plea for funds was all about. Mary's eyes closed almost immediately.

"Thank you. Mrs. Halliday," Tom said as she donned her cape and prepared to leave. "I thank you especially for helping my Mary."

She waved to the children and limped to where Gruver had the carriage waiting.

The following day Sarah sent all the Cranes' laundry to the Paulsons', appalled that the family had so few changes. As she washed their lunch dishes and prepared a meal to leave for their dinner, she thought of all Claire's dresses hanging in the armoire back at the house—dresses that Sarah would never wear, and that would eventually be discarded.

The day after, Penelope, Gruver's wife, helped her pack them all, and Gruver unloaded them in the Cranes' living room. By then Mary was getting around, and she touched the garments with reverence.

"You sure don't want these beautiful gowns, Mrs. Halliday?" she asked, her eyes bright.

"Call me...Claire. They're inappropriate for a widow," she said. Actually they were inappropriate for anyone, but she didn't voice that opinion. Mary had to notice. "You can take them apart and use the fabric for anything you like."

"I'll enjoy that more than you know," Mary said gratefully.

After three days of helping the Cranes all afternoon, hurrying home to feed William, and then working on the plans for guests, Sarah nearly groaned when she saw Nicholas had brought Milos to dinner one evening. She hurried to tell Mrs. Pratt to set another place.

The men politely included the women in the dinner conversation, something Sarah was unaccustomed to with her father and his cronies. She tried to keep her end of the conversation going, but weariness got the best of her.

"Are we boring you, Claire?"

She snapped her head up, and heat rose in her cheeks. "Not at all."

She'd brought William down with her, and Leda had lifted him from his bassinet and now held him against her breast. She turned him to face the men. "Claire's simply tired, darling. It's not easy to do as many things as she does during the day and get up with a baby in the middle of the night. You'll soon be sleeping through, though, won't you, William?"

She kissed the top of his head, adoringly.

"You exhaust yourself during the day, do you?" Nicholas asked, a derisive grin curling one side of his mouth. "The dinner menus have been very good, but hardly a debilitating task."

Sarah gave Leda a placating look. She hadn't revealed to Nicholas where she'd been spending her afternoons, and for some reason she wanted to keep it to herself. "If there's more you'd like done, all you have to do is ask," she said obligingly.

"As long as Mother is rested and happy, that's all I care," he replied in a placating tone. "And she tells me you've taken over many of her tasks."

Sarah glanced at Milos. She shouldn't have been embarrassed—after all, he was a close friend of the family—but she wished he hadn't heard Nicholas's demeaning tone.

Milos lent her one of his generous smiles, however, bolstering her spirits.

A screech sounded from the kitchen just then, followed by the clatter of metal.

"I'll see to that, sir." Mrs. Pratt, who'd been arranging a tray on one of the sideboards, hurried through the swinging door.

Leda paid her no mind, enraptured with the smiles she was coaxing from William, but Nicholas immediately stood and followed the maid into the servants' hall.

"Excuse me," Sarah said to Milos, then pushed back her chair and rushed to the kitchen on Nicholas's heels.

Laughter erupted and Mrs. Pratt shushed and waved her arms in warning. Sarah peered around Nicholas's broad shoulder and caught sight of the tumble of wet skirts and pant legs on the drenched floor. Giggling and not seeing the other servant or their employer, Penelope wrenched away from where her husband had her pinned, grabbed a pan of suds that sat on a work surface and dumped the contents on Gruver.

He sputtered, and roared with laughter, rising as if to retaliate. Penelope shrieked and turned to escape, seeing Nicholas and Sarah for the first time.

The laughter died on her lips, her smile transformed to a wide-eyed expression of dismay.

Gruver staggered to his feet and stood blinking. Soapsuds dripped from his face and clothing onto the soaked floor.

"I—I beg your pardon, Mr. Halliday," Penelope stammered.

"The Hallidays have a dinner guest." Mrs. Pratt's tone was scathing. "Your childish pranks are best saved for your own time and at the expense of your own quarters." She turned to Nicholas. "Sir, I'll handle this."

Nicholas didn't say anything for heart-stopping seconds. Sarah could taste Penelope Gruver's sudden fear. They had solid, well-paying jobs here, away from the toil and poverty of the iron workers. "Forgive us, Mr. Halliday," she begged. "Gruver did a bit of celebrating this evening. It won't happen again."

Gruver wore a repentant but silly expression, and his stance wasn't all that steady.

"What were you celebrating?" Nicholas asked, surprising not only Sarah but the others as well, judging by their expressions.

"We're going to have another baby," Gruver announced.

Penelope's face flamed a deeper shade of crimson. She tried to dry her hands on her soaked apron in a nervous gesture. In the tense silence her gaze flicked to Sarah and back to her employer.

"Congratulations, then," Nicholas said. Sarah wished she could see his face, but she held her position just behind him. He surprised her even more by stepping forward, the sole of his shiny black Wellington splatting in a puddle, and extending a hand to his driver.

Gruver accepted it with a relieved grin. "Thank you."

"See to it she's not the one who mops and dries this floor tonight."

"No, sir," Gruver replied. "I'll take care of it myself."

"And after you're finished, come by my study for a cigar."

"Yes, sir. I'll do that."

"I think we're ready for dessert, Mrs. Pratt," Nicholas said, indicating to all of them that the discussion was finished and the issue settled.

"Right away." She scuttled toward the icebox.

"Thank you, Mr. Halliday." Penelope flashed a grateful smile before she gathered her wet skirts and stepped away.

Nicholas turned back then, and discovered Sarah. He took her upper arm gently and led her into the short hallway that connected the kitchen and dining room.

He stopped there, and Sarah, standing close, examined his odd expression.

His dark eyes met hers. "Stephen used to do that."

"Used to do what?" she asked.

He pursed his lips a second as if searching for the explanation, and gestured with a jerk of his hand toward the kitchen. "Play like that. Do silly things. Spontaneous outrageous things...and laugh."

"A good many people laugh," she replied.

"Do they?"

The confusion in his eyes made the question more than just another of his cynical remarks. "Yes."

"I've never heard you laugh. I've never even seen you smile for that matter."

She could have said the same to him. But she didn't. For some weighty, unexplainable reason, she didn't. "Come some time when William is in his bath and see him splash Mrs. Trent. Or when he tries to study his own fists and only succeeds in crossing his eyes. You'll hear me laugh."

They stood curiously close, their voices low, the sounds from the kitchen a muted backdrop to their discreet exchange.

Sarah's attention dropped to his lips. "Is that an invitation?" he asked.

"I guess so."

"What time does William have his bath?"

"After breakfast."

They both knew he was gone to the foundry by then. But he said, "I'll stop by."

The swinging door behind Nicholas opened and they hurried to the dining room ahead of Mrs. Pratt and her custard.

This unfamiliar side of his personality amazed her once again. The softer side that showed leniency with servants and concern for employees. Was that the side that spoke from his heart every so often? Or was the cynical, acerbic side of him the true side? She didn't think so. Or she didn't *want* to think so.

Which side would be the one that reacted when he finally

learned the truth about her? Would he treat her with the same indulgence he used with his employees? The same tolerance she'd seen tonight? Or had that simply been good business sense: treat employees right, they work harder.

She didn't have much confidence when it came to men's forbearance. It was more likely he would respond to Sarah's deception with the same intolerance she'd been afforded up to this point.

Leda was telling William a tale that had Milos fairly napping. Mrs. Pratt served the custard and Sarah picked up her spoon.

"Tell me about Thomas Crane," Nicholas said, coming to Milos's rescue.

The request gave her a little start. Had someone given her away?

Milos tossed her a subtle glance before replying. "He's doing well. His wife's been sick, but the Ladies' Aid is helping."

Milos knew! The silver spoon slipped from her fingers and clinked against the china dish. She ignored it. If he'd gone and checked on Tom, he'd have known that first Mary and then Elissa were sick, but now nearly recovered. And Tom would have told him about her visits. Was Milos going to say something to Nicholas?

She didn't know why it mattered. She'd actually gone there, in the first place, to do something to help the Hallidays, to pay a debt to Stephen, and perhaps just to assuage her guilt. And yes, she'd wanted Nicholas's approval.

Not now though. She'd lived her entire life in comfort, her first eye-opening taste of reality coming after her father had shunned her. Still, she'd never seen how those who didn't have it as easy lived. And now that she'd seen it, and knew how frightening it was to have nowhere to go and no one to turn to, she simply wanted to help.

Looking at the situation honestly, Nicholas might never

approve of her. But she had to approve of herself. And that had been darned hard to do over the past year.

Nicholas finished his dessert. Mrs. Pratt removed his dish, and he propped his chin on a strong long-fingered hand, his elbow resting comfortably on the arm of the chair. With the other hand he swirled the wine in the bottom of his glass.

His coffee-colored eyes met hers and Sarah couldn't pull her gaze away. "I have a surprise for you," he said.

His shuttered expression revealed nothing. She glanced to his mother and back, waiting expectantly. What kind of surprise could he possibly have for her?

"I know you're already busy preparing for my guests, but we're going to have another."

How did he figure his business associates coming to stay were a surprise for her? "One more will be no problem."

"I didn't think so, either. I wrote her with an open invitation, and I just received a reply that she's coming to stay. Indefinitely."

That last word clued her in that this was no ordinary business visit. *Her?* Did Nicholas have a woman in his life after all? The thought shouldn't have carved a wedge of disappointment in her chest. If he had a woman friend it was not her business. A few more months and Sarah would be erased from their lives. "Are there any special arrangements I need to make?"

"You will know that better than I," he replied.

The cryptic remark brought a puzzled lift of her eyebrows. "I'm sure I don't know what you mean."

He finished his wine, savoring the last sip with a look of self-satisfaction.

Milos, too, seemed to be waiting expectantly for Nicholas to reveal more, and, bolder than Sarah, he asked, "Well, who is this mystery woman who is coming?"

Nicholas held Sarah's gaze and replied to Milos's question. "Claire's mother."

Chapter Eight

Claire's mother.

Sarah's heart tripped an alarmed cadence. Nicholas had questioned her speaking of her mother as though she were dead, and belatedly she recognized another calamitous blunder. Stark terror fogged her brain.

Leda smiled expectantly. "Selfish me," she said, her words somehow sinking into Sarah's benumbed consciousness. "All I've been able to think about is that I'll have to share William."

Claire's mother was alive, and both Nicholas and Leda knew it. Sarah'd been so distracted recently, she'd delayed returning Stephen's letters to Nicholas's desk and securing more. The additional information she could have learned might have helped her in this—another disastrous situation. She berated herself for becoming caught up in helping the Cranes and proving her worth, and thereby delaying finding valuable information that would have helped her— *Wait! Who was this deceptive person she had become?*

"Nicholas sent her funds and invited her to visit for as long as she cares to," Leda explained. "I know how much her presence will mean to you."

Nicholas studied Sarah with a steady assessing gaze she could easily learn to hate. Her head and tongue thick with alarm, she managed to push some words past her lips. "I—I didn't know you were even thinking about this."

Claire had a mother. Claire had a mother. A mother who thought her daughter was still alive.

Sarah's lies had multiplied until they'd trapped her. Tripped her. Suffocated her. *Oh, Lord....*

"I mentioned it to Nicholas right off," Leda explained. "A girl should have her mother to help her through difficult times. We didn't say anything to you, because we didn't want to get your hopes up if her visit didn't work out."

"Well, I—you're so—thoughtful." No other words came to her. At least nothing she could say aloud.

"Dinner was excellent, Claire." Milos pushed his chair back. Nicholas had done the same.

"Join us for a glass of sherry, ladies?"

"I'd be glad to take William up so you can stay," Leda offered, "but I know you're tired."

"Thank you," Sarah said with a nod to Nicholas, "but I'd like to go to my rooms."

"I'll beg off, too, darling. You two talk about whatever gentlemen discuss in private." Leda leaned into her son's kiss, and accepted a peck from Milos as well. "Good night, dears."

"Good night, Mother."

Her mind awhirl with fatalistic thoughts, Sarah followed Leda.

"Why haven't you mentioned your trips to the Cranes to him?" Leda asked as they climbed the marble stairs. She carried William so Sarah could use one crutch and the banister for support.

What was she going to do? The panicked thought of packing her few belongings and rushing out into the night came as her immediate reaction. But then she looked over at her helpless son, and knew there had to be a plan with more sense.

"I just didn't want Nicholas to think I'd done it to earn

his favor," she said lamely, trying to behave normally. "Pride, I guess." Because she *had* been trying to win his favor. And she was afraid she never could.

"He hasn't been very accepting of you, has he?" Leda asked.

Oh, Lord, the woman hadn't seen anything yet! Sarah gripped the oak banister in a white-fisted lock to keep from tumbling to the tile floor at the bottom of the stairs in a pile of quivering panic. "I understand his concern."

"It's the only way he knows," Leda said, as if in defense of her son. "He's been responsible for the foundry, for Stephen and me, since a very young age. He took that responsibility seriously."

Sarah forced herself to concentrate on what Leda was saying. These were things she should know. "How could they have been so different, your sons?"

"Stephen was much younger than Nicholas when my Templeton passed on. Nicholas'd had a year of college, but Stephen was just twelve. I'd had a baby girl in between the two, but she only lived a few weeks."

Sarah thought of those first terrifying minutes in the hospital when she'd awakened not knowing what had happened to her baby. She thought, too, of how much she loved William, and how that love grew with each hour and day and week. Her heart went out to Leda.

They reached the upstairs hall and walked slowly. Sarah's knees now trembled.

"Nicholas came right home and took over everything. I never had a day's worry over the legalities and such. He turned into a man the day his father died. He saw that Stephen finished college, though it was a constant source of friction."

Leda walked Sarah into her room and placed William on the downy emerald counterpane that draped her bed.

"He gave up so much, my Nicholas, even though he never said a word. To this day he would deny he'd sacrificed anything. Such pride.'' She shook her head. ''His own schooling, his own ambitions. And though he claimed he and the girl were merely friends, I believe he might have married the young woman he'd met at school.''

Sarah listened with surprise and new interest.

''He claimed there was no time to nurture a relationship with the girl being in Boston and him here, and I suppose he was right. By the time he had the foundry's affairs in order and had the business once again on its feet, she'd found someone else.

''All Stephen wanted to do was attend the theater, write his scripts and travel. I know Nicholas hoped that Stephen would finish his studies and return to share the load. Nicholas works as hard as his father did, bless his soul. He takes the world just as seriously. I know we wouldn't have all we do if they hadn't been so diligent, but sometimes I wonder...perhaps my husband would still be alive if he'd been a bit more...''

She paused. ''I was going to say a bit more like Stephen, but he's not alive any longer either.''

Tears filled her gray eyes. Sarah leaned her crutches against the armoire and enfolded her in a hug, understanding how Leda had wanted only the best for both her sons.

''Oh, Claire. You're such a blessing.'' Her voice was muffled against Sarah's shoulder. ''I don't know how I would have survived these past weeks without you. Just knowing you're here in the house helps me sleep at night.''

Guilt layered over guilt until Sarah wondered how she could live with its oppressive weight building inside her.

Leda pulled away, dabbing at her eyes with one of her ever-present lace hankies, and stepped to the bed. ''And having William is just the crowning touch. The two of you are so dear to me.'' She sat and placed her finger in William's fist. Her inability to keep from touching him spoke to Sarah's heart as strongly as her direct words.

Her watery gaze lifted to Sarah. ''Sometimes I feel so

selfish. I know your mother must need you, too. But you'd been prepared to leave her, hadn't you? The two of you must have been very close. I can't see how she could bear to part with you for even a day.''

Claire's mother would have to learn that her daughter had died.

It wasn't only Leda and Nicholas and Milos who would be hurt by this horrible mix-up she'd perpetuated. Now there was Claire's poor mother. How many more people would be affected before she had the courage to end it?

Sarah sank to the edge of the bed, reproach squeezing the life's blood from her heart. The woman was probably wondering why her daughter hadn't contacted her. How many more relatives did Claire have that Sarah didn't know about?

What was she going to do? She couldn't just sit here and pretend to be Claire when the woman walked in. Maybe she *should* leave tonight.

''When will she arrive?'' she asked in dread.

''Tuesday, I believe.''

''Oh, dear, that's the night Nicholas's guests will be here, and I've made so many plans.''

''We will just include her, dear. It will be no problem.''

No problem? The woman had no idea of her predicament or its looming consequences! A piercing ache pulsed in Sarah's temple. She raised her fingertips to massage it. What now? What now? *What now?*

Perhaps she could meet her at the train. That was it! And then what? Just tell her that her daughter was dead and expect her to get back in the passenger car and head for home?

Sarah didn't even know the woman's name. She wouldn't recognize her if she danced on her traveling case and sang ''Camptown Races'' at the top of her lungs.

Sarah wrung her hands and racked her brain for a solution.

"Claire, you're positively white! Let me fetch Mrs. Trent to see to William, and I'll help you with your clothing. You've overtaxed yourself with this benevolent business. Your health is important to your son's welfare, and don't you forget that."

"Of course not." She allowed Leda to scold and fuss and summon servants, all the while reeling under the guilt of the woman's concern. Leda loved her and William so desperately. She wanted Sarah's happiness while she feared losing some of her love and attention to this woman now coming. Was that what the selfless love of a parent felt like?

By the time the last servant left and William was full and asleep in his iron crib, her mind still reeled.

She lay staring into the dark, her eyes burning, her stomach a knot of apprehension. Regret and trepidation ate at her soul. She'd been acutely aware of her eventual fate for weeks. She'd known this charade would end and she'd have to blindly make her way into the rest of her life. But she wasn't ready yet.

She still couldn't walk without a crutch. She couldn't even carry William and her bags and manage the crutch all at once, and certainly never long enough to make it to the train station.

Sleep eluded her through the night. Though exhausted, she welcomed William's predawn feeding because it gave her someone to talk to and soothed her chaotic thoughts. Her choices were limited.

She could leave right now. But what kind of life would William have if she ran off without a cent or a means to provide for him?

She could wait and let Claire's mother see her and have her whole masquerade revealed. That scenario didn't appeal either.

Or she could meet her at the station and speak with her

ahead of time. Maybe if she told her the truth and explained the situation, the woman would take pity on her.

By morning she'd settled on the least horrible of choices. She would take her chances with Claire's mother. But how would she learn her name? Had she ever heard Claire's last name? Surely she would have remembered. She would meet her at the station, but she'd have to know her name by then.

It was Sunday. Two days to learn it. And the only way she could think of was to go through the rest of Stephen's letters. Nicholas and Leda had said he'd written home about Claire, so her name would be mentioned. It was the best idea she could come up with.

On Monday morning, Sarah left William napping and made her way to Nicholas's suite. Stealthily, she replaced the letters she'd read and took the rest of the stack, making it back to her room undetected. It frightened her to realize how good she was getting at this treachery! Her need to cover her past sins had overcome her morals. Had it caused her to multiply her transgressions? How low would she sink before this was over?

That afternoon, while the baby slept again, she asked Mrs. Trent to check on the Cranes for her and used the time to read through the stack of letters.

Stephen's tone always came through lighthearted and carefree. Occasionally he mentioned something going on at home or expressed his affection for his mother, but most of his narrative detailed his current projects and friends and the places he'd visited.

After hearing Leda tell about Nicholas's hopes that his brother would come home and help, she had a bit more understanding of how Nicholas must have felt. He'd forgone his own education and desires to take over the foundry.

What all had he given up? As gruff and businesslike as

he seemed, it was hard to imagine him with hopes and dreams. And doubly hard to imagine him as an enamored young man. Had he given up someone he'd truly loved?

He'd seen to Stephen's education and well-being, all the while wanting the best for him, yet wishing he'd share the workload. Stephen's gay tales and unfettered life-style must have been acute reminders of Nicholas's own burdensome responsibilities.

The dates on the letters were months and months apart, as though Stephen wrote only when he could spare the time from his whirlwind social life. The last year or so he'd written five times, the next to the last one describing— Claire *Patrick.*

Sarah zeroed in on the name she'd sought.

Stephen had called her witty and charming, full of vivacious energy and the most beautiful woman he'd ever laid eyes on. Sarah groaned inwardly. No wonder Nicholas hadn't thought she matched the description of Claire.

The last letter announced their plans to marry. Folded into it were three telegrams, one telling of their marriage and planned trip to Europe and another announcing their arrival home.

For long minutes Sarah sat with that telegram in her hand. This was the last time Nicholas had heard from his brother. The brother he had loved and provided for. The brother he had wanted to see happy, yet had yearned to have share his burden.

Undoubtedly the fact that Stephen had married and was on his way to Mahoning Valley had raised Nicholas's hopes that he'd be staying.

The last telegram sent a chill up her spine.

We regret to inform you that there has been a train accident in New York State. Stop. Please come identify the body of your brother at the earliest possible time. Stop. Mrs. Halliday has been taken to the hospital in Newburgh. Stop. She is responding well to treatment and the baby is in excellent health. Stop.

Sarah visualized Nicholas holding this slip of paper, imagined the shock and the horror he must have experienced. She could almost feel what he felt, taste the grief and the anger. And his first thoughts would have included his mother. How would he tell her? How could she bear to lose her beloved Stephen?

With a heavy heart, she refolded the letters. *"A mother should never have to lose her child. Never,"* Leda had said fiercely. At no time had Sarah understood those words as clearly as she did at that moment. Leda had lost a daughter as an infant, and then a son in the prime of his life.

She stepped to the crib, straightened William's blanket, caressed his downy soft hair and assured herself that her son was well and secure as she'd planned. No matter what else, she'd seen to his well-being.

He was still all that mattered. If not for him she would tell Nicholas and Leda the truth that very day. Neither of them deserved the betrayal she'd delivered into their home. She loved them too much for that.

But even though she was much improved, she was still unable to care for him alone—

Love them? Was that what she'd thought?

Love them?

Who couldn't feel a deep affection for Leda? The devoted motherly woman held a place in the heart of all who knew her. Sarah barely remembered her own mother, and she'd come to respect the woman's sweet-voiced suggestions and to depend on her encouraging presence.

As the two women shared tea that afternoon, Sarah tried her best to assure Leda of her affection. Whatever happened, she would regret bringing another loss to the woman.

"Leda?" she said softly.

"Yes, dear."

"I want you to know that sharing William with you has been a blessing. You've made this difficult time not only bearable, but enjoyable."

Leda smiled in shy surprise.

"You've told me many times how much we mean to you. I want you to know how much you mean to William and me, too. You've been here for me when I needed a friend."

"It's been my pleasure."

"So you've often told me. That's why I wanted to tell you. And to tell you that I love you. Whatever happens in the days and weeks to come, remember above all that I do sincerely care for you and appreciate all you've done for me."

Leda took her hand. "I know that, dear."

Yes, she loved her.

But Nicholas? He'd barely said half a dozen civil words to her in the time she'd been there. He was mistrusting and hard-headed, unapproachable and narrow-minded, uncommunicative— She caught herself. If he was all those things, why had she just been empathizing with his grief and his feelings of love and frustration for his brother?

Because he was all those things...and he was more. So much more. She'd thought him remote and supercilious, but she'd seen his interaction with the servants. Her father would have fired Gruver on the spot for his foolish antics and replaced him with someone he could pay less wages to.

She'd seen Nicholas's puzzlement over his servants' play and his sad remembrance that his brother had once had fun like that. If Nicholas never had the opportunity to have fun, or had forgotten how, was he to blame?

And Nicholas had his reasons for being hard-headed and narrow-minded and mistrusting. After all, she was deceiving him. He was absolutely right about her—well, not that she'd married his brother to get to his money, but that she'd come here to take advantage of their ability to provide a home and food.

He treated his mother with tender affection and respect, it was true. He held his employees' safety in high regard. That side of him had been revealed, and it was commendable.

But love? But of course it must be the same familial fondness she felt for Leda. Devotion as toward a brother. She was playing the sister-in-law, after all.

Leda finished her tea and left, and Sarah's thoughts continued to whir. Her mind raced to that kiss they'd shared, and the feelings it had aroused in her. That was not the kiss of a brother-in-law.

If she closed her eyes now she could see his, dark and full of fire and caution. She could see his hands, steady and strong. On any other man, mundane tasks like opening a wine bottle or stoking a fire were colorless tasks, but when Nicholas's hands performed those tasks, the sight gave her an odd little stirring in her middle. Sometimes at night she dreamed of his hands, of his sensuous voice, a sound that sent a shiver across her flesh with its low, soul-piercing resonance.

Those were not impressions one had of a brother. She hadn't even experienced those self-torturing and humiliating thoughts about Gaylen, and he'd convinced her to forfeit her virginity to him! She would have married him!

That thought brought her up short. Had she *loved him?*

Perhaps his flight had been the best thing. One day she would have awakened to a miserable existence and realized she had never loved her husband. The fact that she'd never been as hurt by his rejection as her father's should have told her that long ago.

Sarah sighed, thinking of the letters she'd hidden in the bureau. She would have to return them in the morning before she went to the station to meet her fate at the hands of Mrs. Patrick.

Claire had been a lovely and generous person. She prayed that her mother was the same...and that Sarah would be able to help her deal with the news of her daughter's death.

Sarah had always considered herself an honest, compassionate person. The fact that she was playing havoc with these people's lives did not rest well with her. It was no surprise she spent another sleepless night.

Confident that she knew his daily habits, that she knew the servants' schedule, and familiar with the routine, Sarah hurried to Nicholas's room the following morning. The letters had provided a slim amount of information, and more details would have been appreciated.

This was the last time she would invade his quarters and his private possessions. Nicholas deserved her respect, yet she'd been nothing but dishonest and devious with him. Going through his room had been an added invasion, and she couldn't deal with the shame.

Sarah crossed the space, slid open the desk drawer and lowered the envelopes.

"Exactly what is it—"

A startled shriek escaped her.

"You think—" at her scream, he too jumped "—you're doing?"

Sarah placed her palm over her racing heart. She stared at Nicholas, drawing a blank.

Dressed in only a pair of black trousers, he strode to where she stood frozen. Unaccountably, her gaze fell to the thick black hair that curled on his broad muscled chest and arrowed into his waistband. The tawny, smooth expanse of his shoulders invited her gaze, and when he placed both hands on his hips, the movement accentuated the muscles of his upper arms and the corded strength in his forearms and wrists.

He leaned forward and her heart stopped.

Nicholas lowered his hand and grasped her wrist. Raising it, he brought the stack of letters firmly held in her paralyzed grasp to an inch below her nose. "What are you doing in here, and what are you doing in my things?"

The musky scent of his skin, combined with the spicy smell of shaving soap, teased her senses. Her shame and embarrassment at being caught blended with the sight and the smell of him to blur all other impressions and emotions.

His tobacco-dark gaze bored into hers, ire flaring in its depths. His grip on her wrist was just short of painful.

"There's nothing of any value in my writing desk, Claire. Except a mother-of-pearl-inlaid letter opener, but it's initialed. You might have trouble selling it around here."

Those words provoked her own anger and freed her tongue. "I'm not a thief," she objected firmly.

"Oh, really? Why else does one sneak about another's chamber when they believe the occupant is gone?"

"I was not stealing anything," she said, knowing she was in the wrong and swiftly losing courage. "I was replacing something."

"Replacing?" He frowned and pointedly slid a glance to the stack of letters in the hand he held prisoner. He knew immediately what she held, and his gaze came back to interrogate hers.

The pulse in Sarah's wrist throbbed beneath Nicholas's fingers. Her blue-eyed expression held a staggering amount of fear. What did she think he would do to her?

She moistened her full lower lip nervously with the tip of her tongue, leaving the pink flesh glistening. A faint trembling in her body registered at the point where he held her securely.

Stephen's letters? She'd taken Stephen's letters and was

replacing them? Why? "What had you hoped to find?" he asked.

She shook her head uncertainly.

"Did you find what you were looking for?"

Again she shook her head. Her gaze fell uncomfortably to his chest and skittered away to a point over his shoulder. Nicholas found it difficult to believe she was embarrassed by his state of partial undress, but the color in her cheeks proved it.

Her perfect peaches-and-cream skin amazed him still, as it had from the first time he'd studied her in the carriage on the way home. The clean, devastating scent of her hair reached his nostrils and drew his gaze to the riot of soft corkscrew curls framing her face and lying against her neck.

Everything about her was soft and feminine, from her upswept pale hair and the gray-tinged shade of blue in her eyes, to the way her clothing draped her lush body. The ever-present black of mourning lent her skin and hair a pale vulnerability that drew him like a fat bee to a particularly succulent clover.

He imagined her in something white or pastel, in delicate fabrics and loose-fitting styles.

She would fold against and wrap around a man like a billowy piece of heaven. The erotic thought quickened his traitorous body.

Almost as though she knew what he was thinking, her pulse tripped faster beneath his grasp. Her eyes widened and her lips parted.

"Why did you come in here?" he asked gruffly.

She blinked. "To return the letters."

"Why did you take them?"

"I wanted to read them."

"And how did you know where to find them?"

"It—it was only logical," she stammered.

Had she come in search of letters or had she been rifling

his room? Was she afraid Stephen had written about something she didn't want revealed? "And what did you hope to find in them?" he asked.

"I didn't know." Her voice had dropped to a near whisper.

"What did you find?"

"His enthusiasm," she replied, her voice unsteady. "His lack of regard for anything except his plays and his travel."

He eyed her suspiciously. "Until he met you, of course."

She carefully dropped her gaze to the desktop. "Of course."

In his preoccupation, had Stephen excluded Claire as well? Nicholas wondered. He found that difficult to believe. Their marriage had been the subject of his brother's last two letters, taking precedence even above his beloved plays.

Was it possible that Claire had learned Stephen's carefree nature the hard way? Once again Nicholas wondered if Stephen had been bringing her home because he was ready to settle down. Had this been a convenient layover until the baby came, or had he planned to leave her in Nicholas's care indefinitely?

The susceptible flesh of her slender neck drew him forward. A delicate pulse throbbed beneath the fragile surface. She'd been married to his brother but a few weeks, had slept with him before that. Stephen had found her alluringly beautiful and seductively desirable, just as Nicholas himself did.

But Stephen had never committed wholeheartedly to anything or anyone, and as much as Stephen might have desired her, might have loved her, he could never have given her the commitment and stability that Nicholas would have if—

If she were his...

The tiny lines at the corner of her too accessible mouth

had him imagining a smile on those lips. Had Stephen made her smile?

He relaxed his hold on her wrist, and the letters scattered across the top of the desk. She didn't lift her gaze, nor did she step away.

"When a woman comes to a man's room, she's looking for something more than a few letters." Impulsively, he leaned into the beckoning hollow in the curve of her neck, placed his lips and nose against her skin and inhaled.

Sensation zigzagged through his body, tightening his loins, loosening his grasp on coherent thought. Lord, she smelled wonderful: fresh and slightly flowery, and something more. Something elemental and powerful and wholesome.

He parted his lips and felt a shiver run through her body. He touched his tongue to her warm sleek skin, and a sigh escaped her lips, the heat puffing against his shoulder. His body tensed, nipples drawing tight, and the next instant her palm flattened against his chest. He'd never felt anything quite as wonderful or as exhilarating as her cautious touch.

She tasted as incredible as she smelled, faintly salty, faintly musky, but unique and feminine. Beneath his lips and tongue her blood pounded, evidence of her intense reaction to his nearness and the liberties he took.

A fierce possessiveness gripped Nicholas unexpectedly. He opened his mouth wide on her neck and suckled, flicking his tongue over the cords and tendons beneath the surface. She made a shuddering sound low in her throat and melted against him.

He wrapped both arms around her, one at her waist, the other across her back, and crushed her lush pliant body to his bare chest, relishing the press of her lavish breasts.

Pinning her shoulders with his elbows, he brought both hands up to her hair and plunged them into the mass of curls, bringing her head back and her face to his.

Their gazes met for the barest of moments, hers a wide-eyed look of surprise and anticipation.

He kissed her then, without an inch of space between their bodies, without a care as to her hair or her dress or the consequences. He kissed her with all the appallingly unrestrained need she made him feel.

The kiss was accusatory and inflammatory and as out of control as Nicholas had felt since he'd learned of her existence. It held all the frustration and carnal desire and all-absorbing passion he'd held back since he'd first seen her.

Body trembling, fingers curled into the hair on his chest, she kissed him back.

He touched her lips with his tongue, and hesitantly, she parted them so he could deepen the kiss.

Oh, her mouth was sweet. Her body set him on fire, and the plaintive sounds she made when he tilted his head and fitted their bodies closer, were sweet and erotic and enough to make a man lose control.

The thought of losing control registered briefly. Gently, he eased his mouth from hers, cupped her face and studied her through a haze of dauntless desire. Her lips were pink and gently swollen, her soul-reaching eyes filled with gem-like wonder.

Her palm still lay pressed against his chest. His heart skipped half a dozen much-needed beats she had to feel.

Her other hand rose between them and with one finger she tentatively touched his lower lip.

That seemingly innocent, yet sensual touch ignited more than desire within him. He raised her face, and this time when their lips touched it was with the utmost tenderness and sense-riveting awe.

He'd never kissed a woman like this before.

He'd known passion and fire and even eagerness.

But never a burning tenderness and breathless soul-squeezing hunger that disturbed and quenched, rent and restored all at the same time.

This woman confused and angered him and turned him inside out. And she did it all effortlessly, guilelessly, without plan or remorse.

And she probably did it every bit as well as she had with Stephen.

He wanted his brother's wife.

With bittersweet regret Nicholas ended the kiss. She steadied herself by grabbing his bare shoulder, the warmth a lingering reminder of her heat and vibrancy.

He wanted his brother's *conniving* wife.

Outrage at his helplessness and the futility of the situation rose to the surface.

Claire stared at him with uncertainty and doubt clouding her expression. What did she want from him? What did he have to give her?

The answer came swiftly. A home. The means to live comfortably and raise her child in style.

And she already had all that. Her position had never been in question—except perhaps to her. Maybe she thought securing Nicholas's affections would ensure her place.

"Next time you want something, come to me and ask for it," he said. "Don't snoop about like a thief."

Embarrassment, or perhaps guilt, darkened her already shadowed eyes. He couldn't hold her gaze and deliberately looked away.

It took every bit of fortitude he possessed to stem his anger and claim responsibility for what had just happened here. He would not blame her for his lack of control.

Though she hadn't seemed the least bit reluctant, it would not have happened if he hadn't allowed it.

No matter what he believed Stephen's faults were, Nicholas had no business entering into a liaison with his wife. But it galled the hell out of him that the first woman to stir him in a good many years had to be his brother's widow. And hardly the type of woman he would choose to bring home to his mother.

Claire was nothing at all like the kind of female he approved of or took a second look at. But in some relentless carnal manner, she was everything he desired.

The combination ate at his sanity. And worsened his temperament. Why she even shared his kisses he'd never understand. Unless she feared not to. Or unless it was a part of her plan.

The air grew tense. Nicholas drew in a renovating breath and stepped back.

Where would they go from here?

Chapter Nine

Sarah didn't know which fear was greater, her fear of Nicholas himself, or her fear of her feelings for him. Both had the power to destroy her.

Trembling, she backed away, the feel of his hands still in her hair, the scorching heat of his lips lingering on hers, her heart all but bursting from her chest in its tumultuous thumping.

If that was punishment, she'd gladly have died from it on the spot. Humiliation blistered her skin as effectively as leaping flames. She couldn't resist a glance at the lips she'd kissed, a look at the broad expanse of hair-covered chest she'd been pressed against only seconds before. His face and body were beautiful, his words cruel, and his actions a constant puzzle.

He drew her with his looks and his nearness and his heat, yet repelled her with distrust and cynicism. At least when Gaylen and her father turned her aside and spurned her, she'd known the finality of their intentions by their actions.

Nicholas had her head in a spin with his confusing words and his inconsistent behavior. He'd kissed her like a man starving for the taste of her, yet just as quickly, he'd ended it and seemed prepared to continue their encounter as though the kiss had never happened.

She had no defense for her actions, no explanation for being in his rooms. She stood before him at his mercy, praying he harbored a shred of compassion.

"Did you find what you wanted in Stephen's letters?"

She met his gaze for only the briefest of seconds. "Partially."

"Anything else you'd like while you're here?"

His sarcasm wasn't lost on her. She shook her head.

"Oh, come now, surely there's something else. Don't go away empty-handed."

Instantly the desire pounding through her veins freed itself in a new form. She had no right to feel anger toward him. None whatsoever. This was his home and these were his private rooms and possessions. Regardless, it welled up, a consuming rush of rage that started a new pulse in her veins. "All right," she said.

Gaining new courage, she looked up to find smugness in the glint of his deep brown eyes and the tilt of his freshly-shaven chin.

"I'd like the results of the search you did on my background."

His stony expression revealed nothing. "What makes you think I had your background checked out?"

"Everything I know about you."

He glared at her a minute longer. Had she gone too far? He was unpredictable and his emotions so deep she never knew where she stood with him. But he'd never harmed her. She didn't believe he would.

"Why would you want to see the file?" he asked. "You know who you are and where you came from."

She glanced away, idly noting a pigeon on the sill outside the window. "Because I want to know what *you* know, that's why."

From the corner of her eye, she saw him straighten, as though coming to a decision.

"Very well. I have business to attend to now, and you

have to go fetch your mother. But…I'll have the papers for you later.''

Sarah couldn't have been more surprised. She drew a blank for anything to say.

''Is that all?'' he asked. ''I need to finish dressing.''

''Yes, I—thank you.'' She turned and fled from the room as quickly as her leg allowed, not slowing her pace until she was safely ensconced in her rooms.

The cook had been practicing recipes all week. Nicholas and Gruver packed two crates with delectable meat and vegetable dishes, pastries and sweet breads, and loaded them into the carriage. Nicholas would take the excess food to the Cranes, rather than allow it to go to waste.

The plan also gave him the opportunity to call on his employee and see how the man was faring.

Thomas Crane greeted him at the door, his arm no longer wrapped against his side, but his ribs still obviously tender. A welcoming grin spread across the man's narrow face. ''Mr. Halliday! Come in.''

Nicholas and Gruver carried the cartons into the small house and placed them on the table, which had been draped with a colorful patchwork covering. The splash of color surprised Nicholas, and he glanced around, noting the bright orange kitchen curtains he could have sworn were satin.

Periwinkle blue swagged from the window in the other room. The fabrics were new and shiny, inexplicably out of place, yet adding a festive touch to the Cranes' otherwise drab home.

''Doc says another week, and I'll have this wrapping off and be good as new,'' Thomas said, pointing to his side.

''That's what I wanted to hear,'' Nicholas said with a smile.

''I didn't expect you,'' Thomas said, then turned and called for his wife.

She appeared in a doorway, carrying a tiny girl. When Nicholas saw the child wore a dress made of a deep purple sateen, he glanced at Gruver, then at Thomas, trying not to show his puzzlement.

A grin twitched at Gruver's lips. "I'll wait outside, sir," he said and left.

"Oh, Mr. Halliday!" Mary Crane lowered the child to the floor and self-consciously smoothed her hair into its neat bun. "Would you care for a cup of coffee or perhaps some tea?"

"I—" he started to object, but she cut him off.

"It'll be no problem. The water's hot. Do you like tea?"

"I do. That will be nice."

"Have a seat, then," she said, gesturing to the table. She moved to pick up a crate, but he stepped forward and placed them both where she instructed. He then settled himself at the table and Thomas gingerly sat across from him.

"I thought you might like to invite the other workers over and set out a feast," he said. "Our cook has been practicing on us, and I'm afraid she's gone overboard."

Mary placed three cups on the table, then peeked in the crates with a murmur of pleasure. "What a thoughtful idea!" she exclaimed. "We can have a party! I even have a pretty new dress!"

"That Mrs. Halliday is a blessing," Thomas said. "An angel of mercy, she is. Mary says prayers for her every night, don't you, Mary?"

His wife nodded enthusiastically. "Oh, I do."

"You give her our best," Thomas added.

"Mother?" Nicholas asked uncertainly.

"Of course, her, too," Mary said with a quick wave. "But Tom was referrin' to your sister-in-law."

"Claire?"

"Yes, sweet Claire," she replied. "Why, she came every day while I was down with the fever. She took care of the little ones, and when Elissa caught the fever, too, why Claire did everything a mother would have done for her.''

Nicholas stared at his empty cup.

''We're grateful for the food you sent, too, sir,'' Tom hastened to add. ''And the material she gave Mary to share with the other workers has given all the youngun's new clothes. They're so proud to show up to school in all those fine bright colors. Mary's been savin' her dress for something special, and now she'll have it.''

Mary Crane poured the tea.

Nicholas studied the squares of fabric she'd turned into a tablecloth. Claire had given her all this material?

A dim memory came to him. He'd been dealing with shock and grief at the time, but now he recalled opening the trunks that had been salvaged and stored by the railroad. Dozens of bright evening dresses with low-cut bodices and lingerie of mere lace had confounded him. That was when he'd locked the trunks, instructed the railroad to ship them home and asked the hospital nurses to buy her the clothing and items she'd need for the trip.

Mother had said something about Claire needing new clothing right away, and it had been logical. She'd packed for a honeymoon, after all, not mourning.

She'd given all her clothing to the iron workers' families?

That thought brought him back to the situation at hand. And she'd nursed Thomas's wife and child while they were ill. He felt like an idiot for not knowing. Why had she kept it a secret?

He drank his tea, exchanged pleasantries and hurried out to the carriage as soon as he could make his excuses.

''You knew about all that?'' he asked, jerking a thumb over his shoulder.

Gruver nodded, a smile hiding behind his rigidly controlled set of lips. ''I, uh, brought her here a few times, sir, and—'' he swiped a hand across his mouth ''—and I—uh, I carried the trunks in.''

''Why didn't anyone say anything to me?'' Nicholas asked with a scowl.

''Didn't figure it was my place, sir,'' his driver said, waiting with the carriage door open, his gaze on something in the cloud-filled sky.

''From now on I'd like a report of each place you take Mrs. Halliday.'' He stepped up into the carriage.

Gruver didn't close the door. ''Both Mrs. Hallidays, sir?''

''No, just the young Mrs. Halliday.''

''Yes, sir.''

The door closed, the carriage dipped as Gruver climbed aboard, and Nicholas idly studied the row of shabby houses his workers lived in. Why had Claire possessed all those outlandish dresses? If they were simply her tasteless preference, he'd love to know her reason for giving them all away.

And the fact that no one had told him of her saintly visits irked him to no end. That behavior, combined with finding her in his room this morning, made her as deserving of suspicion as he'd always believed. Claire was trying to pull something.

But what?

Sarah's head swirled with confusion until she could barely think what she was going to do next. Waiting for Gruver's return, she paced the width of the circular drive in front of the house, trying to ignore the ache in her leg, oblivious to the dark clouds gathering overhead.

Nicholas catching her in his room had been her worst nightmare come true. Her collapsing against his bare chest and kissing him had been better than any dream she'd ever had. But it still didn't make sense.

Oh, he'd been angry. Even his kiss had been angry. Why hadn't that repelled her? Why hadn't that stopped her?

Why had he done it?

Of all the days to have everything happen at once! Worry over Claire's mother coming had prevented her from sleeping for the past two nights. Sneaking into Nicholas's office once and his rooms twice had given her a false sense of confidence. She'd thought the return of the letters would pose no problem.

Actually, some tiny little speck of relief presented itself. She'd been discovered. He would never trust her. She'd never be able to do anything like that again.

And she never wanted to.

But the kiss. Lord, the kiss. The first time had been an accident, and could have been forgotten as a slip on both their parts. This one had been no accident. She'd seen it coming by the desire in his eyes and the aggressive stance of his body.

And she'd stepped right into it. Welcomed it.

Enjoyed it.

The sight of his bare torso had made her palms itch to touch him. His scent when he came near gave her the scandalous desire to wrap herself around him and mold herself to him and—

Sarah stopped pacing and placed her palms against her quivering stomach. What kind of woman was she that she desired the man so badly? She'd already gotten herself into more trouble than she'd been able to handle by allowing one man to override her common sense. She'd permitted shameful liberties with Gaylen. Had that and falling from her father's grace turned her into some kind of strumpet?

Her face flamed with shame. Was she one of those foolish women who thought she loved every man she'd ever known? Nicholas wasn't even lovable.

Her fluttering heart contradicted that thought.

She was an idiot to even be thinking of him with wanton

ideas at this moment. She was going to the train station to face the woman who could seal her fate with the Hallidays.

Could they have her thrown in jail for impersonating a family member? Would they?

The clomp of horses' hooves and jingle of harnesses alerted her to the elegant black carriage being drawn up the drive by a lustrous black team. Gruver jumped down and opened the door, lowering the steps. "Sorry I'm not on time, ma'am. Mr. Halliday got a late start this morning."

How well she knew! She accepted his hand. "I know, Gruver. We still have time." Before he could shut the door, she leaned forward. "Gruver. My leg is giving me a problem this morning. I don't know how much walking I can do on it. I'll need you to have a porter page Mrs. Patrick. Once you've located her, bring her to the carriage where I'll be waiting."

He tipped his hat. "Yes, ma'am."

The door closed and she leaned back, her heart hammering. The ride to the station was far too short, even though it was nearly an hour's drive. She rehearsed the words she would say when Claire's mother climbed in looking for her daughter.

Gruver left her waiting and went in search of their visitor. Sarah feared she would faint or throw up. She opened the shade and gulped in heavy, rain-laden air. Beneath her uncomfortably stiff corsets and black gabardine suit, she perspired.

The black bonnet would keep the woman from seeing her face until she'd been settled and Gruver had climbed aboard and pulled them away from the station.

She heard the porter's page. His voice rose above the other station sounds and rang in her head like a death knell.

She peered into the throng of people on the platform, heard the hiss of steam from an engine. The sound of crashing metal and the lurching sensation of that awful night came back to her in a rush, and she closed her eyes against a sense of vertigo.

Forcing herself to breathe deeply, she didn't open her eyes until she'd quashed the nightmarish memories. Two men in black with an oddly draped form between them broke apart from the crowd, and Sarah hurriedly latched the leather shade and sat back against the seat.

Boots on cinders outside alerted her to their nearness. Her stomach quaked.

The door opened.

She looked at her lap.

Someone grunted.

Another male voice grunted, and a strained curse followed.

Fabric rustled, the carriage rocked, and Gruver's black-clad rear end appeared directly in front of Sarah's face.

At that she looked up.

He had backed into the carriage and, with both hands under the woman's arms, pulled her inside while a profusely sweating black porter tried to wrestle her limp legs through the opening.

Was the woman dead?

Sarah stared at their awkward burden. Gruver's hat fell off, and the porter stepped on it as he got her lower body inside the coach. They hauled her onto the opposite bench, and situated her there, her legs stacked on the leather seat, one arm fallen and her hand nearly touching the floor.

Immediately the porter backed out. Gruver stepped to the stairs, picked up his hat and, winded, used his thumbs to pop out the crown.

The woman's hat hung to one side, her gray-shot wild red hair tangled in the ribbons. Her mouth gaped open, and an unladylike snore gusted forth. The smell of liquor assailed Sarah all at once, and she gaped from the drunken woman to Gruver.

He appeared decidedly embarrassed—for her!

He thought this was her mother, of course.

Sarah looked at her again, trying to see some resemblance to the young woman she'd met so briefly on the train. Same brassy red hair. Same pale, freckled skin.

Claire's mother was *intoxicated!*

"Uh, I'm sorry, Gruver. Is the porter still out here?"

He glanced aside. "Yes, ma'am."

She fished in her reticule and pulled out a few coins. "Tip him, please."

Gruver took the money.

A minute later, the sounds of luggage being strapped on the back became evident. Mind awhirl, she stared at the unconscious woman. Gruver placed the step inside, his worried gaze darting to their passenger, and closed the door.

The rank smell of liquor drifted to Sarah and turned her stomach. Perhaps the poor thing didn't travel well and drank to dull the experience. Her unconscious state didn't suggest someone who'd had a few nips for the road, however. But it could be worse, she assured herself. At least no one but Gruver had seen her like this.

After nearly an hour of listening to her irritating snore, they arrived home.

Gruver appeared in the doorway in his misshapen hat, a look of dread on his face. "Upstairs?"

"I'm afraid so," she replied. "I'm so sorry," she said again.

"It's not that she's fat or nothin', ma'am," he said. "It's just that she's such—"

"Deadweight?"

He nodded.

"If there were some other way..." she said. "But I don't want to leave her here—or downstairs—until Nicholas comes home."

"No," he agreed sympathetically. "Don't you worry,

Mrs. Halliday. I can get her, and Mr. Halliday will never have to know."

"Thank you, Gruver."

She helped him maneuver her out of the coach and as far as the foyer. There, he shot Sarah an apologetic glance before awkwardly hoisting the woman over his shoulder. He clamped both forearms securely beneath her ample derriere and carried her up the stairs, her head and arms dangling, her hat flopping.

Sarah raced ahead to the room they'd prepared, and flung open the door. Mrs. Patrick landed none too gently on the mattress seconds later.

Gruver straightened and grimaced, the back of one hand in the hollow of his back, and watched Sarah remove the woman's shoes. "I think I'll rest a few minutes before I bring the trunks up."

"Of course! Bless you! I'll see that Penelope and Mrs. Pratt fix you something special for dinner—for the rest of the week."

He grinned and backed from the room.

Sarah turned and stared at Claire's mother in abject horror. Now what?

By late afternoon, the woman still hadn't awakened, and Nicholas's other guests began arriving. The Gallamores arrived first: Monty and Ellen, a couple in their sixties. Sarah had them settled just as Mrs. Pratt announced the Kleymanns. Quinn was several years older than Kathryn, and they were expecting their first child.

Monty Gallamore and Quinn Kleymann ensconced themselves in Nicholas's study, and their wives rested from their trips.

Sarah was in the kitchen double-checking on dinner when Nicholas arrived unannounced.

"Evenin', Mr. Halliday," Mrs. Pratt and Penelope chorused. They'd hired extra help for the week, and two new women studied Nicholas surreptitiously. He obviously held a reputation in his town.

"Good evening. Have the guests all arrived?" he asked Sarah.

"The McCauls aren't here yet, but the others are settled. The gentlemen have been in your study most of the afternoon."

"And your mother?"

She tasted the soup and complimented Mrs. Pratt before replying. "I'm afraid she's under the weather."

"She's ill? Is it something contagious?"

"No. It's not contagious. She should be fine by tomorrow. Or at the very least the next day."

"Is she prone to these spells?"

"Lord, I hope not."

"What?"

"No. She'll be just fine. It's just that—she doesn't travel well. See to your guests. I have everything under control."

"You're sure?"

"I'm sure. Dinner will be served precisely at eight."

He glanced around the kitchen. "*Nothing* had better go wrong."

"Your confidence is rewarding."

He shot her one last glance and left.

Sarah turned to Penelope. "I'd like to leave a tray in my mother's room in case she wakes. Perhaps just biscuits and jam or something that will keep. And coffee. Lots of black coffee. I'll take it up."

Penelope fixed the tray.

"Did Gruver tell you about my mother?" she asked from close beside her.

"Yes, ma'am. I won't tell Mr. Halliday."

"Thank you. Will you check on her from time to time, then?"

"I will. I'll have a headache powder for her, too."

Sarah gave her a grateful smile and took the tray.

Mrs. Patrick hadn't moved a muscle that she could tell. Sarah set the tray nearby, added a log to the fire and hurried to her room to get ready.

The extra maids had brought hot water and towels to all the occupied rooms, so she spared the time for a quick bath, hoping to feel refreshed. She'd only seen poor William long enough to feed him all day, and took a few minutes to cuddle and talk to him.

"Did Leda visit William today?" she asked Mrs. Trent.

"Mrs. Halliday never misses a morning or an afternoon," she replied. "He will be the most spoiled child in all of Ohio."

"Good." She dressed in one of her loveliest bustled fashions, sick to tears of black, and wishing she had something to relieve the tediousness. She clasped on her emerald bracelet and pinned a lacy white handkerchief to her breast in a fan shape.

Hurrying to Leda's door, she rapped and at the soft reply, entered. "I've missed you," she said honestly.

Leda was just slipping on her shoes. "Did you have a grand reunion with your mother?" she asked, accepting Sarah's brief hug.

"I'm afraid not. She's quite ill."

"Oh, dear. Here I left you both alone to visit. I should have seen if there was anything I could do."

"No, there wasn't. There isn't. She'll be better tomorrow."

"Whatever do you think is wrong?"

"Probably the train ride. I know I get sick just hearing the steam or a whistle now."

"That fear will pass with time," Leda assured her. "Let me know if there's anything I can do to help with her care. I won't have you working yourself sick. I've already warned you. Do you like this dress? I am sick of wearing drab colors," she admitted. "I wore black for ever so long after Templeton died, and now again."

"It's a lovely dress."

"I don't carry off black quite like you do, though I can't wait to see you in something else. Isn't it strange the things we do for the sake of appearance? I have a rebellious streak," she whispered, leaning into Sarah. "See?"

Leda raised her black skirt to expose a bright red petticoat. "Shocked?"

Sarah laughed. "Not at all. I am wondering, though, why we didn't order one of those for me. Shall we greet our guests?"

Sarah locked her arm through Leda's and they strolled downstairs to the formal parlor where drinks and appetizers had been laid out.

The Kleymanns were already seated on a divan. Quinn stood. "Good evening, ladies."

Leda and Kathryn had met before and exchanged pleasantries.

"We haven't had a chance to tell you before how sorry we are about your son," Quinn said, and then turning to Sarah, "and your husband."

"Yes, none of us is quite the same," Leda replied. "It's as if a part of me is missing. Just like when my Templeton passed on. But then that pain lessened with time...I'm sure this one will, too."

No one spoke for a few minutes.

"I do hope we'll get to meet your son soon," Kathryn said, and Sarah looked over to see she was speaking to her. "I've been looking forward to it."

"We'll have his nurse bring him down after dinner," Leda said. "He is a handsome fellow. He will make you eager for your little one."

"Oh, I know that," Kathryn replied with a smile. "I'm already eager."

Quinn cast her a loving smile and placed his hand over hers, and a niggle of envy dipped in Sarah's chest. It was replaced by sadness when she remembered the last time she'd felt just this way: when Stephen and Claire had looked at each other and he'd spoken to her so lovingly. She'd thought then what a lucky baby they were having. What a lucky woman Claire was.

But that hadn't been so at all. Fate had stepped in.

Or was she wrong in thinking that way? Yes, their lives had been cut short. Their child had never even taken his first breath. But they'd all been loved so much and they'd all left this earth together. As a family.

Leda must have sensed her heavy-heartedness, or perhaps she'd let it show on her face, because the older woman took her hand and pulled her down to sit on a divan beside her. Sarah thought of the red petticoat, and her mood lightened.

Gruver appeared in the doorway just then. "The McCauls have arrived, Mrs. Halliday."

Sarah started to stand, but Leda pulled her back down. "I'll see that they're settled. You stay."

Sarah gave her a warm smile of gratitude.

"She thinks the world of you," Kathryn said after Leda excused herself. "I think you're just what she needed."

"Well, the feeling is mutual," Sarah replied.

"I hope you and my wife will have some private time together," Quinn said. "Katy is too loyal to complain, but she doesn't have many young friends, and I think she's dying to ask you a hundred questions."

"We'll make some time together," Sarah assured them both. Not that she knew the least helpful thing to tell the poor woman. She'd been alone and frightened when she'd been pregnant, and unconscious when William had come into the world. Perhaps the older women were Kathryn's best choices for confidantes.

Nicholas and Milos appeared then, and the conversation changed to the upcoming storm and the lack of rain for the season. The McCauls joined them as they entered the dining room, and Nicholas made introductions.

The staff had outdone themselves, and Sarah observed that even Nicholas was impressed with the fare and the service.

"Why don't we gentlemen retire for a smoke, and then we'll join you lovely ladies in the parlor," Nicholas suggested.

Pleasantly full from an exquisite dinner, the party moved to the foyer where the men started toward Nicholas's study.

A sound at the top of the stairs apparently alerted the men, for one by one they turned back. A loud voice singing an off-key version of "Buffalo Gals" echoed down the curved marble stairway. The hair on the back of Sarah's neck stood up, and she looked up in horror.

Oh, no! Good Lord, no! Not now! Not like this!

"—won'tcha come out tonight, come out ton-night!"

The silence among the guests at the bottom of the stairs seemed as loud as the squalling from the woman at the top. She appeared on the stairs, her step unsteady, wearing a bright green satin dress with a matching bow on her mop of flaming frowsy orange curls. She flipped her skirts and attempted a cancan, revealing a revolting length of veined and freckled calves and knees, as well as the fact that her shoes didn't match.

Panic roared in Sarah's ears. Not only was the woman awake, but she was still drunk—or drunk again! What on earth would she do when she discovered Claire wasn't here? Sarah had considered locking her in the room, but the thought had seemed too cruel and too unsafe. But now...

Mrs. Patrick descended a step unsteadily, her song ending, her eyes narrowing as she tried to focus on her rapt audience below. "Where's Claire?" she called, her voice cracking.

Here it came.

One by one, Sarah sensed each head turn in her direction, and she allowed her gaze to scan the faces, their expressions ranging from shock on their guests' and amusement on Milos's to sympathy on Leda's and—outrage on Nicholas's.

The skin against his starched white collar turned a livid red. His eyes bored into Sarah's with scathing intensity.

Sarah wanted to vomit. She didn't know if that frightened little sound of alarm had escaped her lips or if it had been inside her roaring head.

She glanced up at Claire's mother once again, foolish regret gripping her. She should have stayed with her. Should have assigned one of the servants to her. What had seemed like unprofitable use of their time only a few hours ago, now would have made all the difference in the world.

She should have bolted the door.

What would Mrs. Patrick say to Nicholas—in front of all these people?

Sarah met his eyes again and his fury permeated to the very depths of her pathetic and doomed soul.

He had warned her.

And it was worse than even he could have imagined.

Sarah's days in Mahoning Valley were numbered.

Chapter Ten

As though in a slower-than-life motion, with all other sounds faded into the background, Sarah watched in horror as Claire's mother reached one of the landings and stumbled toward the banister where an enormous fern sat in a ceramic pot on the oak ledge that was part of the banister's decoration.

From the servants' hall below, Penelope appeared, laden with a silver tray and tea service. She caught sight of the throng of guests and paused hesitantly.

Just as Penelope glanced upward to view the subject of everyone's riveted attention, Claire's mother tripped and slammed against the base of the blue and white container. The leaves shimmied. The pot turned over. And the weight of the plant propelled it over the side of the banister.

The women gasped.

Nicholas lunged forward, snagging the servant across the front of her chest and knocking her over. She fell to the floor beside him, the silver service banging across the tiles.

The huge planter careened to the foyer floor and smashed with a deafening crash of ceramic pot and imported floor tiles. Shards shot in all directions, and black dirt and pebbles spread in a starburst spatter, showering Nicholas and the stunned Penelope, and reaching the toes of the horrified guests.

One of the women next to Sarah emitted a squeal.

Sarah couldn't move for what seemed an eternity. The deafening sound still echoed in her ears. From above came slurred laughter and a loud "Whoops-ie!"

The woman had fallen in an undignified and embarrassing spraddle-legged sprawl on her fanny and elbows, her skirt hiked around her fleshy thighs, her bright hair and the ridiculous bow askew. As if in a daze, she blinked and blew a hank of disheveled hair from her face. One shoe dangled from her toes.

If Sarah could have had one prayer answered immediately in her entire lifetime, it would have been the one right then and there to have the floor open up and swallow her whole.

Nicholas assisted Penelope to her feet and they brushed dirt from their clothing. Nicholas leaned forward and ruffled his hair. Particles fell out and bounced on the floor.

Sarah couldn't face him or his guests or his mother.

Forcing her numb legs and feet into action, she gathered her skirts and climbed the stairs as quickly as her tender leg would carry her.

The murmur of Leda's soothing voice rose, taking control of the situation with the guests, urging them on to the activities they'd planned.

One of the men chuckled.

The horrible woman looked up as Sarah approached. Sarah converged on her before she could say or do anything more. She'd already caused enough damage. Wanting nothing more than to grab her around the throat and squeeze the air from her, Sarah took her firmly by one arm and urged her to her feet and up the stairs.

"What the hell—" the woman objected.

"Hush, Mrs. Patrick," she shushed her. "You've made

enough of a spectacle of yourself already. You're going back to your room."

They'd reached the upper hall, away from the eyes and ears of those below. The woman jerked away from her. "Where is my daughter?" she asked. "I came to see my daughter."

Sarah pushed her along the hallway. "How would you even know if you've reached the right place? You've been drunk or passed out since you arrived."

"Ain't I at the right place? Ain't this the Hallidays'?"

"Yes, it's the Hallidays'." They reached the lavender room, and Sarah guided her in and closed the door.

The woman made her way over to the bottle on the stand beside the bed and poured a tumbler half-full, sloshing liquor on the wooden furniture.

Sarah grabbed a towel and wiped it up.

"So, where's Claire?"

"I have something to tell you about Claire, but I can't tell you like this."

"Like what?"

"Like—" Sarah gestured at her "—*this*. Like you are."

"And how am I, sweetie?"

"You're *drunk!*"

She took a long swallow. "Hell, this ain't drunk. I still know what I'm doin'."

Sarah shook her head in frustration, thinking of Penelope's close call, Nicholas's anger and Leda's embarrassment.

"So where's Claire?"

Sarah gave her a long assessing stare. What would happen if she took all the liquor and came back when the woman was sober? It could be worse. She'd heard of men who went berserk when they couldn't get drink. And the woman did have to learn about her daughter.

"Mrs. Patrick, I think—"

"Celia."

"What?"

"My name's Celia. Or Cele. But don't call me Mrs. Patrick."

"All right, Celia. I'm afraid I have some very bad news for you about Claire."

Celia dropped onto the edge of the bed. "I knew it. The no-good bastard dropped her like a hot potato, didn't he?"

Sarah blinked. "Who?"

"Stephen Halliday, the great playwright, of course. Who else did she marry?"

"Well—no one that I know of. No, he didn't drop her, Celia...Stephen is dead. Didn't you know that?"

"Yeah, I knew. I thought maybe he ditched her once they got back to the States or somethin'."

"Why would he do that?"

"We ain't exactly cut from the same cloth," she said with a smirk, and Sarah remembered Claire saying the same thing when she spoke of her concern about the Hallidays not liking her. Perhaps her mother had instilled that fear in her.

"My Claire's a pretty thing," she went on. "Great legs. Knocked her up, he did."

Sarah looked aside in disgust.

"I figured he'd take his jollies until she was fat, and then he'd look for somethin' new."

"Well, he didn't," Sarah said with increasing irritation. "He loved her very much."

Celia snorted into her booze. "So what's the bad news, then? Squander all his money, did he?" She set the glass down with a thunk. "Who are you, anyway?"

"That's what I need to talk to you about."

"Well, I guess I ain't goin' anywheres. Talk." She sat on the bed and flopped against the headboard.

Slowly, carefully, Sarah began by explaining her situation. She told Celia how she'd been riding the train westward in hopes of a job and somewhere to stay where she could have her baby and find work. She explained about meeting Stephen and Claire. And she told how she'd awakened in the hospital with the doctor and nurses calling her Mrs. Halliday and how it had all snowballed from there.

Celia stared at her with blurry eyes, drunk, but cognitive. She squinted hard at Sarah. "What are you sayin', girl?" She sat up straight. "Are you sayin' what I think you're sayin'?"

She lunged to the edge of the bed and refilled the glass, taking several fortifying gulps.

"I'm afraid I am," Sarah said plaintively. "Claire died in that train wreck."

"What about her—her body?" the woman asked, with a jerky motion of her head.

"I have no way of knowing," she confessed, all the guilt and anguish brought vividly to life. "Stephen was found and Nicholas had to identify his body and send him home for burial. If no one was looking for Claire's body since they all thought I was her, I don't know what happened to her."

"What about your old man? Would they have known you were on the train?"

Sarah nodded. "My luggage was in the baggage car. I had papers and books that would identify the belongings, and they would have shipped them to my father. I think."

"Maybe they sent her body to him, thinking she was you."

Sarah hadn't thought of that before. Maybe her father thought she was dead! Maybe he thought that was what she'd deserved.

"How can you even be sure Claire's dead?"

Sarah studied her now, reading the numbed awareness. "If she were alive she would have contacted you or the Hallidays. Wouldn't she?"

Celia nodded, tears glittering in her already glassy eyes. The hand holding the tumbler trembled. "She was good to me. She loved me. I was a rotten mother, but she loved me.''

Sarah didn't know how she could feel pity for the woman after what she'd done earlier, but sympathetic tears prickled behind her eyes.

"Ya know I ain't really surprised?" she said. "I had a horrible feeling about all of it—her marryin' him, all of it. I knew nothin' good was gonna come of it. She went and got herself killed."

"The train crash was an accident, Mrs. Patrick. It was a terrible thing, and many lives were lost, but it was just an accident. No one had any control over it or knew it would happen."

"Don't call me that, I said. Pattie was a no-account son of a bitch, and I'd like to forget he ever existed."

"I'm sorry. Celia. And I'm sorry about Claire. She was one of the kindest people I've ever met. Really."

Celia's face scrunched up and her shoulders shook for several heart-stopping moments. It was a wonder how this woman had produced a daughter like Claire. Sarah considered whether or not to cross over and put her arms around her, but Celia's face and back straightened before she could decide.

"I wasn't cut out to be no grandmother, anyhow," she said, her voice low-pitched, and Sarah couldn't argue with that one. "Wasn't cut out to be no mother, neither. But Claire woulda been a good mother."

Sarah nodded.

"She took care of me, she did." She teared up again and blubbered into her liquor. "Who's gonna take care of me now?"

Sarah stared at her in shock. Her meal ticket was gone! Was that all she thought of her daughter? And now she cried over who would take care of her—meaning supply the money for her indulgence. She bit her tongue. And thought.

For nearly half an hour, Celia swung between bouts of tears and self-pity and feeble anger. Celia's behavior wasn't a one-time thing, she concluded. She was a drunk, pure and simple, and until Claire had married Stephen, she'd taken care of her as best she could.

The tears Sarah had mistaken for tears of grief were tears of self-pity. All Celia cared about was where her next bottle came from. Maybe somewhere inside was a lovable person, for Claire had loved her, but her lifetime relationship with the bottle had destroyed that woman somewhere.

Celia was exactly what Nicholas believed Sarah herself was. And Sarah was going to help hide it from him.

"Well," she said, finally knowing how to reach her. "I can take care of you as long as I'm here."

Celia blinked up at her.

"As long as they think I'm Claire, they'll think it's normal for me take care of you."

The woman's eyes narrowed. "Yeah?"

Sarah hated herself for adding more deception to the already staggering amount she'd amassed. But what were a few more weeks added on?

"You mean I could stay here?" Bleary-eyed, she glanced around the room.

It had to be the grandest place the woman had ever seen—not to mention the food was excellent and the liquor free. "For a while, anyway," Sarah replied. "As long as they think I'm Claire."

"That'll be a stretch, for sure," Celia said, looking her over.

Sarah held her ground and met her eyes.

"But not impossible."

"You'll stay up here when you're drinking," she said, laying out the conditions. "Which will obviously be the greater percentage of your time."

Celia snorted.

"You very nearly killed one of the servants down there,

you humiliated the Hallidays in front of important business clients and you made a fool of yourself. You will stay in this room unless I say you can go downstairs or out. If you stop drinking, however, that's a different story.''

Celia leaned her head back and looked at Sarah through half-slitted eyes. ''You know, maybe it won't be so hard to pretend you're Claire, after all.''

After saying that, her chin quivered. ''That girl loved me, she did.''

''Do we have an understanding, then?''

''You're Claire. I stay right here until you let me out, sweetie.''

Could she trust her to stay put? ''You go out there,'' she said, pointing to the door, ''and let it slip, and we'll both be kicked out of here. Maybe you can go back to where you came from, but I can't. It doesn't appear to me you could hold a job, so you'd just better stay put.''

''I'm a drunk, sweetie, not an idiot. I'll stay here and have my own private party. I do like to read the newspaper. Could I get papers, do ya think?''

''I'll see that the papers are sent up each day after Mr. Halliday reads them. I believe he receives several. They should keep you busy.''

''What about—you know—*them?*''

''The Hallidays?'' Sarah's heart skipped a beat at the thought of facing them. ''I'll talk to them. I'll apologize.''

''Act real ashamed of me. That always gets 'em.''

Sarah turned away. As if Claire had ever had to act! What the poor girl must have gone through she could only imagine. Sarah had always felt robbed of a mother, especially after learning to know and love Leda, but having a mother like Celia would be...exceedingly *difficult,* to say the least. ''I left biscuits and jam here for you. Eat them and drink the coffee. I'll have fresh tea sent up.''

''See what kinda booze the rich people stock, will ya? I might as well drink in style, too.''

Sarah eyeballed her with disgust and left the room.

Gruver was sweeping dirt and rock from the foyer floor when she descended the stairs. He'd already hauled away the pieces of the broken crock. He looked up, and an expression of empathy crossed his features.

Sarah stepped closer and studied the cracked and broken floor tiles with a sick feeling in her stomach. "How many of them are ruined?"

"Looks like five. Mrs. Pratt said these were imported from Italy back when the old Mr. Halliday had the house built."

She caught herself biting her lip. "I wonder if they'll be replaceable?"

He shook his head. "I don't know."

"What about the pot?"

"That was something Mrs. Halliday brought back from a trip to India."

"Oh, great." She wrung her hands. "Gruver?"

He looked up.

"I'm going to need your help."

"Anything, ma'am."

"Celia—don't call her Mrs. Patrick by the way—mustn't be allowed out of her room unless I'm with her. I can't take the chance of anything like this happening again—or something worse next time."

"I'll alert the staff," he said in understanding. "We'll take turns seeing that she's kept out of the way."

"Thank you. Has tea been served to the guests?"

He affirmed that it had.

"All right. See to it the new help knows the procedure for preparing the guests' rooms for night, and that it's taken care of before they retire."

"Yes, ma'am. Ma'am?"

"Yes, Gruver?"

"His bark is worse than his bite, Mr. Halliday's, and just

you keep in mind he's an honorable man. He always does the right thing.''

The right thing in this case would be to toss her out on her ear, and her baby with her. That drunken woman up-stairs had more right to be here than she did; *she* was Claire's real mother, after all. "I'll remember that. Thank you."

Somehow, she had to save Nicholas's reputation with his friends and clients. She smoothed her skirts and paused in the servants' hall to check her hair in the mirror. Her curly mop was hopeless as usual, a few tresses wilder than nor-mal, but nothing she could fix without going to her room and starting over. Her cheeks didn't need pinching. She looked as though she'd stood in the sun all day.

Resigned, Sarah straightened her shoulders, ignored the throbbing at her temples and in her leg and headed for the formal parlor.

Nicholas refilled the men's brandy snifters and motioned for Mrs. Pratt to freshen the ladies' tea. Jane Marie McCaul had accepted a glass of sherry, but declined a refill.

The conversation had been stilted since the fiasco in the foyer. He burned with ire at the scene Claire's mother had created in front of his guests, and hadn't done much himself to improve the atmosphere. Mother, bless her, had valiantly apologized and moved them into the parlor.

Kathryn and Jane Marie discussed a play they'd seen in London the season before. Nicholas observed his guests moodily, wishing he could charge up those stairs, jerk those women from whatever they were doing and set them straight.

He'd expected nothing better from someone who came from Slay Street. But he'd expected Claire to keep her seedy background and her lush of a mother from his guests. She'd known what could happen, and she should have been prepared. If she'd alerted him or the servants, they could have prevented the calamity.

The thought of tearing up those stairs and giving her a piece of his mind struck him more than once.

Leaning against the mantel, he sipped his brandy. From the corner of his eye, he caught a movement and turned his head.

Claire entered the room with a swish of black satin, her limp more pronounced than usual as the evening grew long. Her cheeks were flushed a becoming rosy shade, and she appeared breathlessly lovely, as though she'd just danced a waltz instead of dealing with a drunken mother.

Having the guts to show herself to his guests, to him, was more than he'd anticipated. Nicholas fought the spark of admiration that flickered.

One by one, the others tried not to make an issue of her arrival, but gave up and glanced uncomfortably from one Halliday to the other.

Leda started to stand and go to her, but Claire halted her with the palm of her hand and a soft command. All eyes focused on Claire.

"I'd like to take responsibility for what happened earlier," she said, her voice a little quavery. "I'm quite embarrassed. I don't wish for my mother's behavior to reflect on Nicholas in any way. He had no idea that she has a drinking problem."

She glanced solicitously toward him, and he continued to stare.

"I won't apologize for her. She's been that way, well, for a long time. Since my—father died. But I apologize for my lack of responsibility, and the fact that I should have taken better care. I know Mrs. Gruver could have been seriously hurt or killed." Her voice cracked on that word. "I can assure you that the rest of your stay will not be interrupted with any further unpleasantness."

She looked at Leda. "Nicholas and Mrs. Halliday have been nothing but kind and gracious to me and my son. I owe them a great deal, and I'm sorry to have let them down.''

Her voice had grown soft. Those enormous blue eyes turned directly to him. ''I hope you all can find it in your hearts to forgive me.''

Nothing could have taken the wind out of his sails faster. He detested being caught off guard. He hated not being in control of a situation. And this one was totally in her hands. She'd just won the hearts and the sympathy of each person in the room with her sincere voice and those big watery eyes.

It was damned near impossible to resist a plaintive appeal like that.

He'd appear the heel if he drew out her anguish. Oh, she was a sly one: confront him before all these people so he couldn't rant and rave as he desired. The words and the fury boiled deep inside him.

And admitting her transgression right out loud to everyone concerned! Refusing to accept responsibility for her mother's problem, but assuming liability for the woman herself. Clever.

Milos cleared his throat, an obvious call to action on Nicholas's part.

Leda did get up then, and rush over to enfold her daughter-in-law into her cushioned embrace. ''We're going to forget all about it, arcn't we?'' she said, hooking her arm around Claire's waist and leading her forward. She ran a persuasive eye over each of the guests.

They nodded and made appropriate sounds of agreement.

His mother's intent gaze fixed on him, and Nicholas knew he'd been bested. He gave a curt nod.

Leda beamed and urged Claire to sit on the love seat beside her. Claire arranged her skirts, and slanted him a dubious glance. She knew it wasn't settled with him. But she'd gracefully saved face for all concerned.

''Mrs. Pratt, will you have Mrs. Trent bring William

down to meet our guests now?'' Leda turned from instructing the servant to speak to Kathryn. ''Just wait until you see our precious boy. He and Claire have brightened the Halliday house. I don't know what I'd do without them.''

Once Mrs. Trent brought William, the women gathered around him and spoke in silly voices and oohed and aahed. The men drew off to one side, and a discussion of shipping prices ensued.

Ellen Gallamore spilled tea on her skirt, and Claire hurried to bring a damp cloth. Nicholas trapped her as she returned it to a tray in the hallway.

''We are not finished discussing what happened by any means,'' he said, grasping her wrist.

She brought her startled blue gaze to his face, the high color draining from her cheeks. Her attention deliberately dropped to his mouth, and he could have sworn the pulse under his fingers leaped. ''All right,'' she said. ''Would you like me to come to your study later?''

''I have no idea how late the others will remain up,'' he said. ''My study is open to the men at all hours.''

One pale brow rose in question.

''I'll come to your room. Wait up for me.''

She nodded her consent. Her gaze dropped away.

Nicholas released her wrist and she hurried back into the room.

He would have to be careful not to touch her like that. Not to get close enough to see the fire in her eyes or smell the arousing scent of her skin and hair.

Even when he was angry with her, even after she'd allowed her mother to humiliate him, even though he saw through her manipulations, she set him on fire. Allowing himself to weaken would be a terrible mistake.

Yes. He would have to be careful.

Chapter Eleven

After a day's work and an evening of entertaining, Nicholas grew ready to call it a night long before his gentlemen guests. They finally left him and headed upstairs, and he threw open the drapes and the remainder of the study windows to air the now stuffy room.

The men would be traveling to Youngstown with him in the morning, and daybreak would come all too soon. He climbed the stairs, determined to take Claire to task without further endangering his resolve.

Carrying a large envelope, he tapped lightly on her door. Mrs. Trent and the baby would be sleeping. She opened the portal immediately and stepped back.

Nicholas strode into the room, which smelled like her, and cursed himself for coming to her on her ground.

No! He pulled his thoughts together. There was no "her ground" here. This was *his* home, every inch of it! She had only as much as he allowed her.

Guiltily, he walked forward. She was Stephen's wife. She had as much right to the house as he did. He only bolstered his flagging confidence by telling himself otherwise.

"Do you mind if I sit?" she asked.

He turned. Her pale face revealed her weariness. She lowered her gaze to the envelope as he replied, "No."

She sank into one of the wing chairs and raised her foot to the upholstered stool.

He glanced down. She wore both shoes. He hadn't paid attention until now. "You got the cast off."

"The other day."

He could see her stockings above her shoes, one ankle visibly larger than the other. "Your foot. It's swollen."

"It does that after being on it all day."

"You should have removed your shoes."

"I knew you were coming."

He'd told her to wait up, and of course she hadn't undressed. He felt like an absolute beast. He set the packet of papers aside, leaned over to unlace her soft-soled shoe and raised her foot. She drew in a breath.

"Did I hurt you?"

She shook her head, her lips in a strained line.

He removed the slipper, gently lowered her foot to the cushion and did the same to the other. "You should have put some ice on it."

"I sent the servants to bed. They have to be up early."

He thought of the melting ice in the silver bucket in his study. "I'll be right back."

He returned with the bucket, poured ice into a towel and wrapped it around her ankle. "Better?"

She had closed her eyes and leaned her head back. "Let's talk about what you came to discuss."

Of course. She needed to sleep. "It can wait," he decided.

Her eyes flew open. "You had me wait up, and now you say it can wait?"

"We're both tired, Claire. Perhaps it would be better if we talked another time." That smoky hint of gray in her eyes concealed deep emotion. He wondered what thoughts dwelled behind those eyes. "I kept my promise."

Warily, she took stock of the envelope on the table.

"The papers you wanted," he clarified.

She didn't make a move.

He picked up the envelope and tossed it in her lap.

Finally, she looked up. "Thank you."

She could barely keep her eyes open. She'd probably checked on her mother, fed William and sent the servants to bed all since he'd seen her last. And then she'd waited for him to come rant at her.

"Lean forward."

She eyed him uncertainly, but complied.

He slipped one arm behind her and another beneath her legs, and her scent assailed him as he picked her up. A little floral, a little earthy. A lot woman. *Dangerous.*

He placed her on the bed and stepped back, his seditious body already responding. "Go to sleep."

Abruptly, he turned and left her room.

Sarah removed the ice from her foot, opened the unsealed envelope and slid the papers onto the bed. All the facts of Claire's life lay before her, some scrawled in spiky longhand, others printed neatly. Of course he'd hired the Pinkerton Agency, nothing less for Nicholas Halliday, so the information had been recorded with detailed accuracy and a list of sources.

Claire's limited schooling, her friends, her parents, all the details of her brief life were described on the pages. Celia drank before her husband died. Theirs had been a rough and rocky marriage. Claire had had a brother who had been killed in a street brawl.

Struggling to keep her eyes open, Sarah read of three men with whom Claire had kept intimate company before she'd met Stephen. Perhaps those men had been the reason Nicholas questioned Claire's motives where his brother was concerned. But Nicholas couldn't know of her love for Stephen. He'd never observed them together.

If there'd been men before Stephen, there certainly

would never have been any after. Sarah had never known two people in love before. But she'd recognized it when she'd seen it.

So Claire had led a rough life. She'd lived in a slum area and worked in a sweatshop until she'd met a man involved in the theater and gone to work as a seamstress and costumer. That didn't make her the gold digger Nicholas believed her.

Too tired to do more than slip out of her dress and stockings, Sarah unpinned her hair and slid between the sheets in her underclothing.

His challenge to ask for anything she wanted had prompted her boldness in asking for the papers. But he had agreed to provide them. And even after the fiasco with Celia, he'd kept his word. Why? It seemed too much to believe he had a conscience in there somewhere where she was concerned. Maybe he'd experienced a twinge of guilt for having his sister-in-law investigated. She doubted it.

Closing her eyes, Sarah prayed William wouldn't wake too early. But exhausted as she was, sleep eluded her. Self-recriminations rolled through her mind more acutely than the dull throb in her leg.

She'd told one person the truth that day. Celia. She'd always thought that telling the truth set a person free; however, she was anything but free now. Celia's knowing who she really was bound her more securely to the lie. Now she had to double her defenses and her efforts to keep Nicholas from finding out.

Claire hadn't deserved to die. No matter how unpleasant her past, no matter who her parents were, she'd loved Stephen and would have made him a good wife.

Celia hadn't deserved to hear the truth about her daughter like she had. It might have been better than an impersonal telegram, and there was no good way to announce a loved one's death, but she hadn't deserved this.

Sarah's stomach ached with the depth of her deception. What would all this lead to?

Before long, she would gather William and leave. At this point getting away from Nicholas and his suspicions, running out from under the stifling web of lies she'd woven for herself should come as a relief. But she didn't know how she would she do it, what she would say. Just take off? Leave a letter, confessing?

Leda had been warm and welcoming, and the dear woman loved William so much. How could Sarah just leave her and Nicholas to deal with the shock of knowing Stephen's true wife was dead and that Sarah had done nothing about it?

Even Celia must think her a monster for allowing Claire's body to go unclaimed, undiscovered. The horror of that had plagued Sarah from the first.

She rolled to her back and stared at the shadowy ceiling. As a Halliday, she had resources at her fingertips. The Hallidays would spend their money finding Claire, so there was no reason she shouldn't do it for them.

Obviously sleep was for those with clear consciences.

She scrambled to the side of the bed, found the tin of matches and lit the rose-painted glass oil lamp. Fumbling through the papers, she found the name of the investigator Nicholas had hired. She would hire a different agent to assure he would not contact Nicholas. Here was something she could do before she left. It wouldn't make up for the lies, of course, but it would be a way to make up what she'd done to Leda and Nicholas when they learned the truth. Perhaps, too, it would be an atonement to Claire's mother.

Carrying her small lamp, Sarah slipped down the hallway to the lavender room, and stealthily opened the door.

Celia's frizzy head could be seen above the back of one of the chairs. "Are you awake?"

"I'm awake."

Sarah slipped around and sat on the footstool. "I've made a decision."

"What's that?"

"First thing tomorrow I'm sending a wire to the Pinkerton Agency and arranging for them to find what happened to Claire's body." Perhaps Sarah would have a small measure of peace if she knew, if she could bring Claire to lie beside her husband in the Mahoning Valley cemetery.

"That make you feel better?" Celia asked.

"I was hoping it would make you feel better." Celia would have something tangible to grieve over. If she could find it in her selfish heart to grieve. Or if she stayed sober long enough.

Sarah admonished herself for her unkind thoughts.

"It's the least I can do," she continued. "Actually it's all I can do."

Celia shrugged, a careless gesture Sarah hoped was intended to cover her feelings.

"I just wanted you to know."

"Okay. I know."

Sarah glanced at the bed. "Why don't you get some sleep now?"

"I'll sleep in a while."

"Good night." Sarah slipped from the room and padded back to hers. Everything she did had an effect on so many other people. Coming here had had an enormous effect, and leaving would have an even bigger one.

Leda would be the one to suffer the most. William was the joy of her life—the baby she believed was her grandson and the descendent of her beloved son and husband. The sooner Sarah ended the deception, the better. Each day her love for Leda grew stronger.

And each day her love for Nicholas took on deeper and more frightening proportions. Her inability to resist him even though he cared nothing for her was shameful. Removing herself from his presence seemed the answer to more than one dilemma.

Once the authorities knew what to look for it shouldn't take them long to locate Claire's remains. Nicholas's guests would be here a few more days, and Sarah had the obligation of caring for them.

Perhaps in another week or two she'd have the information about Claire. By then, she'd be able to stand and walk for longer periods, and her time here would be over. Until then she'd have to keep Celia quiet.

Snuffing the light, she climbed into bed. She would be glad to get away from Nicholas, she had to tell herself. In a hundred lifetimes she'd never meet another man who at the same time angered and puzzled and excited her as he did. Of all the things that could have happened, of all the places she might have been heading, and the trains she could have been taking, she'd boarded an ill-fated one that had introduced her to Stephen and Claire and Nicholas and Leda.

Fate had entwined their lives.

And desperation still drove Sarah to astounding lengths.

She prayed her resourcefulness carried her into the coming weeks, into finding a job and a place to live and a way to care for her son.

Sarah snuggled into the covers and disciplined herself to sleep.

The following night's dinner was more elegant than the first, with candlelight and crystal, courses chosen to complement one another, and Claire a lovely and cordial hostess.

After dessert, she gently invited their guests into the music room, where a string quartet and pianist performed a chamber concert for them. Even the music had been chosen with eclectic tastes in mind.

Nicholas observed her from his position on the opposite

side of the room. No one could carry off unrelieved black like Claire. This evening she'd done something different with her curly mane of hair, a cluster of long sausagelike curls hanging against her neck.

Occasionally Ellen Gallamore on her right, or Milos on her left, spoke to her, and she'd lean in to hear the whisperer. She said something back to Milos, one of the curls brushing his shoulder, and he replied with a tilt of his head.

Claire graced him with an amused smile.

That faint smile played havoc with Nicholas's senses. She'd casually invited him to attend William's bath one morning if he wanted to see her smile, not mentioning he might observe her smiling at his friend at any given moment.

Nicholas crossed his arms over his chest. He didn't care if she grinned herself silly at Milos.

He studied them, her the picture of grace and femininity with the sheen of the gas lamps illuminating her pale hair, Milos the only friend Nicholas had ever known. He couldn't help but wonder at what they spoke of so easily. How did Milos know what to say to bring a smile to those lips?

Her watchful gaze touched upon the guests, checked the clock, the coal fire in the grate and in passing stumbled across Nicholas's stare.

Against his will he wished she had a smile for him, one that spoke of intimacy or friendship or even tolerance. But then why should she? He'd been nothing but critical and accusing since she'd made his acquaintance. And as much as he'd wanted to think it, she just didn't seem the type to wile her way into his good graces with feminine posturing.

Her attention to this evening's meal and entertainment showed more savoir faire than even his mother had ever displayed. Claire possessed polished sureness when it came to social manners and activities. He could find no fault in any of the preparations or her dress or comportment.

After last night's fiasco, he'd thought his guests would pack and leave, or at least hold themselves in reserve, but they had seemed to sympathize with Claire's embarrassment and had dismissed the incident. She'd won them over with her gentle beauty and seemingly sincere apology.

But he had to wonder how she had come by this innate sense of dignity and ability. It made no sense. Fortunately, the Galamores and Kleymanns and McCauls didn't know she'd come from the back streets of New York, that her father had been a penniless factory worker, so they'd overlooked her mother. Even a family of quality had its skeletons.

But Nicholas knew better. And he couldn't deduce how she'd pulled it off. She never referred to him as anything other than Mr. Halliday in front of the guests. And though she was smart as a whip, she hadn't larded conversation with references to literature or science, but instead practiced quiet reserve as a true lady would. She even handled the servants as though she'd done it all her life.

The musicians ended their set, and Claire gently guided the guests toward the parlor for coffee and liqueur. Nicholas followed behind as she walked with her hand on Milos's sleeve.

Even if she'd learned it all in preparation for marrying Stephen, she'd have bungled something by now. Yet she behaved as though she'd done this dozens of times, as though she were born and bred to the life.

And he'd been patient. He'd watched and given her all the rope she needed to hang herself.

He truly hadn't expected this.

He'd expected his mother to do all the work and Claire to take credit. But he knew it wasn't so. In fact his mother had never been so rested, so relaxed, so happy.

Grudging respect wormed its way into his attitude toward Claire. If she'd gone to such lengths to win Mother over,

Nicholas could only imagine what she'd done to win Stephen.

They'd reached the parlor, and the guests seated themselves, the drone of conversation picking up. Claire moved toward Nicholas. "Will you be serving the liqueur, or shall I ring for one of the servants?"

"I'll do it."

She nodded. The dress she wore revealed the generous swells of her ivory breasts. Another woman would have worn a priceless gem around her neck to display her wealth and draw attention to those lush features, but Claire herself was the jewel, needing no adornment. Crafty as she was, she'd no doubt used that to her advantage.

Without another word, she slipped back among the guests.

Nicholas poured spiced brandy and discussed the day's business with Monty Gallamore. But his attention never left Claire. If she felt she needed to stay in his good graces, to what extent would she go to please him?

The question sent a rippling wave of heat through him. She'd passed the test with the food and the entertainment. But what if he were to test her loyalty rather than her abilities?

Anyone could learn tasks or fake knowledge.

But one couldn't pretend love and fidelity.

If she loved and adored Stephen the way his mother believed, the way she pretended, she would not fall into another man's arms.

She'd already allowed him to kiss her. Did she think kissing him would secure her place?

The thought sickened him.

The idea intrigued him.

The image enticed him.

The true test of her love for Stephen. Afterward there would be no doubt.

Nicholas couldn't wait for his guests to leave.

Chapter Twelve

Somehow, between directing the servants during the day, entertaining Nicholas's guests each evening and catering to Celia's demands, Sarah found the time to travel into Youngstown and send messages and a retainer to the Pinkerton Agency. She instructed the telegraph office that any return messages were to be held for her and not sent with anyone from the Halliday house who might make the trip to town.

During one of their afternoons together, Sarah and Kathryn Kleymann played with William on Sarah's bed. Over the past few days they'd spent many pleasant hours together and Sarah had grown fond of the young woman. The sweet woman deserved the affection she shared with her husband, and Sarah prayed for their happiness.

"Perhaps next time we visit we'll have our little one along," she said happily. "You can visit us in Virginia, too. The children can be playmates."

Sarah smiled at the wistful thought. If only that were possible.

After five full days and nights, the guests took their leave. Sarah was so bereft to see Kathryn go, she ran up to her room and cried.

Leda followed, entering without knocking, and sat on a chair near where Sarah perched on the window seat.

"What's wrong, sweet girl?" she asked tenderly.

Ashamed, Sarah dried her face and blinked into the sunlight streaming through the glass panes. "Nothing."

"I see. You don't want to tell this old lady."

Swiftly Sarah moved to sit at her feet. "It's not that. I just don't want you to think me foolish."

She took Sarah's hands. "I've never thought you foolish."

Sarah spared her a smile, and accepted a violet-scented hankie to wipe her nose. "It's just that I grew so attached to Mrs. Kleymann, I hated to see her go."

"Why, that's perfectly natural," Leda assured her. "Women need other women their own age to talk with. All you've had for months is me."

And now the horrible mother confined to her rooms, Leda probably thought. "I love you," Sarah said quickly. "Please don't think I don't appreciate your friendship."

Leda stroked her hair from her temple. Tears shone in her gray eyes. "I don't think that. I understand loneliness, child. But you'll see Kathryn again. We meet up with the Kleymanns at least once a year."

Sarah nodded, feeling no better knowing that next time the families gathered, Kathryn would learn of Sarah's treachery.

"I think you should nap," Leda suggested. "I'll wake you for dinner."

Sarah nodded. Leda unbuttoned her dress before leaving her alone.

She slipped out of her shoes and the black crinoline dress and rested atop the counterpane. Within moments she slept.

The next day Sarah took Celia her dinner tray. "I've heard you're not eating well. The servants are concerned."

"What the hell do they care?" Obviously Celia hadn't

washed her hair or bathed for days. She sat in a chair, dressed in her worn and wrinkled wrapper. "All they have to do is leave the papers."

"I'm concerned, Celia."

Her red-rimmed eyes rose to Sarah. "Why?"

"Because I hate to see you doing this to yourself. You bathe and get dressed tomorrow, or I'll bring the maids in here and we'll do it for you."

"You wouldn't."

"Don't push me, Cele."

She glared back, but conceded with a shrug.

"I'll have the water sent up in the morning."

She tucked her bare feet beneath her. "You do that."

Sarah uncovered the tray and sat with her until she'd eaten most of the dinner.

"So, what's that baby of yours look like?"

The question caught Sarah off guard. "William? Well, he looks like me, I guess." She urged Celia to drink her tea. The woman's silence prompted her to think over her words and consider her train of thought. "Would you like to see him?"

Celia shrugged noncommittally.

"You start bathing and dressing and I'll bring him to see you."

Celia nodded as if she didn't care, and Sarah wondered if she'd misread her.

"Did you send the telegram?"

"I did. I expect it'll be a while before I hear back. I've asked the telegraph office not to send my messages with anyone but me, so I'll have to keep checking. Of course if you were up and able to take trips into town, you could check."

"Don't depend on me," she said. "I'd only let you down."

Sarah glanced at the clock on the mantel. Her own dinner was ready. "Have you let down very many people?"

Celia avoided her gaze. "Some."

"None of us like to do that," she said. She removed the tray and wished Celia a good-night.

Changing her clothing quickly, she carried William to the dining room and placed him in the bassinet Leda insisted be kept there for him. She'd been enjoying having no guests to entertain in the evenings.

"I'm well pleased with the way the visit with my associates went," Nicholas said after they'd eaten, surprising Sarah. He hadn't mentioned anything until now. But then he'd been working late hours. "You ladies outdid yourselves with the meals."

"I can't take credit for that," Leda said. "Claire handled the menus and the kitchen servants. I took care of baths and laundry and rooms and such."

"Well done, Claire," Nicholas said.

Warmth crept through Sarah's chest and curled itself into an unfamiliar little ball of gratification near her heart. At his expression of appreciation, her cheeks grew warm. He had no idea how much those two words meant to someone who'd never expected to hear them. She'd done her best simply because that was what she did. She'd learned long ago not to count on her best being enough.

She curled her fingers in her lap and didn't dare look up. In her years of experience with her father, he'd never once tossed her a bone of encouragement. Even when she'd done her best to please him, he'd found something to fault her for.

She waited, breath held, for Nicholas to say something about Claire's mother, about Sarah's irresponsibility and his humiliation, as he hadn't broached that subject yet, but her waiting was for naught.

"Each of our guests expressed to me privately how impressed they were with you, and with your attention to every small detail of their comfort, even though you were, yourself, in mourning. I must commend you."

Sarah's chest expanded to near bursting. She didn't know how to reply. Words became stuck. "Th-thank you," she managed finally.

"Thank you, Claire. Stephen would be proud of you."

She met his eyes then, eyes dark and enrapturing and filled with a mysterious glint. An ache blossomed in her throat. *Stephen would be proud of you.* She wasn't sure how to take that statement, though he could mean it no other way than how it sounded.

Would Stephen have been proud of Claire for doing the things Sarah had done? Or would Stephen have even cared? Nicholas had been the one concerned over details pertaining to the foundry.

"Our Claire is a blessing," Leda said cheerfully. "Even if she didn't know her shrimp fork from a hill of beans I'd still adore her. Stephen made a wonderful choice when he married you."

Sarah gave her a feeble smile.

"I'm off to play cribbage tonight, dears," Leda said, finishing her wine and standing. "Unless you need Gruver for anything, I've given him the night off after he delivers me to the Austins'. The Dextrixhes' driver will drop me home."

"That's fine, Mother. Unless Claire has plans."

Sarah shook her head, surprised to be included in the discussion.

"Don't forget the picnic next Saturday," he said before she turned away.

"Is it that time already?" Leda asked. "Does Claire know about it?"

"The Halliday Iron picnic," he explained.

"Nicholas provides food and fireworks for all the foundry employees," his mother added. "It's quite fun to watch the games."

"I'll look forward to it." Sarah waved her off.

"Claire," Nicholas said after his mother had left.

She looked over expectantly.

"Would you mind bringing William to my study this evening?" At her pause, he added, "I just thought he and I might as well get to know each other."

"I'd be happy to," she replied.

After William had been fed and changed, Sarah instructed Mrs. Trent to come for him at his bedtime. She carried him downstairs and approached Nicholas's study with uncertainty.

She opened the doors without knocking and entered. A cradle had appeared since the last time Sarah had been there.

"I found it in the attic and cleaned it up myself," he said at her questioning look. "Penelope helped with the mattress and bedding. I thought he might like a change of scenery occasionally. I won't light a cigar while he's here."

His gestures couldn't have surprised her more. She stood nearby, saying nothing.

"I had tea brought for you."

She glanced at the tray on the corner of his massive desk.

He stepped close and observed the child in her arms. "I've never been around a baby before."

She gave a little shrug. "Neither had I."

"Well, I guess I can't hurt him with ignorance then, can I?"

She shook her head, and tentatively handed her son over.

Nicholas accepted the infant gingerly, his arms and chest seeming to swallow the baby, and held him against his fine black coat. Sarah prayed William wouldn't get an air bubble and spit on his clothing.

"Fix your tea," he said.

She complied, pouring, adding lemon and cream. "Would you care for a cup?"

He shook his head and seated himself in one of the wing chairs. "Well, William, what's life like with all those women about upstairs? You'll need to come down often so they don't mollycoddle you.''

Repressing a smile, Sarah carried her tea to the divan and sat.

"I don't see how you women attribute familiar characteristics to a wee baby. He has a tiny nose, tiny ears, a tiny mouth...what color are his eyes?''

"They're blue. Your mother says they may change, but I don't think so.'' She sipped her tea.

Nicholas observed William like a man seeing an infant for the first time. He caught one of his flailing fists and studied his fingers.

The tea, Nicholas's soothing voice and his unthreatening mood relaxed her. She leaned back and enjoyed the tranquillity of the moment.

"His hair is so fair,'' he said minutes later, bringing Sarah's attention back. "It seems to pick up a little gold in the firelight just as yours does.''

The observation impelled her heart to leap. He'd noticed the firelight in her hair?

He moved the baby to his knees where he could study him and have his hands free. "And I guess he does have your mouth. With that little bow right there.''

He'd become familiar with the shape of her lips?

With a long finger, he touched William's lip, and the baby moved his head and opened his mouth, seeking.

Nicholas chuckled.

Sarah stared.

He brushed one cheek gently. "I've never felt anything quite so soft,'' he said, amazement in his tone. Then his head snapped up, his wonder striking her. "He smiled!''

She nodded, understanding the powerful effect of William's enchanting, toothless smile.

As though captivated, he studied William for the better part of an hour, talking to him, stroking his cheek. Nicholas's agreeable behavior, his attention to William, lulled her into imagining what it would have been like to have a husband—a real family. Someday Nicholas would have children of his own. His wife might sit here just like this and watch him with their baby. Maybe she'd knit. Maybe she'd sing.

Maybe they'd go up to their rooms together afterward and tuck their baby in.

Mrs. Trent arrived on schedule, conveniently interrupting Sarah's wayward thoughts.

Nicholas looked from the woman to Sarah. "He doesn't have to leave now, does he? Couldn't you change him or whatever you need to do and leave him?"

Sarah nodded at Mrs. Trent, who left and came back with clean linens. Sarah excused her for the night and changed William in the cradle, blushing while Nicholas looked on.

"That's all there is to it?" he asked.

"For now."

He picked him up and held the baby a few minutes longer until he fell asleep. "I think I bored him."

Sarah placed him in the cradle and covered him. "It was his bedtime," she replied, laughter in her voice.

Nicholas came over to stand behind her, and she sensed his warmth, smelled the starch in his shirt, the tang of tobacco on his clothing. She couldn't turn, for if she did, they would be face-to-face.

He reached from behind her, his chest pressing her shoulder, and smoothed William's hair with long gentle fingers. His breath fanned her ear and sent shivers along her shoulders and down her arms. "He's beautiful."

Tears sprang to her eyes, and she blinked furiously. Somehow it was different from having Leda say it, from hearing Kathryn say it, from thinking it herself. When Nicholas said her son was beautiful, it was a proclamation. He wasn't a woman swayed by emotion, he wasn't Stephen's mother, prejudiced by her love; he was a hard-edged man who didn't even like or trust Sarah.

At his nearness, her heartbeat quickened to a wild, unsteady rhythm. She was a fool to feel anything for this man. Up until this instant he'd never shown her a moment's kindness. Or had he? He'd been tender in his own way, seeing to her comfort, concerning himself with her swollen ankle and carrying her to ease her leg. She could easily melt back against him and lose herself in his heat and his scent. Her reaction humiliated her, and she prayed he'd move away before he recognized what he was doing to her.

"I meant what I said earlier," he said against her ear.

Her knees weakened, but she didn't move.

"You made me very proud."

"But—"

"Are you going to mention your mother?"

She nodded.

"Don't."

She'd expected him to rail at her over Celia. The fact that he hadn't gave her the impression of waiting for the other shoe to drop, and she didn't like it.

"But the floor tiles—"

"Gruver found extras in the carriage house."

"Oh. Your mother's planter?"

"I always thought it was rather gaudy anyway."

"But she must have—"

"No more," he insisted. "We're going to let the subject rest. *Permanently.*"

"All right," she whispered.

"Perhaps you can persuade her to have dinner with us one evening soon." His breath rustled against her hair. A tremor ran down her spine. Her head spun with turmoil. She didn't want Nicholas around Celia, but how could she be so cruel to the woman?

"Your hair has driven me crazy since the first time I saw it," he confessed in a low intimate tone.

His words soaked in and numbed her thinking. If he touched her, she'd dissolve into a puddle.

"I've wanted to test those tight curls beside your face and along your neck. See if they spring back when I tug them."

She tipped her head and touched her curls self-consciously.

"When I get within a foot of you, I can smell your hair, and I want to bury my nose in it."

Sarah's brain dealt with his words slowly. "You think all that about my *hair?*"

"Not just your hair."

Oh, Lord. Her eyes drifted shut against her will, as if closing them could protect her from the sensory onslaught of his voice. A rush of anticipation sluiced through her veins.

"It's the way it lies against your neck, and how pale and soft-looking that skin is. So delicate. And it feels as soft as William's."

Her skin tingled everywhere. The thought of him touching her again gave her nerve endings vibrant expectancy. She couldn't think past the heat and the tension.

"Right now I can see your pulse at the base of your throat. I could feel it if I placed my lips there. What's making your pulse race so, Claire?"

Sarah thought she might faint. She reached for something to steady herself, and his strong hand came up from beneath and clasped hers. She clung to it.

With his other hand, he tested the curls beside her face with gentle tugs, did the same along her neck. He leaned closer and inhaled, and she was sure she heard him groan.

"May I?" he asked in a hoarse voice, releasing her hand.

She nodded, and when she reached back, she met his fingers, already plucking pins. Hands trembling, she helped him until her hair was free. He thrust his fingers into it, buried his face in it, pushed it all to one side and pressed his lips to her neck so gently they might have been the radiating heat of the fire.

Heat skittered down her body, setting it atingle.

He kissed her neck, traced the shell of her ear with his tongue, then turned her with gentle hands and ran his tongue along her throat, down to the pulse point, up to her chin.

She faced him now, her head fallen back; her loose fists rose helplessly. He delved his fingers against her scalp and held her head fast, bringing her mouth to his.

Sarah grabbed his shoulders before she collapsed, and welcomed his mouth upon hers. His kiss inflamed as staggeringly as his words had, his lips warm and pliant and hungry for the taste of her. She wanted to absorb him, have him for herself. She kissed him back, a hungry, greedy kiss that left her modesty in tatters and her composure in shreds.

He settled her against his body, and Sarah lost all sense of time and place and propriety. Her swollen breasts welcomed the hard plane of his chest. Their thighs pressed together through their clothing, his long and muscled, hers trembling.

"I want you," he said against her mouth, and the proof pressed against her belly. The intimacy shocked, yet excited her. She should push him away. She should put a stop to this. But he ran his hands down her back and cupped her bottom through layers of dress and petticoats, and all Sarah could think of was what that would feel like if she were unclothed.

Apparently Nicholas had the same thought, for he turned her and unbuttoned the row of tiny buttons from her neck to her buttocks, all the while, his breath fanning her neck.

Shamelessly, she helped him peel the bodice forward, and her chemise followed, but caught on her corset and her arms.

He didn't care. He turned her toward him and rested his blazing dark gaze on her breasts.

Sarah blushed, her body tingling. She'd never had a man

look at her like this, and her breasts were full and heavy now, her nipples swollen.

"Will I hurt you if I touch them?" he asked, apparently as concerned as she, yet considerate enough to ask.

She shook her head. "I don't think so."

"You'll tell me?"

She nodded.

He cupped a palm beneath one breast, more gently and reverently than she'd expected from his passion moments before. He rubbed the sensitive skin, tested the weight, ran his thumb over the crest of her nipple and watched it harden.

He kissed her again then, more tenderly this time, more worshipfully but with every bit as much fire and dedication.

Gaylen Carlisle had given Sarah a baby, but he'd never set her on fire or shown her passion. What she'd done with him could not be compared to this.

She didn't think there was a comparison for this.

Desperately needing to touch him, Sarah raised her hands, but her arms caught on her chemise. "Nicholas," she said against his mouth.

At his pause, she looked down and unlaced her corset, allowing it and her chemise to fall, then liberating herself of the stiff layers of petticoats.

With her arms free, she cupped his face, touched her palms to the warm, slightly rough skin of his cheeks, and pulled his face back to hers while he shed his coat.

He kissed her, but urged her to the divan, where he laid her back against his coat and ran his palms over her shoulders and breasts.

Sarah sighed her pleasure, hooked an arm behind his neck and raised herself to his ministrations. He slid his fingers over one nipple, up the side of her neck, caught her chin and kissed her hard.

He pressed kisses against her eyelids, her chin, her neck, the valley between her breasts, touched his tongue to her nipple, and she shivered. He looked up at her then, his eyes dark with passion, and she caressed his cheeks and his brow.

He lowered his head to her breast and suckled. She savored the rush of sensation until she felt her milk let down. Embarrassed, she pulled his head away. He gave her a quizzical glance, but respecting her unspoken wish, allowed her to stop him without question. He kissed her lips, his tongue invading and drawing hers to kiss him as deeply.

Sarah's insides turned liquid. She pulled him against her, running her hands over his back through his damp shirt, the scents of starch and man strong in her nostrils.

He slid a hand along her hip, caught her against his hard frame and ground himself against her, emitting a frustrated groan.

Sarah clutched at his shoulders, wild with the fire of his kisses and the near-ecstasy of his touches.

Nicholas slipped his hand between them, cupped her through her pantalets, and she gasped. He parted the placket in the material, and his gentle fingers found her folds, quickening her with sure steady strokes, and instinctively she raised her hips into the pleasure.

Her exquisite feminine responses had Nicholas tied in a knot. He buried his nose in her hair, felt the tightening of her lush body, gloried in the breathless gasps against his ear and gave himself the gratification of feeling her pulse against his hand. Could he bury the shame of seducing her by pleasuring her and denying himself?

Somewhere along the line his plan had backfired. How would he know if she were doing this just to ingratiate herself with a wealthy man or if he'd approached her at a vulnerable time and said and done all the things she'd needed to hear?

These responses weren't faked. That he knew.

But worse than even those thoughts was the seed of doubt he couldn't close his mind to. Perhaps he reminded her of Stephen. She was lonely. If she had truly loved his brother, she might be drawn to Nicholas because of the physical similarities.

She held herself still and quiet. Waiting.

He wanted to take her now. Sink into her and lose himself in her lush and lovely body. He fought against taking her as quickly and harshly as he desired. He clenched his jaw. Hard.

"Nicholas?" she asked tentatively.

He smoothed his hand up over the cotton covering her hip. "What?"

"Aren't you going to—?"

"No," he said, and it was the hardest decision he'd ever made.

"But—but…" Clearly, she didn't know what to say or think.

"You've just had a baby, Claire."

At that she tensed. "It's been months," she replied.

"But you don't need to have another one," he argued logically.

She had no reply for that. She pulled away slightly, her passion-bright gaze taking in his still fully clothed body. Crimson stained her cheeks in the firelight. Lord, she was beautiful.

"It's perfectly all right, Claire."

Her blue eyes seemed to turn more gray. "It doesn't feel all right."

He reached for her face, but she turned it aside so he couldn't kiss her. He wanted to kiss her. More than he wanted to bury himself in her and slake his desire for her, he wanted to kiss her. Reassure her. What had come over him to even care what she thought or felt? He could have had her. Right then and there, and it would have been better than anything he'd ever known.

He still could. If he spoke to her now, reassured her,

stroked her silken limbs and kissed her, he could still have her.

But he wouldn't. He was too ashamed of himself. Merely pumping his seed into her for the sake of proving that he could was not the conquest he'd imagined it would be.

He'd proved nothing.

Except that he was incorrigible.

And that she was vulnerable.

And that he wanted her like nothing he'd ever known or needed in his life.

He deserved to lie awake all night. He deserved the sick, gut-punched feeling that gripped him where it hurt, and twisted.

Whether that was Stephen's baby over there or not, this was Stephen's wife, and he was a no-good son of a bitch for seducing her. Wanting her was bad enough. Following through was worse.

Mixed with his desire for her came the overpowering sense of abasement. No matter what her purpose, he still had his honor.

He calmed her with gentle strokes along her hip and her bare arm. He gently threaded her hair from her face and kissed her temple, all the while holding her, relishing the hard crush of her breasts and the delicate wisp of her breath against his neck.

He became aware of her hand against his shirtfront, urging him back. He loosened his hold, and she pulled away, hurrying to turn her back and pull on the white cotton chemise she found crumpled on the floor.

Her great skein of multitoned tresses bunched beneath the fabric, and when he reached to assist her, she pushed off his hands and stepped away, grabbing for her discarded black dress.

"Claire...?" he questioned softly.

Her chin came up at that, and she looked him in the eye. Tears glistened on her golden lashes. Shame shone clearly on her delicate features. "Please don't say anything," she pleaded, her blue eyes more eloquent than her words. "Just let me go to my room."

He didn't know what he would have said. That he was sorry? He wasn't. Oh, he shouldn't have planned to seduce her, certainly, but would he take back what had happened? Did he wish he didn't know how her skin felt or how her mouth tasted or the smothered sounds of desire she made when he touched her?

Humiliation burned in the depths of her hurt gaze. He was not sorry he'd aroused her and pleasured her. He was only sorry she'd belonged to Stephen first, and that he had no right to be lusting after her now.

In obedient silence, he took a step back, watched her gather her corset and petticoats and her sleeping son and flee from his study as though demons pursued her.

Nicholas stared at the scattering of hairpins around the foot of the cradle. He picked them up and closed his fingers over them. No, he wasn't sorry for what had happened.

He only regretted he'd ever heard of Claire Patrick Halliday in the first place.

Chapter Thirteen

Sarah had begun to wonder what it would be like to fall asleep without fears or worries or regrets plaguing her long into the night. It had been a year since she'd slept the peaceful sleep of a young woman without taxing concerns.

And all because of her rebellious nature, and her dubious character. It wouldn't have killed her to marry one of those promising young men her father had paraded before her. Perhaps accepting secret invitations from Gaylen had simply been a means to strike back at a demanding father who never had time for her, but imperiously ordered her life about.

It was all well and good to look back now and say she'd been rash and foolish, but perhaps the truth was that she'd chosen Gaylen because he wouldn't really care for her, just as her father had never cared for her, and just as Nicholas Halliday didn't care for her. What was it about her that sought the affections of men who could not respond in kind—men who didn't even like her? Whatever dark need inside, whatever warped characteristic, it sickened her.

She hadn't been able to place William in his bed. She'd kept him beside her where she could see his slight form in the low-burning firelight, smell his baby-sweet fragrance and touch him each time the hurt washed over her anew.

She had William. William. He was hers and hers alone. No one could take him from her or come between them. No matter what else befell her in this lifetime, she had her son.

Tears trickled across her temple and into her hair, and an ache like the ponderous encumbrance of a boulder sat upon her chest. She was not the best mother a son could have had. She had to admit that. But she loved him fiercely, and she would do her best for him. She'd made another big mistake tonight. She'd endangered William's welfare.

If Nicholas had not stopped short of fulfilling the act they'd begun, she could have found herself expecting a second child! Did she never learn? She hadn't been able to provide for one child, let alone two!

She had no illusions about Nicholas Halliday. He might desire her as Gaylen had desired her, but he was every bit as eager to rid himself of her. The longer she stayed, the harder it would be to leave. There could never be anything between them. Her deceit had seen to that.

The muted sound of glass shattering in the hallway drew her upright. She dried her eyes with the bedsheet and tiptoed to the door. Moonlight flooding through a floor-to-ceiling window on the landing revealed a hunched form sitting at the top of the stairs. Sarah hurried forward.

Pain pierced the bottom of her foot. She stifled a cry and limped the rest of the way to where Celia sat on the top step. "What are you doing? Do you know what time it is?"

The woman bobbed her mane of wild hair and swiveled toward her, and Sarah regretted her words. She'd learned Celia had no sense of time. When she woke, she drank. When she was drunk enough, she slept.

"I was hungry." Her thick voice betrayed the effects of the liquor, but she appeared coherent.

Sarah crouched down beside her. "One minute I have to threaten you to eat, the next you think you're starving."

Just then yellow light flickered across the walls, sending their shadows into deep relief across the wallpaper. Nicholas climbed the stairs in only a pair of trousers, carrying a lamp that reflected a dark puddle on the polished wood floor near the wall and shards of glass scattered to the middle of the wide hallway. He stood towering over them. "Who's hurt?"

His immediate question caught Sarah by surprise until she saw the blood on the carpet runner. "Your carpet!" she said with dismay.

"The hell with the carpet," he said with a churlish growl. "Which one of you is bleeding?"

Sarah cringed. "I'm afraid it's me."

"Show me," he demanded.

She sat beside Celia and, holding her nightdress primly around her calf, raised her foot for his inspection.

Shirtless, his dark hair mussed, Nicholas lowered the lamp to the floor and raised Sarah's foot. Celia's glittery-eyed gaze traveled from Nicholas's broad, golden shoulders to Sarah's pale foot and up to her face. A hint of acknowledgment flitted across her florid features.

Sarah swallowed hard and tried not to stare at the dark swirls of hair curling across his chest. She closed her eyes and tried not to remember seeing him stark naked in his bath or feeling the sensation of his aroused body pressed intimately against hers or the effect his hands and mouth had on her.

"Ouch!" she cried, her thoughts immediately jolted elsewhere.

"There's a piece of glass in there," he said. "Just a small one."

Celia cast her an apologetic glance.

"Celia's hungry," Sarah explained. "She was going down to find something to eat."

The woman nodded. "I didn't have any dinner."

"Penelope brought your dinner. You just slept through it and she cleared it away," Sarah said calmly.

"I didn't want the whole blamed house up," she said, unsteadily getting to her feet. "I just wanted somethin' to eat!"

Nicholas stood, grabbed an embroidered linen scarf from a decorative table nearby and knelt again.

"Don't—" Sarah objected too late. He'd already wrapped it around her foot. "It will be ruined."

"Sit there," he said, ignoring her concern and scowling at them both. "Don't either of you move until I get back. Understood?"

They nodded in unison.

He descended the stairs into the darkness below on silent bare feet.

"You two got somethin' goin' on?" Celia asked when he was out of earshot. The old bird wasn't too snockered to observe their stilted interaction.

"No," Sarah said firmly. "How stupid do you think I am?"

The woman cocked a brow and gave her a sidelong glance. "I don't think that would be stupid at all. I think if you played your cards right, you'd have yourself a dandy little setup here."

"Well, I don't want a 'dandy little setup,'" Sarah denied. "And I certainly can't afford to stay here any longer than necessary."

"You could do worse," Celia said, and rested her head against the oak banister. "Never had servants wait on me before."

"And what?" she asked, unable to hold the irritation from her tone. "You play my mother for the rest of our lives?"

Celia's head came up, and she fixed Sarah with a glassy stare. "You're the one pretendin', darlin'. I *am* Claire's mother."

Sarah clamped her lips shut and turned to peruse their two long shadows on the wall. After several minutes, she whispered, "You're right, you know. I've brought this all on myself, and I have no right getting angry with you. In fact I owe you an apology. I'm sorry."

Celia's brows shot up. "For what?"

"Shh. For playing this part. For getting you entangled in it."

Celia stared at her lap for a few minutes. "Don't see as how I'd have done any different if I'd been in your place. Claire probably would have, too."

That thought took Sarah by surprise. "Well, we got off to a bad start, you and I. I don't know how I can fix it now, because I don't know what I'm going to do, but I just want you to know how sorry I am about Claire. When I find her body, I'll see that she's buried here by Stephen. You'll be able to visit her grave then."

"I got plenty of things I'm not proud of, too," the woman said, keeping her voice low.

Sarah took that as an acceptance of her apology, and felt a measure of relief.

The shadows dipped and swayed, and she turned to see Nicholas approaching with the lantern and a tray. "Don't move. Which room are you in?"

He'd asked Celia, but Sarah answered for her. "The lavender room. On the left there."

Skirting the glass, he disappeared with the tray and returned for Celia. "Come on. I was having a midnight snack myself, so I knew there was chicken and a turnover left."

His glare indicated Sarah was to wait, and he returned for her. "Pick up the lamp and hold it steady," he ordered. She did so, and he lifted her into his arms. "That foot's on your bad leg, isn't it?"

The heat of his chest scorched right through the flimsy fabric of her nightgown. One arm banded tightly about her back, the other behind her knees, just as he'd carried her many times before. "Yes."

"You favor that leg, so I think it prevented you from placing all your weight down and embedding the glass too deeply."

They'd reached Celia's room, and Nicholas deposited Sarah on the chaise, turned up the lamp and lit another.

Like a queen, Celia sat upon a tufted brocade chair, picking apart her chicken and licking her fingers as contentedly as a cat with a fresh flounder.

Nicholas carried the supplies he'd gathered and urged Sarah to place her foot at an angle where he could see it. At his touch on her bare ankle, she fought her automatic response and the embarrassment it created each time.

Gently, Nicholas cleaned the area and extracted a small sliver of glass. The alcohol he poured on a cloth and pressed against the cut stung so sharply, her eyes watered.

"I'm sorry," he said softly.

Their eyes met, and the words took on a whole new meaning. They stared at each other. With all her heart, Sarah wished she were someone else, someone with a clean conscience and an unscarred past. Someone who hadn't already made too many mistakes and lied about them all.

Someone a man like Nicholas could love.

She blinked away the tears and the foolish thought.

"I'll wrap it and it should heal in a day or two," he said.

"I need to wash this down," Celia said from across the room.

"I brought you a glass of milk, there," Nicholas said, turning to address her.

"Can't stand the stuff," she said and huffed a little burp. She stood and found the bottle she'd left on the bedside table.

Nicholas looked to Sarah as if for advice. As if she knew what to do about the exasperating woman. Or *for* her. Sarah shrugged.

"I can't have you breaking any more glasses, Mrs. Pa—"

"Don't call her that," Sarah advised softly. "Call her Celia."

"Don't need a glass then," Celia said, sitting on the bed and tipping the bottle to her lips.

Muttering a low curse, he strode from the room, his feet soundless on the thick carpet.

"Nicholas has asked that you join us for dinner," Sarah told her. "You're going to need to pull yourself together for that."

"What's he want me at dinner for?"

"It's customary for people to dine together, engage in conversation."

"I don't have anything to say that he'd want to hear."

"You don't know that. Maybe you'd be entertained hearing what he has to say. And Leda is delightful. It's not healthy for you to stay shut away up here. I'll come help you dress for dinner. *Be prepared.*" She hoped her last words were understood as "don't be drunk."

Nicholas returned with a silver stein.

"Pretty fancy," Celia said, turning it to squint at his engraved initials in the lamplight.

He took the bottle from her and poured a healthy portion into the metal cup. "Stephen sent it from one of his journeys," he said matter-of-factly. "I'll feel better knowing you're not strewing broken glass up and down the halls. Speaking of which," he said, slipping the bottle in his pocket and tossing all the rags and supplies on the tray, "I'd better get that cleaned up before someone else walks on it."

"I can see to it," Sarah said, rising.

"No, you won't," he argued with a raised palm. "Tell your mother good-night."

She gave Celia a concerned glance. The woman had

slumped over on the bed. A light snore parted her lips. "Sweet dreams, Mother."

Nicholas raised Celia's feet to the mattress and covered her with the thick counterpane before walking toward Sarah.

"I can walk," she said quickly.

"Your foot hurts." He plucked her into his arms as though she weighed no more than William.

Sarah balanced herself with a hand splayed against his chest. Her fingers met soft springy curls and the undeniable heat of his skin beneath. It had only been a few hours since she'd kissed him, touched him, wished for him to remove his clothing....

Swiftly he carried her to her dark room and strode to the bed.

"Careful," she warned. "William is lying there."

He identified the baby's form in the darkness and placed her beside him.

"Thank you, Nicholas," she said before he moved away.

His tall outline stood motionless.

"Thank you," she repeated softly. "For taking care of my foot. I'm sorry about the glass...and the stain on the carpet."

"See that you take care with it," he said. "If it looks at all inflamed, send for the doctor."

"I will."

Still he didn't make a move to leave.

She felt the need to apologize for Celia, too. She wasn't really her mother, but he believed she was. And that made her feel responsible.

"You know, Claire," he said in that seductively low voice that always sounded as though it were meant for her ears alone, "that you are welcome for as long as you wish to live here. Forever if you desire. Your mother, too."

Sarah stared at his shadowy form in surprise.

"I can't fault you for her behavior. I'm sure you've done

your share of covering up and making up for her in your lifetime. You don't have to do that here. We'll make arrangements and cope with her together.''

Together. Words failed her. Coherent thought failed her. This was far from anything she'd expected him to say. More than she'd hoped for. But she knew it could never be. She and Nicholas would not be doing anything "together.''

His kindness was far more difficult to accept than his derisiveness or his anger...because she didn't deserve it. "But why?'' she asked finally.

"She's your mother,'' he answered simply. "She's William's grandmother.''

Sarah closed her eyes and braced herself against the tidal wave of guilt that slammed into her. Just when she thought she had him figured out, just when she'd prepared all her defenses, he did or said something that proved what a small, selfish person she'd become.

She had no one to blame for her situation. She'd expended a great deal of energy on blaming her father, and Gaylen's memory had been a sound whipping board for months, but the truth of the matter was she'd caused all the grief herself.

Resigned, she opened her eyes.

He was gone.

Bereft, she curled up on the mattress, touched William's head for reassurance and ignored the dull throb in her foot and the hollow ache in her heart.

There was no choice. There never had been.

She had to leave soon.

Chapter Fourteen

The following morning Nicholas arrived at Claire's door early and rapped softly. She called out for him to come in.

Her expression told him his presence had caught her off guard. She wore a white apron over a deep green day dress, the first time he'd seen her in anything other than black, and the dress surprised him.

"Good morning," he said.

"Am I in time for William's bath?"

"We were just preparing it," she replied.

"Had you forgotten you'd invited me?"

"No, I…"

"Just didn't think I'd take you up on it," he finished for her.

"Well, I know how busy you are."

"I don't want to get in the way." Now he wondered if it had been a good idea to come.

"You won't be in the way." She gestured for him to follow them to the dressing area where she poured hot water into a basin, cooled it with water from a nearby pitcher and checked the temperature. "When he was first born and the weather colder, we used to do this in front of the fire." She turned. "It's ready, Mrs. Trent."

The woman tucked William firmly beneath one arm and

poured water over his hair, turning it a dark gold against his pale scalp. Claire handed her the soap and she lathered and rinsed. Claire blotted his head dry, and Mrs. Trent propped him upright in the ceramic basin, holding him beneath one arm and supporting his back and head.

It seemed a routine the women and baby were familiar with, but Nicholas watched with fascination. Imagine handling a slick squirming infant in such a confident manner! As soon as William was seated in the basin and Claire sponged water over his shoulders and round little belly, he kicked and flailed his arms. Water splashed in all directions.

Claire laughed.

Nicholas laughed.

"My, but you're a strong boy," she crooned, laughter in her voice. "Handsome, too."

"We'll have to be watchful of you at the picnic tomorrow," Nicholas added. "You'll catch the eyes of all the girls."

She laughed and met his gaze, the smile softening her exquisitely feminine features and adding a glow to her skin and eyes. She had promised he'd see her smile if he attended William's bath. That was why he'd come.

And the sight took his breath away.

The smile revealed her straight white teeth and a curved line at each corner of her lovely lips. Her cheeks were flushed with pleasure, and a drop of water clung to her chin. Huge wet spots dotted her dress and apron.

Her radiant joy at motherhood became her as much as the exultant flush of passion. And he'd seen them both.

William gave a healthy kick and splattered even Nicholas. He laughed out loud.

The surprise in her eyes gave him pause. But of course, she'd never before heard *him* laugh, either.

Claire placed the baby on her bed and dried him. His hair stood in pale spikes atop his head, and Nicholas laughed again. She had William diapered and dressed within an amazingly few minutes. Her wet clothing must be uncomfortable, and she needed to change.

"We'll be leaving at about ten tomorrow morning," he said.

"We'll be ready."

"What about your mother?" he asked.

"Don't worry about her. I've arranged for Mrs. Trent to watch her while we're gone."

"I wasn't worried about her. I thought you might like to take her along for the outing."

Her pale eyebrows drew together, and he regretted chasing the content expression from her face. "I'll ask her," she said.

Sarah watched him exit the room. Just yesterday, she'd tried to take Celia for a carriage ride, and the contrary woman had complained the entire time. Sarah hadn't allowed her to take along her liquor, so she'd pouted and whined, and finally become belligerent, and Sarah had brought her home posthaste.

Her erratic behavior worried Sarah.

Nicholas's concern touched her deeply, however, and added to the burden of guilt she carried daily. Each day she learned a little more about him—just enough to raise him in her esteem and lower her opinion of herself even further. What tonight and tomorrow held, she could only imagine.

Sarah had helped Celia dress, making sure her shoes matched, and that she didn't carry a flask on her person. She'd spent hours coaching her on appropriate behavior for her first appearance at the Halliday's dinner table, and prayed things went smoothly. Nicholas and Leda were waiting for them in the dining room.

"You didn't bring William?" Leda asked.

"No, he was napping soundly, and I didn't want to disturb him." Actually she had wanted to avoid any extra complications.

"Good evening, Celia," Nicholas greeted the woman, obviously remembering the title she preferred.

"Evenin'" Celia replied, seating herself beside Sarah.

"I understand you're quite handy with a needle and thread," Leda said, breaking the ice.

"I've done a bit of sewing in my time," Celia agreed.

"And you've taught Claire the skills," Leda said. "That's lovely."

Celia reached for her wineglass. Sarah and Nicholas exchanged a look as she took a swallow. "Actually, Claire always wanted to do something else," Celia replied.

"Did you see a lot of the plays Claire sewed for?" Nicholas asked.

"Some."

Tension knotted Sarah's shoulders. What on *earth* would they converse about that wouldn't be a dangerous topic? She recalled all those newspapers Celia went through, and racked her brain for a newsworthy item.

Finally thinking of something she'd overheard Monty Gallamore and Nicholas discussing, she brought up the amendment currently going through the senate and—with surprising intelligence—Celia bantered it back and forth with Nicholas until the dessert was served.

She and Leda shared a smile, and Mrs. Pratt poured coffee.

"We're attending a picnic tomorrow," Sarah said, broaching the new topic gently. "Nicholas told me he'd like you to join us."

Celia polished off another glass of wine, and declined the coffee. "I'd rather stay here."

"It would be a good chance for you to get some air," Sarah coaxed. "Enjoy the weather."

"You know how I get along with air," she replied.

The matter was settled. Sarah glanced at Nicholas. "Just so you know you're welcome," he said.

Celia appeared embarrassed by his words. "I'm not good around people. Trust me. You wouldn't want me there."

"We'll leave that up to you," he replied. "Excuse me, ladies."

"Do you have any opinions on bustles?" Leda asked.

Celia cocked an eyebrow at her.

"I've been trying to decide on a dress for an upcoming event, and I can't make up my mind about the bustle. Maybe you'd look at the pattern for me."

"Sure," Celia said with a shrug.

Leave it to Leda to try to make her feel more welcome, and not to hold any bad feelings about what had happened that first day. Sarah accompanied them to Leda's chamber, and later took Celia to her room.

"You'd think I was really somebody the way that woman treats me," she said, letting Sarah help her from her dress.

"She's quite a woman," Sarah agreed. "She's worked hard in her life, too, and she doesn't consider herself above others."

"Her sons, too, huh?" she asked.

Her sons? Yes, Stephen had been much like Leda. But Nicholas? He treated his employees well, and that spoke volumes for him, but he hadn't thought Claire was good enough for Stephen. She couldn't tell Celia that, though.

"Her sons, too," she agreed.

"Could you find me a drink?" Celia asked.

"Don't you think you had enough at dinner?"

"I'll let you know when I've had enough."

Sarah brought her a bottle and left her alone.

Saturday couldn't have been a nicer day for the outdoor festivity. The sun shone bright and warm, but not hot enough to spoil the outing. The number of makeshift tables spread with cloths and laden with baskets and crates amazed her. She'd never attended anything as informal, as all of her father's business acquaintances were stuffy old bankers and investors. Even her own school activities had been formal affairs, and a ride through the Boston Common the closest she'd been to nature.

"Come see the trophy we made for this year's competition!" Several men, all talking at once, gathered around Nicholas.

"Don't worry, we didn't do it on company time," someone else laughed.

"Claire?" he said over his shoulder as they ushered him off.

She smiled and waved. "Don't worry about me."

Leda had found a spot in the shade to visit with a group of chattering women working on quilting squares, and Sarah wandered about the area on her own.

Children ran and played, laughter ringing across the lush green countryside. Booths had been constructed with carnival like games, and she watched in fascination as children of all ages tried their skill at tossing rings over bottles and throwing balls at stacked cartons.

"Mrs. Halliday! Claire!" Sarah glanced around.

Mary Crane, with a rosy-cheeked David on her hip and Elissa clinging to her purple and blue taffeta skirts, hurried toward her. Sarah admired the dress Mary had cleverly designed from two of Claire's dresses, using both to come up with enough material to make the garment modest and lovely.

"Hello," Sarah said, greeting the three of them.

"Have you had something to drink yet?" Mary asked. "You must be thirsty after your long ride."

"I'd love something cool," Sarah replied.

"Follow me." Mary led her to a spot beneath a towering oak where two barrels sat stacked on top of others so that the spigots were accessible. "That one's lemonade, and this one's tea. Or if you're inclined the men have brew over yonder."

"Lemonade sounds good." They filled tin cups and drank.

"Come on, I want you to meet some of the others."

Sarah walked beside her, and Mary introduced her to the wives of the iron workers. Several of them wore dresses made over from Claire's clothing. Even the children wore bright-colored shirts and pinafores. Sarah smiled, and hoped Claire would have been pleased to see her clothing make so many people happy.

A sharp-chinned young woman named Vella crooned at William and chatted with Sarah and Mary. "Your brother-in-law is the dearest man," Vella exclaimed. "We look forward to this picnic every year. My sister's husband works at Neligh Ironworks, and the workers don't have it near as good as we do here."

"Is your husband an iron worker?" Sarah asked.

"I'm not married yet." She blushed. "My daddy is one of the furnace foremen."

William got cranky, and Mary found Sarah a place to sit in the shade, where she fed him within the circle of young mothers and beneath the concealment of a flannel sheet.

He fell asleep immediately.

"Leave him here, and I'll watch over him," Mary said. David had fallen asleep, too, and Elissa and another little girl played with scrap dolls on a nearby coverlet.

Sarah glanced at the circle of pleasant-faced women.

"Please," Mary said softly. "It's the least I can do for you. You can enjoy yourself while he naps."

"Well. If you're sure you don't mind."

"Watching over a soundly sleepin' baby isn't nearly as tough as carin' for a whole sick family," she replied. "And I know you don't want anything in return, but, well, I feel like we're friends now. Friends do things like this."

Sarah blinked back her surprise. And smiled. She could use a friend. "Thank you, Mary. I'll wander for a while."

Mary beamed.

Feeling quite liberated, Sarah walked among the families of the iron workers. It seemed everyone knew who she was. Of course they hadn't seen her before, but her black mourning dress stood out from the clothing of the other women. Time after time, others stopped to share their sympathies or thank her for the material, or tell her they'd heard about her coming to the Cranes' aid.

Surprisingly, they never made her feel like an outsider, and before long she recognized why. Whenever she observed Nicholas, she found him within clusters of the workers, sipping foamy beer, exchanging joking remarks or just sitting companionably in their groups. Even Leda remained with the older women most of the morning, sewing and visiting.

Sarah had seen the side of the Hallidays' life-style that reminded her of her father's, but she'd never seen this side—well, perhaps just a glimpse from time to time, such as Nicholas's interaction with the Gruvers. Each person here today was in Nicholas's employ, yet he walked among them like an equal.

Their livelihoods depended upon him. But Nicholas obviously believed his livelihood depended on them as well.

The iron workers were not wealthy. They lived in tiny shacklike homes, but their children were loved; they weren't treated simply as small humans who should be ignored until they grew up. The concept warmed Sarah's heart.

And Nicholas had afforded all this for his people. It was more than generosity. They earned adequate wages and had time off to spend with their families. He provided them with a sense of community and gave them the opportunity to share this carefree day. A new sense of pride and appreciation blossomed within Sarah.

A new level of excitement ran through the crowd, and the men congregated on a gently sloping bank near a shallow creek. The woman traveled that way, too, and Sarah returned for William so that Mary could join the others. He was awake and watching the leaves overhead in fascination.

"I thought you might like to see what they're doing," she said to Mary.

"You come, too. It's a tug-of-war."

Sarah changed William, found her parasol and followed.

The men were dividing into teams. About half, Nicholas among them, crossed the stream via a small bridge upstream and gathered on the opposite bank. He'd removed his jacket and rolled back his sleeves, and his shirt gleamed white in the sunlight.

The sight of him from this distance, tall and handsome and well respected, gave Sarah an odd proprietary feeling, and for a brief moment she wished she had the right to think of him in that manner. But she didn't. She had no rights at all where Nicholas Halliday was concerned. But she wouldn't ruin her day with self-disparaging thoughts, so she shook them off.

A long fat rope came into sight. One of the men tied a huge knot in the end and tossed that end across the stream. Nicholas caught it and men lined up behind him, taking their places along the length of rope.

The same formation took place on this side of the water, and the rope drew tight across the expanse.

A shot rang out, and the men on both sides pulled in opposite directions, some leaning clear back, all straining and grappling for footholds.

Shouts went up from the women. Several had run down to the bridge to watch.

Sarah had never seen anything like it. "Oh, my goodness," she said, gripping the handle of her parasol. "If one side doesn't pull hard enough, they'll be dragged into the water!"

"That's the idea," Mary said with a laugh. "The winners are the ones with the dry shoes."

Sarah laughed. "What fun!"

It seemed so strange to see Nicholas and Milos partici- pating in the iron workers' games.

The women and children around them shouted and cheered, calling out for their husbands and sons and fathers.

Dozens of pairs of feet dug into the creek bank, slipping, creating divots, grappling for footholds. Sarah held her breath and watched as Nicholas strained in tandem with the other men, the muscles beneath his shirt bunching, his face red and perspiring.

He worked frantically to keep his footing, losing inches at a time and doubling his efforts.

His team now toiled to keep Nicholas from the water's edge. They gained a foot to the pleasure of the crowd, but then lost it again. A groan came up from the onlookers.

Sarah felt the tension in her own body. She clenched her fingers on the parasol and bounced on her strong leg in excitement.

She'd never seen people interact in quite this way before. She'd seen horse races and polo games and had played croquet, but this was different.

The man directly behind Nicholas lost his footing on the bank and slid, knocking Nicholas's feet from under him. Nicholas clung to the rope, but couldn't regain his footing. A third man stumbled and released the rope before he fell atop the men in front of him.

The woman went wild with screams and cheers.

Nicholas gained his feet only to have the rope drag him, laughing, into the water, followed by half a dozen of the men behind him. They slapped him on the back and he bent over with his hands on his knees, gulping air.

The men on this side of the stream hauled the rope in and the others released it before their feet, too, hit the water. The end of the rope dragged through the stream and came up on the bank. The smelters raised a cheer and slapped one another on the back.

Nicholas and his team made a production of stomping

through the calf-high stream, splashing and sending water flying up the bank ahead of them.

The winners extended their hands and hauled them up the bank in easy camaraderie.

Sarah followed Mary and Vella and sat with the children while the women set the meal out. The task was accomplished in no time, and Sarah went in search of Leda. She discovered Nicholas with her, his white shirt damp and wrinkled. She glanced down.

A dark patch of mud stained the seat of his trousers, and he wore a worn pair of wet brogans she'd never seen before.   –

He turned his attention to the baby in her arms. "Did you like the tug-of-war, too, William?" he asked. "Soon as you get a few pounds on, you'll help me."

Leda handed Sarah a blanket to spread and took William. "You have to let him stay with me the rest of the afternoon. We old ladies need a little entertainment, too."

They prepared plates from the huge spread of enormous dishes that had been laid out, and back at their blanket, they settled and ate. The food was delicious, and Sarah ate until she could hold no more.

The Cranes waved from a blanket nearby.

Sarah waved and observed their close-knit family for a few minutes. "Where's Milos?" she asked.

Nicholas glanced across the crowded area unconcernedly. "Found someone to dine with, I'm sure. Here, I brought you a piece of pie."

Sarah groaned. "I can't eat another bite."

"At least try it."

He extended his fork, a succulent bite of red filling and flaky crust on the tip. Sarah had no choice but to accept the offering. She opened her mouth, and he fed her the bite.

She caught a bit of crust with her tongue. It melted in her mouth, and she savored the sharp tang of rhubarb. "Mmm, it's wonderful," she said appreciatively.

His eyes darkened and his gaze focused on her lips.

Sarah's heart skipped a beat.

Heat flooded her cheeks.

She met his eyes and knew he was thinking of the in-flaming kisses they'd shared. She remembered her reactions to his touches, and embarrassment scorched her face. She glanced at Leda, but the woman had finished her meal and was playing with William.

"Want another bite?" he asked.

Sarah shook her head and lowered her gaze.

"I guess I'll have to finish yours then." He finished eating and sat relaxing, one arm resting on an upraised knee. Leda chattered to William. After a few minutes, Sarah relaxed and placed the sultry moment out of her thoughts.

"Are you enjoying yourselves?" a female voice asked.

Sarah glanced up and discovered pale green eyes set in a vaguely familiar face, framed by the underside of a white parasol. She felt she should know where she'd seen the woman before. She clung to the arm of a muscular young man with chestnut-brown hair and eyes.

"Yes. It's a lovely day," Sarah replied.

"Sorry," the woman said, and extended a hand to Leda. "We haven't met before. I'm Judith Marcelino."

"Of course," Nicholas said, his voice not altogether welcoming, and Sarah understood he hadn't recognized her at first either. "You didn't move on with the theater group?"

That was it! They'd met her at the restaurant in Youngstown after the theater.

"No. I decided to stay a while." She patted the young man's arm.

"J.W.," Nicholas acknowledged.

"Mr. Halliday," the young man returned with a polite nod.

She'd stayed because she'd met an iron worker?

"Well, it's nice to meet you, Judith," Leda said. "And you know Claire?"

"Oh yes. We go back a long way. Don't we, Claire?"
Sarah merely blinked.

"I knew Claire in New York. Before she ever met Stephen, of course. She did the costumes for *A Midsummer Night's Dream.* I had a lead."

"O-oh," Leda said with interest, making the word two syllables.

"Claire designed a lovely blue gown with hundreds of seed pearls." Judith's piercing green eyes held a silent message. "*Remember,* Claire?"

Her eerie inflection made the hair on Sarah's neck stand on end. The food she'd eaten turned to a hard ball in her stomach. Panic rose in her throat, and her heart thudded a few sluggish beats as though it would stop altogether.

What was she saying? Good Lord, what was her purpose? If she knew Claire and meant to expose Sarah, why hadn't she done it the last time they'd met? She obviously expected Sarah to go along with her taunting questions.

"I—I..." she stammered.

"It was a cobalt blue," Judith prompted.

"I—yes, of course I remember that dress," she replied. Nicholas looked at her curiously.

"And who is this?" the girl asked, kneeling gracefully beside where Leda sat holding William.

"This is my grandson, William Stephen Halliday," Leda said proudly.

"Oh!" Judith looked him over. "William Stephen Halliday," she repeated, rolling the name from her tongue as though she were trying it out. "Well, what do you know?"

Sarah wanted to jump up and push the woman away from her son, but she commanded her body to stay put. She set down her plate.

"Do you think he looks like Stephen?" Judith asked Leda.

Sarah's heart jumped.

"Somewhat," Leda responded with a rich smile. Anyone

who took an interest in William won her over. "But he's the very image of Claire. All that pale hair, and see his chin?"

"Oh, yes," Judith agreed as if it really were important to her.

Nicholas and the fellow he'd called J.W. exchanged a look. "Will you join me in getting something to wash down that meal?" Nicholas asked.

A smile spread across the young man's face as though he were honored. "Sure."

The two of them headed toward the area where barrels of beer sat on the tailgate of a wagon in the shade.

"You go enjoy yourself now," Leda said to Sarah. "William and I have some ladies to impress."

Sarah helped her to her feet and watched helplessly as she walked back to the sewing circle.

With trepidation weighing her heart, Sarah turned back to the young woman who had made herself at home on the blanket. Judith patted the spread beside her. "We may as well catch up on old times, don't you think, *Claire?*"

Sarah's knees shook, so she sat quickly. "What are you doing?"

Judith appeared stricken. "What am I doing?" She splayed her hand over her chest dramatically. "Why, I'm just being an old friend!"

Her smile gave Sarah a cold shiver.

"And authenticating your story, of course."

"You know as well as I do that I'd never seen you before that evening at the restaurant."

"You and I know that. But the Hallidays don't." She raised a haughty brow and looked at Sarah through her kohled lashes. "Yet."

Sarah couldn't catch her breath.

"And I assume you want it to stay that way."

Sarah stared at her. "What is it you want?"

Judith adjusted a ring on a finger of her right hand,

straightened her bodice and patted her hair. "Why the same things you want, of course. A rich husband. Lots of fine clothing and jewelry."

Heat rose in Sarah's face. She was sure it must appear that way. "What do you want *from me?*"

Judith looked her square in the eye. "I'll be happy to have the Hallidays go on thinking you're their precious Claire. If that's what you want, then that's what I want."

Sarah waited.

"I'm sure you'd be more than happy to support the arts this season. A donation toward the refined things we both love."

"I have no money of my own," Sarah said bluntly.

"Of course you don't. Isn't that why you're here? But you have a good thing going with the Hallidays. If you play your part well, you'll have his ring on your finger before you're out of those widow's weeds."

"I mean—" Sarah glanced around "—I don't have any money to give you. Can't you just leave us alone?"

"How stupid do you take me for? They think you're a *Halliday,* for crying out loud! I'm confident you can handle it. Until you figure out the cash, there's that lovely emerald bracelet...."

Stricken, Sarah stared at her. "That was my mother's!"

"I'm sure she'd think it was a good cause. There'll be plenty more where that came from, after all."

"Please, you don't understand—"

"Oh, I understand. I understand quite well. And if you don't want your fish on a hook—Nicholas there—to understand, too, then you'll do exactly as I say." She stood.

Sarah stared up at her in horror, unable to make her body move.

"I'll come calling morning after tomorrow. And I'll leave richer than I came. Got that?"

Sarah nodded dumbly.

"And if I don't—Mr. Halliday will have his eyes opened. Opened *wide*. Got that, sugar?"

Sarah nodded again.

Judith straightened her skirts. "Well, I must go after my amusing partner. He doesn't have money, but his robust, homespun talents almost make up for it."

She opened her fringed parasol and sauntered away.

Sarah didn't know whether to cry or faint.

The sounds of conversation and children calling blended into an accusing drone in her ears. She was being blackmailed. Only murderers and thieves were blackmailed. She pressed her fingertips to her temple.

No. Someone with something equally ugly to hide could be blackmailed. And she had a secret. A big one. An ugly one.

Each day had been leading her a little closer to this moment. She'd been on stolen time since the minute she'd arrived. It was only a matter of time until Celia blundered or she herself did something to give the ruse away.

But she would not steal from the Hallidays to pay Judith. And the bracelet was her only means of providing for William's future; she certainly wasn't going to turn that over.

She had to leave.

Sarah pledged that her last day in Mahoning Valley would be a day to remember, a day to hold close to her heart when the days ahead grew long and lonely. She threw herself into the festivities, joining Milos in a ringtoss competition and watching the fathers and sons run three-legged races.

She watched and she laughed and she forgot for a few hours that she was Sarah Thornton, and that tomorrow she'd be totally and completely on her own, and that everyone here would remember her only as the woman who'd deceived them all.

Chapter Fifteen

She wouldn't be able to leave on Sunday. She'd be discovered. Gruver always drove them to church and then had the afternoon off with his family. Sarah spent Sunday carefully laying her plans for stealing away after Nicholas left for the foundry the next morning. That would give her all day to travel and be as far away as possible before he came home.

She would leave Leda a note saying she'd gone to the Cranes' for the day and taken William.

Somehow she struggled through her last hours with them on Sunday. She and Leda made a cold supper, and they shared it with Nicholas in his study.

She avoided his eyes and never allowed herself to be alone with him. Leda came to her room that night, and Mrs. Trent brought them tea.

"This is generous of you, Mrs. Trent," Sarah said. "Now you go rest. I'll clear this away and see to William if he should wake."

"Thank you, ma'am."

"Your leg is much stronger," Leda commented. "I noticed at the picnic that you hardly favor it any longer."

"It's much better. It only aches a little at night."

"It's probably still healing."

"I'm sure that's so."

"You know how dear you are to me, Claire," Leda said.

Sarah tensed, praying Leda wouldn't go on about how she and William were her life source. She didn't think she could handle the remorse tonight. She nodded.

"You've become like my own daughter." She hurried to say, "I don't mean to offend you. I know you have your own mother."

"I'm not offended. I know what you're saying." Leda was the closest thing she'd had to a mother in many years. Leaving her was nearly as difficult as leaving Nicholas.

"Since you know how fond I am of you," Leda continued softly, "I don't believe you'll take this wrong."

Sarah prepared herself. "What is it?"

"I loved my Stephen as much as any mother could love her son. As much as you love William."

"Of course you did."

"I overlooked much of his foolishness. At first I forgave him because he was young. And after that because Nicholas treated him like a child. And after that I forgave him simply because he was Stephen. Just as I forgive Nicholas for being domineering and aggressive. Because they are my sons. A mother turns a blind eye to those things she doesn't wish to see."

"I think I understand, but I don't know what you're trying to say."

"That's because I'm doing it poorly. It's just that—you don't seem suited to Stephen to me. There, I've said it."

Sarah blinked and absorbed the woman's quickly spoken words.

"Oh, I know opposites attract and all that, and I'm not saying Stephen didn't have a hundred reasons to admire and love you. Heaven knows you're easy to love.

"And I'm not saying Stephen wasn't easy to love, either—everyone loved him. But he could be a difficult person to be around. He was…overstimulating. One had to be on one's guard and ready for anything. There wasn't much relaxing to be done when he was about.''

Sarah didn't know what to say.

"I haven't hurt your feelings, have I? I didn't want to say it all wrong."

"No, Leda. You could never hurt my feelings." She leaned forward and closed her hand over hers. *But I will surely hurt yours.* She lowered her gaze before Leda could see the betrayal in her eyes. "I understand perfectly."

They sat in companionable silence a while longer. Sarah wanted to reassure Leda somehow. Stephen had been a kind, generous man. It was because of his goodness that he had died. Finally she gathered her chaotic thoughts to speak. "Leda, I told you once that Stephen was the kindest man I'd ever met. That was the truth. Please don't ever forget that."

Stephen, though unknowingly, had made the ultimate sacrifice out of the goodness of his heart. "He was a good man. Kind. Generous. And he had so much love in his heart. I know he loved you dearly."

Tears pooled in Leda's soft gray eyes. She turned her hand over and clasped Sarah's firmly. "I know he loved you very much, too, dear."

"Don't ever forget how grateful I am to you and your sons," Sarah said around the lump in her throat. "And always remember that I'm here because of Stephen's good heart."

"I'll remember." Leda patted her hand and stood. "We need to rest now. I'll see you tomorrow."

Fighting tears, Sarah gave her friend a lingering hug. She would never forget her kindness. She'd learned much about love from Leda. Much about being a mother. Much about being a woman.

Leda patted her back and pulled away, and Sarah let her go. She wouldn't understand if Sarah broke down and clung to her. Closing the door, she covered her mouth with her fingers and sat on the edge of the bed. It wouldn't do to lose control now.

William woke and she changed and nursed him. She wouldn't have another opportunity, so she carried him with her as she went to check on Celia.

The woman sat in her usual chair by the fire, a stack of rumpled newspapers at her feet, a glass of amber liquid on the nearby table.

She looked up as Sarah entered. "That the boy?"

Sarah nodded. "This is William."

Celia leaned forward and inspected him. She didn't seem terribly drunk this evening, but Sarah hung on to her baby all the same.

"Don't look so fierce," she said. "I ain't gonna snatch him and drop him on his head."

Sarah ignored her comment and sat across from her.

"I can see why they're so all-fired crazy over him," she said. "He's a fine-lookin' one."

"Thank you."

Celia gave a nod. "I had a boy once."

Sarah recalled reading the Pinkerton's report about Claire's brother, who'd been killed in a street fight.

"His name was Walt."

Sarah waited for something more.

"Named him after an old beau. I think that jinxed him, though. The first Walt was killed, too."

She met Sarah's eyes, and Sarah remembered Leda's words vividly: *A mother should never have to lose a child. Never.* Celia had lost a son. Sarah couldn't help wondering if that loss had anything to do with the woman's inability to cope with life in a sober state. And now she'd lost another child.

"New York ain't no place to raise kids." She sipped from her glass.

"I imagine not."

"This here. This'll be a fine place to raise your boy."

"Yes." Safe. Secure. If only she were staying. Mahoning Valley would be a good place to live. "What about you, Cele? You could live and work here, too. You could probably have a job as a seamstress if you wanted one. It would give you something to do."

"I'm too old to start something like that."

"You're not too old. Afraid maybe."

"What do I have to be afraid of?"

"You tell me."

They stared at each other.

"It's not fair you've lost both of your children," Sarah said. "You have a right to your feelings. But you're still alive. And in order to live, you've got to pull yourself together and go on."

"You're a fine one to give advice. You're doing so well with your life."

Sarah accepted the criticism with grace. "I didn't mean to condemn. I just want what's best for you."

"I guess I know what's best for me."

"Okay. Do you have everything you need?"

"You see to that."

She couldn't worry about what would happen after she left. Nicholas and Leda would care for Celia. The woman was, after all, Claire's mother. "Good night, then."

"'Night. Thanks for bringin' him."

"You're welcome." She hurried back to her rooms and put William to bed. He fussed for a few minutes, then fell asleep.

Sarah stacked the flannels and gowns and blankets she would take for William and made a list of everything she could fit into two bags.

Sitting at the small desk, the weight of her secret good-bye pressing on her heart, she dipped the pen in ink and wrote the note she'd been planning for weeks.

Nicholas and Leda,

I know what I have done is unforgivable, so I don't ask for your forgiveness. All I ask is that you do not hate me. I planned to tell you the truth from the very minute I awoke in that hospital. But when I saw your grief, Nicholas, and when you offered protection and shelter for my son, I could not bring myself to speak the words. I thought perhaps they'd be more easily spoken to your mother.

And then, dear Leda, when I saw your tears, and your expression as you looked at my son, I could not bear to say the words then, either. I am still too much of a coward to speak them to your face, so I am leaving this letter.

I am not Claire Halliday. I was never married to your Stephen. I only met him that night of the train wreck. He took me in out of the rain and he and Claire gave me food and dry clothing and shared their berth with me.

If they had been in that compartment that night, they might still be alive. So you see, I am responsible for their deaths. That is something I will live with for the rest of my life.

That and the lies. I lied to you and pretended to be Claire so that I could take advantage of you until my leg was healed and I was able to make it on my own.

Enclosed you will find a list of all the items I have taken with me. As soon as I am settled and have a job, I will repay you for the clothing and food and the time spent in your home.

I can never repay you for your kindness, nor for the sin of lying to you and for the loss of your son and brother. I can only tell you how very ashamed and sorry I am.

I don't know if you can find it in your hearts to not hate me. For the things I have done, I hate myself.

You have no reason to believe me, but now you

must see I have nothing left to lose, so I want you to believe this: Stephen was a good man. He knew how to love. He was a son and brother to be proud of. I was but a stranger, and he and Claire showed me kindness. You would have liked Claire, I know. Cherish their memories.

Sincerely, Sarah Thornton.

Sarah folded her letter with the list inside and sealed them in an envelope. On the outside, she carefully penned Nicholas and Leda's names, then tucked it under her pillow.

As soon as Nicholas was gone in the morning and Gruver returned, she'd place the note in plain sight and leave.

Nicholas arrived home early, in a good mood and hungry.

"Mr. Halliday, sir," Penelope said. "Your mother requested that I ask you to join her in the parlor as soon as you arrived home. She has a guest."

To his surprise, he found Judith Marcelino. His mother appeared decidedly uncomfortable.

The young woman wore a vivid green dress, something resembling all the fabrics Claire had given to the iron workers' wives. The bodice bore a plunging neckline, and he drew his eyes from the area she strove to accentuate to her pale green cat eyes.

"Mr. Halliday," she said, offering her ungloved hand. "I've been waiting for Claire most of the day. We had an appointment."

"And she's not here?" he asked.

"She left me a note that she'd gone to the Cranes'," Leda said. "But she always returns by now. And she's taken William with her, which is unusual."

"Well, she is his mother," he stated.

"Yes," she agreed. "And the Cranes are no longer sick,

so I guess it's normal for her to go calling and take him along. She does enjoy visiting them.''

"But she's always back by now?" he asked.

"Yes. She always oversees dinner. And it's odd that she's forgotten her appointment with Miss Marcelino. That's unlike Claire.''

His mother seemed truly upset over Claire's lateness. To set her mind at rest, he'd summoned Gruver.

"Gruver, did you have a time agreed upon to bring Mrs. Halliday home from the Cranes'?''

"I didn't take her to the Cranes'. But I did take her to Youngstown.''

"Youngstown! And when were you supposed to return for her?''

"She said she arranged for transportation home, sir.''

"Where, specifically, did you drop off Mrs. Halliday?''

"Specifically?'' He swallowed. "At a jeweler's.''

"Why there?''

"She asked me if I knew where she could sell jewelry for the best price.''

Nicholas's mind ran in circles. What jewelry was she selling? And why? She had no need for money. The whole thing sounded so bizarre—as though she were running away. But why would she?

If she was all he'd originally suspected, had she met someone and run off with him? But why would she keep it a secret?

He turned and looked at his mother. She stared at him in disbelief.

"Oh, you poor dears,'' Judith said. "I was afraid of this. I came to warn you, but it appears I'm too late.''

Nicholas moved to stand before her. "What do you mean?''

She stood and moved her body directly beside Nicholas's. "I knew Claire back in New York, and she always went with the fellow with the most to give. Don't take it personally." Tucking her arm through his sympathetically, she allowed her generous breast to brush his coat sleeve. Nicholas couldn't help but get an eyeful when he looked down at her.

He moved away.

"I'd check for the silver and jewels," she added with a knowing sidelong glance.

"Why, Claire wouldn't—" Leda began.

"Wouldn't she?" Judith cut her off. "You didn't think she'd run out without so much as a by-your-leave, either, did you?" She moved to sit beside Leda and take her hand. "Oh, you poor thing. I know how distressed you are." She touched the fingertips of one hand to her own chest in a dramatic gesture. "And rightfully so. I can't bear to think of that dear sweet baby with that irresponsible woman."

Leda's gray eyes opened wide, and she stared from Judith to her son in shock. "You don't think—oh my…"

Nicholas sat beside his mother, placed his arm around her shoulders and glared at Judith over the top of her head. "You've seen her with the baby, Mother. You know she'll take good care of him."

"Oh, yes, I'm sure she'll take care of the Halliday heir," Judith said quickly. "He's worth a fortune, after all."

"What was your business with Claire?" Nicholas asked her quickly, before she could say more to upset his already distressed mother.

"She owed me some money. I can see I'm not going to get that now."

"What did she owe you money for?"

"I made her a loan to help her out of a scrape back in New York. She kept saying she'd repay me."

"How much?"

She eyed him consideringly. "Let's not worry about that right now. You have enough on your mind, what with the baby missing and all. I'll leave you to—to tally your valuables."

Nicholas tried not to let his mother feel his distress. The Marcelino woman rubbed him the wrong way. Or was it his own humiliation rubbing him raw? He'd been deceived but good, and the fact rankled.

"Gruver, see Miss Marcelino out."

Gruver directed a scathing look at the woman. "My pleasure."

"Now, do call on me to do anything I can," she said in a sugary-sweet voice, and patted the reticule she'd been holding snugly beneath her arm. "I will be praying for your little William's safety."

Nicholas waved her off and Gruver ushered her from the room.

"I can't believe Claire would have done this, Nicholas," his mother said shakily. "Can we be sure something dreadful hasn't happened to her?"

"You heard Gruver, Mother. She left of her own free will."

"Perhaps there's some mistake. Perhaps she'll be here soon."

He didn't hold much hope of that. Nicholas took his mother's arm. "Come with me."

"Where?"

"We're going to check your jewelry case."

"No!" she insisted.

"Then I'll do it."

She stood and took his arm. "All right."

He threw open her door and entered her violet- and camphor-scented room. "Where do you keep them?"

"Here," she said, her voice quivering. She pulled open a drawer and unrolled a satin jewelry bag.

Tears began in earnest. She sobbed into her hankie.

"What! What the hell is missing?"

"M-my rings. The emerald necklace your father gave me. The diamond bracelet that you bought me for my birthday."

Nicholas cursed and slammed his fist against the top of the dresser. "I knew it! I knew that damned woman was trouble from the minute I heard her name!"

Mother wilted onto the bed's edge and cried brokenly. "How could she? How c-could she do this to us? And W-William!" she sobbed, sounding as though she couldn't catch her breath. Her voice grew hysterical. "We must find him! We can't let anything h-happen to William!"

Nicholas heard the grief and hurt and panic in his mother's words and with deliberate effort stopped his own outraged ranting. He sat beside her and pulled her against his chest. "There, there. You're a goodhearted person. She took advantage of that."

He had no words of comfort for her. She would mourn her grandson as she mourned her husband and her son.

"Will you go after her?" she asked. "For the jewelry?"

He stroked her hair. "I'll go buy your jewelry back at Grambs'."

"I don't care about the jewelry. I care about William!"

"I know, Mother—"

"You must find William. I want my grandson!"

Hurt and anger boiled up in him. He never wanted to set eyes on Claire again. He hoped she'd run as fast and as far as her legs and his money could take her. But his mother wanted her grandson back. "All right," he promised. "I'll look for him."

"Thank you, Nicholas. Thank you. I just don't understand." She sobbed. "Why would she steal from us and run off?"

"A conniving mind never makes sense," he replied.

"But what little she could get from the sale of that jewelry is nothing compared to what she could have had staying here. All she had to do was ask."

She was right. It was illogical. "Unless she was biding her time here, and needed a few dollars to get her to a bigger and better conquest."

She shook her head. "No. I don't believe that."

After Nicholas calmed her down, sent for the doctor and had his mother sedated and resting, he approached Celia's door. Claire had run out on her mother, too. But maybe the woman knew something.

Nicholas received no reply to his knock. He pushed open the door.

The woman slumped in a chair by the dormant fireplace. An empty bottle lay on the carpet at her feet, and another, half-full, stood on a nearby table. The room smelled stale.

"Celia!" he said sharply.

She didn't move.

He opened a window, carried her to the bed and filled a waste can with all the bottles—full and empty—before he carried it out and closed the door behind him.

He instructed the servants not to bring her liquor without his permission, checked on his mother and finally closed himself in his room.

Nicholas stared at the cognac decanter on his desk, thought better of it and shrugged out of his shirt. He'd been the man of this house for many years, but at that moment he'd have given anything to have someone else make decisions for a while.

He didn't want to find Claire.

But his mother wanted her grandson.

Even as he checked his personal belongings and discovered a diamond stickpin and a watch missing, he had to agree with his mother that Claire's running off made no sense.

He turned down the wick in the oil lamp and leaned back on the bed. Her betrayal ate at him. He'd been right not to trust her. She'd married Stephen for the Halliday money.

And until he himself married and produced a child, she was the mother of the only Halliday heir.

She could have had so much more here.

The light burned out and darkness enfolded him.

He cared about the money. He was livid over the jewelry. Nicholas folded his arm over his eyes.

Unbidden, an ugly nagging suspicion crept into his mind. *Milos.* Nicholas tried to bury the thought deep, but it persisted until he allowed himself to examine it. The two of them had seemed comfortable with each other. He'd seen them absorbed in conversation from time to time. They'd shared private smiles.

Nicholas hated himself for distrusting his friend. Milos wouldn't betray him. He was too levelheaded to let her steal his good sense.

But hadn't Nicholas always believed that about himself, too? And look how easily he'd been fooled. She could fool the best of men.

No. He took control of his thoughts. He was torturing himself. Milos was a good-looking man, but he wouldn't be rich enough for Claire's tastes. Besides, he was decent and loyal, and would not run off with his employer's sister-in-law.

What was wrong with him? He hadn't behaved like himself since he'd gone to bring Claire home.

Humiliation crept over him and settled in his chest. He'd never entertained such degrading thoughts. He'd never wanted a woman so badly before. Oh, he'd fancied himself in love years ago, but that had been nothing like the all-consuming need and passion he'd felt for this woman. He'd been drawn to her from their first meeting. His feelings had shocked him, made him feel disloyal to his brother, and he'd fought them.

That was her ploy, he realized with bitterness. Whereas Judith Marcelino's obvious seduction tactics sickened him, Claire's had reeled him in. That air of provocative innocence was her trump. And she'd had him.

She could have had it all. He couldn't understand why she'd fled when her artifice had been so successful.

But she was gone. And that was all he had to go by.

He never wanted to see her again. But he would honor his mother's wishes.

The following morning he stood before Gramb and Sons' door as Howard Gramb arrived. The portly gentleman unlocked and unbolted the door and ushered Nicholas inside.

"Have you come for a gift?" he asked.

"No, I've come for the jewelry that a young woman sold yesterday."

"Ah. Yes." He bent, opened a floor safe and withdrew a satin box. "A lovely piece."

Nicholas stared at the emerald bracelet. The one he'd seen on Claire's wrist at least twice. "What about the rest? An emerald necklace, several rings, a diamond bracelet—"

Howard Grambs shook his bald head.

"A diamond stickpin, a gold pocket watch?"

He shook his head again. "This is the only piece I bought all day."

"But she offered you others?"

"No. This was the only piece she had."

"Very well. How much did you give her for it?"

"I would not be a shrewd businessman if I told you that, now would I? Then you would know enough to barter the price until I made no profit."

Nicholas scowled, and the man's expression flattened.

"I don't give a damn about your profit margin. I want to know how much you gave her for this bracelet."

"One hundred and twenty-five dollars," he admitted.

"It's worth four times that."

"Not to me. I'll be lucky to get two-fifty for it."

Nicholas opened his jacket and plucked bills from his flat leather wallet. "Two-fifty it is."

He reached across the counter to take the bracelet from the surprised man. "If she comes back, notify me immediately."

He dropped a card on the glass counter.

"Yes, Mr.—Halliday! I will. Thank you for your business."

Nicholas dropped the bracelet into his pocket. "How many other jewelers are in Youngstown?"

"Seven, I believe."

Nicholas exited the store.

Shortly after ten, he concluded she'd either taken the rest with her or she hadn't left town yet. He left a card with each business owner, along with instructions to notify him if someone came in with the items described.

That night at dinner he pulled the bracelet from his pocket.

His mother, who hadn't eaten a bite, stared at the winking emeralds. "It's Claire's."

He shrugged. "Or something she stole from someone else. She sold it to Gramb."

"The rest?"

He shook his head. "Not yet. I wired every jeweler in five states, Mother. I'll get your things back."

She nodded. She didn't care about the jewelry.

Dinner was silent. She stared at the bassinet until Nicholas ordered Mrs. Pratt to remove it. Finally, she excused herself.

"Good night, Mother." He waited until she left the room before he shoved his plate away, planted his elbows on the table and wearily covered his face with his hands.

Damn the woman! Damn her to hell! Hadn't she caused enough upheaval in this family by marrying Stephen? Did she have to hurt his mother, too? For the life of him he couldn't imagine what she had to gain by it.

And what about him? *Them.* What about the kisses and caresses that had passed between them?

Yes, what about those?

What had he been thinking? Every self-preserving instinct he possessed had cried out to him to be wary of her.

He'd been wary. And he'd been fascinated. Captivated. Stupid as hell.

She was the perfect deceiver. Beautiful. Passionate with an air of innocence. And he'd been drawn to her as a moth to a flame.

"Are you finished, sir?"

Nicholas looked up to find Mrs. Pratt clearing the table. "Yes, thank you."

His voice didn't sound like his own. He stood. His home didn't feel like his own. Nothing was as it should be.

And he still had to face her mother.

Chapter Sixteen

"What do you know about Claire leaving?" Nicholas asked her mother the following day.

Celia moved slowly, as if it hurt to use her muscles. She opened a drawer, looked in a cabinet, glanced around the room. "Leaving for where?"

"That's what I'm asking you."

"Where's the bottle I had here last night?" she asked herself.

"I'll answer that after you answer me."

She squinted at him and sank onto a chair. "All right. Get it the hell over with. I'm thirsty."

"I want to know where Claire went and why she left."

"Left?" Celia repeated.

"That's right."

"You mean packed up, took off, left?"

"Precisely. Well, she didn't actually pack up much, but she's gone. Sold the bracelet she said you gave her."

"What bracelet?"

"The emerald bracelet. She claimed you gave it to her."

"Humph." Celia pushed a hank of her frizzy red hair back from her face.

"Did you give it to her?"

She looked him in the eye, hers clearer than he'd hoped.

"What do you think? I look like the emerald bracelet type to you?"

"Claire never mentioned leaving?"

"She didn't tell me she was going, all right? Pretty damned inconsiderate of her, if you ask me."

"And you know nothing of the bracelet."

"Back to that damned bracelet."

"Was anything she ever said to me the truth?" he wondered aloud.

"She ever say she was in love with you?"

"What?"

"Well, that woulda been the truth."

"You're a crazy old woman."

"That might be, but I know what I know. And I want to know where the hell the bottles are."

"And what you do know is that she was in love with me."

"Yeah."

He laughed scornfully. "Well, she was a damned good actress anyway."

"She was a poor actress, she was. Never had me fooled for a minute."

"That's because you're her mother."

She rolled her eyes. "Okay."

"I can see you're all choked up about her being gone, so I'll leave you to your misery." He stepped to the door.

"You do that," she said. "And tell that damned maid to bring a bottle and the newspapers!"

He stared at her for a long minute. Claire had been far too lenient with the woman's poor disposition and despicable habits. "The servants have been ordered not to bring you a bottle. You may have wine at dinner. I'll expect you dressed and downstairs at eight this evening."

Her eyes widened as though they'd pop from her head. "What the hell—?"

"And you'll curb your language in front of my mother."

She opened her mouth as if to object again, but he cut her off. "If you want to eat, you'll be there. I don't pay my staff to wait hand and foot on someone capable of bringing herself to the dining room."

He shook his head and closed the door on her cursing. *Thank you very much, my dear Stephen.* Lord help him if he was stuck with this woman for life. But if he was, there were going to be some changes made. He'd see to it.

Fort Wayne, Indiana

Sarah stared into the darkness overhead. She hadn't known she possessed the strength to board that train back in Youngstown. But she'd done it. And she'd kept her bags and William possessively in her grasp the entire five days.

She hugged William to her side, grateful for the crowded boardinghouse room because she was lying down to sleep for the first time in days, and because she no longer had to listen to the droning rhythm of the rails and feel the tremulous rocking of the passenger car.

The talk around her had centered on factory jobs and restaurant work, and she'd listened unobtrusively. She received frowns of disapproval from more than a few of the women. The proprietress had warned her that if William so much as cried out at night, she would have to leave.

She'd hastened to assure her that William never cried. And she would spend the entire night with him affixed to her breast if need be. She had to sleep. Her leg ached from being unable to prop it, from walking, from climbing the metal stairs on the train cars, from running to get a seat after stopping for food and water. Her back ached from carrying the bags.

But inside, deep inside, was where the true ache yawned. Her deception ate at her. Her lies and the hurt she'd caused the Hallidays were worse than any physical pain. Missing them tore at her heart and brought tears that she fought constantly.

Loneliness and shame created an ache far worse than hunger or fatigue or mending bones.

"That baby got a daddy?" came a softly spoken question from the darkness beside her.

"No," she replied.

"Shame. Baby should have a daddy."

Tears rolled down her temples into her hair. Lies, lies and more lies. "He died."

"Oh. Shame."

"Yes." What had become of her life? Would she ever be able to speak without being on guard?

"Need a job?"

"Yes."

"Can't take a baby to the factory."

"I know."

"Don't pay as good, but I know somebody lookin' for help."

"You do?"

"Shut it up!" The loud voice startled Sarah, and even William jumped in his sleep. She soothed him with loving pats.

"I'll tell you in the morning." The voice came as a whisper this time.

"Thank you," she replied, grateful there were a few kind people in the world.

She purposely relaxed each limb and muscle in her body, thinking of her downy canopy bed back in Boston, the luxurious four-poster at the Hallidays'. But she no longer led that kind of life, lived in comfortable homes as before or slept in beds as privileged people did.

Worse, she thought of William's lovely iron crib with the high sides and the taffeta skirt that fell to the floor. He'd been so comfortable in that bed Leda had provided for him.

Her choices had changed their futures. She was of the working class now. And she might as well get used to it.

Morning came way too soon. The other women went about their routines of dressing and leaving for their various jobs. The woman who'd spoken to Sarah the night before came to stand at the end of her cot as she changed William and worried where she'd wash out his flannels from the previous night.

"That position I told you about?"

She looked up. The woman wasn't much more than a girl, with wide violet eyes and honey-colored hair pulled back in a neat roll. "Yes?"

"It's working for Mrs. Hargrove over at the Hotel Gold."

Someone behind her chuckled. "And you think the war wagon's gonna let her bring a baby?"

"One of the other girls has a baby."

"Well, she ain't gonna last."

"What does the job involve?" Sarah asked, worried it was something she wouldn't know how to do.

"Hotel maids is all. Making beds, heating water and such. Trouble is nobody will put up with Hargrove when they can make more money at the factory."

"Well, I can put up with her. I can put up with whatever I have to." She had no choices.

"I think you can."

"Hotel Gold, you say?"

"It's a fair walk from here. On the nice side of town. I'll point you out the way."

"I appreciate your help."

By seven, she stood nervously in the kitchen of the Hotel Gold, waiting for Mrs. Hargrove. The cooks and other servants bustled about, barely sparing her a glance.

At seven-thirty, the woman appeared, looking nothing at all like Sarah had expected a tyrant to look. She had mousy-brown hair shot with gray, and a tall, wiry body. Everything about her appearance was stark, from her bland expression to her black dress and white collar.

"You want a job?" she asked tersely in front of the others.

She ignored those who couldn't help but listen. "Yes."

"What can you do?"

"Anything you ask of me."

"That your baby?"

"Yes. His name's—"

"What are you planning to do with him?"

"I need a job where I can have him with me. He never cries. He's no trouble at all."

"What's your name?"

She had no reason to lie about that now. No one would know the difference. And it was one thing she could say that was the truth. "Sarah—Sarah Thornton."

Mrs. Hargrove looked her over critically. "You a widow?"

"Yes, ma'am."

"How long?"

"Almost four months."

"I guess I won't have to worry about you consorting with the guests then, will I?"

Sarah felt her face grow warm. "No, ma'am."

"I'll try you today. If you don't measure up, no pay, and you're out. If you work out, you'll get two uniforms that you'll launder and press yourself, one meal a day, and the starting wage. Do you accept that?"

She had no choice. "Yes."

"There's a schedule by the desk. It tells which rooms are occupied, and what times the guests wish to have them cleaned."

Sarah nodded.

"Speak your understanding," she said harshly.

"Yes, ma'am."

"I will inspect the rooms you've done. I expect square

corners on the beds and not a speck of dust. The chamber pots must be emptied and washed, the chimney lamps cleaned, and fresh towels placed on the hooks.''

''Yes, ma'am,'' Sarah said hurriedly.

''Now come with me. If you can't read the schedule, you will have to—''

''I can read.''

She raised both eyebrows. ''I'll show the book to you.''

As Sarah turned to follow, she glanced at one of the girls standing at a nearby table, and the girl flashed her an encouraging smile.

Mrs. Hargrove explained the schedule to her as succinctly as she'd explained everything else. Then she turned and left her on her own.

Sarah fashioned a sling from two of William's blankets, and tied him to her chest. By one o'clock she had cleaned seventeen rooms. The Gold was an enormous and well-appointed hotel. Sarah had stayed at a few hotels with her father when he'd allowed her to accompany him on business trips, and this was as splendid as any her father had patronized.

Mattie, the young maid who'd smiled at her in the kitchen, showed her how Mrs. Hargrove preferred beds made, and Sarah needed to be shown only once.

She'd never dusted or swept or done any of the things she did that day, but doing them gave her a sense of satisfaction. It was honest work. She would earn her pay.

When Mrs. Hargrove found her at dinner with the other servants, she spoke to Mattie, rather than Sarah.

''Sarah did her rooms adequately, Mattie. Give her uniforms.''

She left the room as abruptly as she'd arrived.

''That means you passed the test,'' another maid named Hannah said. ''The uniforms are black, as you can see. I've worn black for so long now, I don't know if there is another color. I had a husband who was killed in a mining accident before my baby was born."

Hannah seemed so young, it was hard to believe she'd been widowed already. "I'm so sorry," Sarah said, wondering where the young woman's baby was now.

Hannah nodded. "It's hard. My folks are gone, and I only have my sister. Sometimes I want to leave this place and take my baby and run away, but I don't know where I'd go that would be any better."

"The first days are the hardest," Mattie said to Sarah. "After that you'll get used to it."

"I'll do just fine." Sarah assured herself more than anyone else. Anything was better than riding the train day and night and sleeping sitting up.

"Where did you work before this?" Mattie asked.

"Well, I...." She considered the truth, but decided they wouldn't accept her if they knew she'd never worked a day before. "I worked for a family in Ohio. I took care of their house." It was partly the truth. She had run the Halliday home for the past few months. The thought prompted her to wonder how Leda was getting along without her help. Nicholas had been adamant about his mother needing help so she could rest more and see friends.

Perhaps he'd have to entertain less. Or find himself a housekeeper...or a wife....

"If you carry the baby on your back, it will hurt less," Hannah said.

She listened, glad for the distraction. "Oh?"

"I can show you. I have a little girl."

"Where is she?"

"She's with my sister right now. I hated to leave her, but she's getting too big to keep with me. My sister lives on a nearby farm, so I see her on my days off."

Sarah wanted to cry for her. What would *she* do when William got too big to carry? She didn't want to think about it. She *refused* to think about it.

"Mrs. Hargrove could fill our jobs in a minute, though," Hannah explained. "The hotel is always shorthanded. Girls either leave to get married or take factory jobs. Girls at the factory leave, too. I'd be long gone from this sorry place if some farmer or rancher would ask me."

Mattie laughed. "Me, too."

"You'll marry again too, Sarah," Hannah said. "You're the prettiest one I've seen since I've been here."

"Oh, I don't know," Sarah said, then stopped her denial. She would not give up William. If she had to marry someone in order to take care of him, she would do it.

Immediately, her thoughts turned to Nicholas. Could she bring herself to marry a man she didn't love for William's sake? She swept his image from her mind and finished her dinner. There was still water to heat and carry for the guests as they prepared for bed.

"We can leave at a quarter to ten," Mattie explained. "And we get either Saturday or Sunday night off. We take turns so we can keep company with our young men."

"For me it's time with my baby," Hannah added.

"Doesn't matter to me," Sarah offered. "I will take Sundays so others can have free time on Saturday."

Mattie and Hannah grinned and thanked her.

By the time she snuggled William against her on the cot, her body ached worse than it had the night before. But she'd come this far and she'd found a job on her own. Once again she wondered how long she'd be able to keep her baby with her all day while she worked.

And again Nicholas's image swam behind her closed eyelids, and she remembered him as she'd seen him the very first time. She recalled the strength in his arms as he'd carried her, the smell of his hair and his clothing.

The vivid memory of his inflaming kisses and the warmth of his sleek skin would be with her always. She could see him as he'd been the day of the picnic, smiling, his always perfect hair mussed by the wind. He'd become a man the day his father died, Leda had told her, and Sarah understood. That was why he'd been demanding of Stephen, that was why he'd been wary and severe with her.

And if she hadn't already been in love with him, watching him that day would have made her fall. Oh, but there wasn't a man who could compare.

There might be handsome men out there. There might be perfectly nice ones who could provide for her and maybe even love her. But there was not another Nicholas. And for that reason she could not marry. She could not live with a man, sleep in his bed, give him children, and love Nicholas for the rest of her days. He was the one she loved. The one she desired and the one she could never have.

If she had to she would move on, find work farther west.

Sarah drifted into exhausted slumber. She dreamed of a man with black hair and eyes as dark as strong coffee. And awakened an hour later to startling screams and the choking smell of smoke.

Chapter Seventeen

Sarah stood outside with the other boarders, a blanket wrapped around her for modesty. The summer night was unpleasantly warm, and her cotton nightdress clung to her damp body. Against her shoulder William's head lay drenched with perspiration.

She held him protectively, watching and listening as volunteers found the source of the smoke somewhere behind the row of buildings. Her body trembled with fatigue and anxiety.

"This is going to be a short night," one of the other women grumbled.

The boardinghouse owner appeared in a frilly wrapper, oddly out of place on such a plain woman. "Okay, girls, head back upstairs. The fire was in the living apartment behind the shoe store next door. It's all taken care of."

Sarah followed the complaining boarders up the creaking set of outside stairs and back into the stifling upstairs room. The stuffy space still smelled like smoke.

The fire could have spread to the boardinghouse. Or the smoke could have overcome them all. She and William could have died here. Alone. With no one knowing where they were or who they were.

Creating a pillow of her blanket, she tried to make herself

comfortable on the cot and give William space. She didn't allow herself to think of Mahoning Valley, the Hallidays' home, Nicholas or the security any of them represented. As miserable as it was, this was her life now.

If she'd died, they would have placed her body in a grave beside the bodies of strangers. Would her father ever have learned of her death? Would he have cared? Or did he already think she'd been killed in the accident? Thinking of that, she wondered if the agent she'd hired had found news of Claire's body. She regretted being unable to give that information to the Hallidays. She supposed she didn't deserve any better conditions than she was living under now.

Because of her, Stephen and Claire were not together. Worse yet, because of her they hadn't been in their compartment where they might have survived the accident.

Loneliness and guilt would be her closest companions for a good long time. She might as well become used to them.

Nicholas's office boy rapped on his door and entered. "Miss Marcelino is here again, Mr. Halliday. She wants to see you."

"Did you tell her I'm busy?"

"I told her, sir. She's not an easy person to put off."

"You're telling me. This is the third time in a month. Tell her—"

"Tell me nothing. Tell me yourself," she said from the doorway.

The youth gave Nicholas a stricken look.

"It's all right. I'll handle this." He waved him into the outer office, then stood, rolling down his sleeves, and shrugged into his jacket.

Without waiting for an invitation, Judith seated herself on one of the chairs across from his desk. "If I didn't know better I'd think you were avoiding me."

"I have a foundry to run, Miss Marcelino."

"Surely you could spare time for lunch."

"No, not really."

Her green eyes narrowed. Today she wore a fashionable turquoise dress with a bustle and a low-cut bodice, and sported a perky hat to match. Gracefully, she got up and moved to perch on the edge of his desk, where she leaned in to him.

He remained where he stood. Her heavy floral perfume assailed his nostrils.

"You seem the type of man who would appreciate a bit of diversion during the day." She ran a finger across his lapel and pressed her breasts against his chest. "We don't have to eat."

Nicholas stepped back, and she had to catch her balance. High color rose in her cheeks.

"If this is about the money you claim Mrs. Halliday owes you," he said, "why don't you just let me pay the debt?"

Her chin notched up. Taking obvious offense at his constant refusals, she narrowed her eyes. "You are dense, do you know that?"

He raked his gaze over her straining cleavage and back to her irritated expression. "Not as dense as you believe. I caught on two visits ago that you had set your cap for me. But short of bluntly spelling out that I have no interest in pursuing a relationship, I have no idea of how to handle you delicately, except to refuse your offers."

Her neck and cheeks blotched with embarrassment—or was it humiliation? *Anger,* he realized, as she drew a breath that threatened to spill her from the dress and stood. "You arrogant son of a bitch. I suppose you think you're too good for somebody like me? You think I'm theater trash!"

An unattractive vein appeared in her temple. "Well, guess what, Stephen's wife was theater trash, too. She wouldn't have cleaned up any better than I do."

Her rush of words struck him as odd. "Wouldn't have?"

"Look at you. Pompous is written all over you. You hold me in contempt."

"Not because of your upbringing or your occupation."

She shot forward and raised a hand to slap him, but he caught her wrist.

"And what about your precious 'Claire' you were so proud to take to the theater and to dinner and show off?" she asked, placing contempt in the name. "Do you think she's a better person than I am? Do you think she has any more class than the real Claire had?"

He held her wrist firmly. "Wait a minute. The 'real' Claire? What is that supposed to mean?"

"Your dainty little blonde was a phony." She laughed, jerking her wrist from his grasp. "I knew Claire Patrick back in New York. And your sweet little number wasn't her."

"What are you talking about?"

"Claire had brassy red hair and freckles, long legs and a tight little fanny. That soft little thing wasn't Claire. And *that*, Mr. High-and-Mighty Halliday, is how dense you are." She poked him in the chest for emphasis and turned to leave.

He caught her arm and jerked her around to face him. "Oh, no, you don't. You're not going to say something like that, and then just walk off."

"Okay, I'll spell it out for you so. That little number you were so hot over is not Claire Patrick. I don't know who she was, but I'd never seen her before that night at the restaurant. And I knew Claire. I knew Stephen, too. He wasn't the stuffed shirt you are." With deliberate control she softened her voice. "He knew how to appreciate the finer things in life."

He stared at her, noting the lines around her eyes and mouth that she'd artfully tried to disguise with makeup. "Why should I believe you?"

"You don't have to believe me. Doesn't matter to me." She pulled out of his grasp and walked only a few steps before stopping. "On the other hand, how much would proof be worth to you?" she asked over her shoulder.

"What kind of proof?"

"Proof positive."

Obviously she wasn't going to tell him what the proof was. "I'll pay you whatever Claire owed you."

She turned back. "A thousand dollars."

He turned and flipped open the ledger on his desk, dipped his pen and wrote out a bank draft.

She reached for the slip of paper, but he pulled it out of her range. Her eyes narrowed into an unbecoming hateful scowl.

He blew on the ink and stood slowly, enjoying taunting her. With his other hand he beckoned. "The proof first. Then the money."

Judith opened her bag, withdrew an envelope and sailed it across the room. It hit the wall and fell to the floor.

"What is it?"

"A farewell note."

He walked to where the envelope lay and picked it up. His name, along with his mother's, had been written neatly across the front. The flap had already been torn open. Nicholas pulled the sheet of parchment out and unfolded it.

Nicholas and Leda,

I know what I have done is unforgivable, so I don't ask for your forgiveness. All I ask is that you do not hate me. I planned to tell you the truth from the very minute I awoke in that hospital.

His heart dipped. He extended the bank note, glad to be rid of her. With a derisive smile, Judith snatched it from his fingers.

His legs suddenly unable to bear his weight, Nicholas carried the letter to his desk and sat. He read on.

But when I saw your grief, Nicholas, and when you offered protection and shelter for my son, I could not bring myself to speak the words. I thought perhaps they'd be more easily spoken to your mother.

Anyone could have written this, Nicholas thought angrily, denying the emotion the words drew from his soul. Judith could have written it herself as a means to hurt him or get a thousand dollars from him.

And then, dear Leda, when I saw your tears, and your expression as you looked at my son, I could not bear to say the words then, either. I am still too much of a coward to speak them to your face, so I am leaving this letter.

I am not Claire Halliday. I was never married to your Stephen. I only met him that night of the train wreck. He took me in out of the rain and he and Claire gave me food and dry clothing and shared their berth with me.

If they had been in that compartment that night, they might still be alive. So you see, I am responsible for their deaths. That is something I will live with for the rest of my life.

That didn't sound like something Judith would think to make up. Did it? Those words sounded like—"she" was blaming herself for Stephen—and Claire's death. But if the woman he'd brought home hadn't been Claire, who was she?

A sick feeling permeated his chest. He looked up to see Judith's gloating smirk. "Where did you get this letter?" he asked.

Her expression flattened. "It—it doesn't matter where I got it."

Nicholas wondered if his feelings of confusion and betrayal were written all over his face. He couldn't bear for this woman to watch him read this letter and see what it was doing to him.

"Get away from me," he said through his teeth.

Her left eye developed a tic. She raised her chin, spun on her heel and fled his office.

Without sparing her a second thought, he picked up where'd he'd left off. *That and the lies,* he read, imagining Claire's soft voice as she would say the words.

I lied to you and pretended to be Claire so that I could take advantage of you until my leg was healed and I was able to make it on my own.

Enclosed you will find a list of all the items I have taken with me. As soon as I am settled and have a job, I will repay you for the clothing and food and the time spent in your home.

Nicholas read over the list of clothing and articles for the baby. Inconsequential things, material things that didn't add up to a hundred dollars. Exactly the things Mrs. Trent had said were missing. No one else could have known that.

But what of the jewelry she'd taken?

His fingers trembled on the parchment.

I can never repay you for your kindness, nor for the sin of lying to you and for the loss of your son and brother. I can only tell you how very ashamed and sorry I am.

I don't know if you can find it in your hearts to not hate me. For the things I have done, I hate myself.

You have no reason to believe me, but now you must see I have nothing left to lose, so I want you to believe this: Stephen was a good man. He knew how to love. He was a son and brother to be proud of.

Tears burned beneath Nicholas's eyelids.

I was but a stranger, and he and Claire showed me kindness. You would have liked Claire, I know. Cherish their memories.

Sincerely, Sarah Thornton.

Sarah Thornton.

Perspiration trickled down his back beneath the shirt and jacket. He swiped an impatient hand across his eyes. Who in the hell was Sarah Thornton?

Actually, much of this explanation made sense. When he thought back over her avoidance of speaking of Stephen, when he remembered her desperation to see the Pinkerton's report, it made sense.

Yet so much didn't.

How could he know for sure?

Immediately, the answer came to him.

"I'll be out the rest of the afternoon," he called on his way through the outer office.

He rented a horse at the livery and rode like hell toward home.

Celia and his mother were sitting in the shade on the verandah when he rode up.

"Nicholas!" his mother called. "You never come home early."

"Pardon my appearance, Mother," he said politely, referring to his windblown hair and the dust on his clothing, then turned abruptly to Celia.

"What do you know about this?" He shoved the letter under her nose.

"What is it?"

"A letter. From Sarah Thornton."

She blanched and reached for her glass, only to realize it was lemonade and push it away.

"You know, and you're going to tell me," Nicholas insisted.

"Oh, my," She waved a napkin to stir the air around her.

"Nicholas, what is this all about?"

He handed his mother the letter. "I'm not sure, but I'm going to find out. Do you recognize the handwriting?"

She studied the piece of paper. "It's Claire's."

He turned back to Celia. "Start talking."

"I—I don't know—"

"Yes, you do. When did you find out your daughter wasn't here?"

"After—after that night I tripped on the stairs. She came to my room and she told me."

"Who came to your room?"

"Sarah."

Sarah. "And what did she tell you?"

"That Claire had been killed in the train accident, and that everyone believed *she* was Claire."

"And what did you do?"

"Why, I cried of course."

"And after that?"

"And after that she said she'd see that I was taken care of as long as I stayed to myself and didn't let on."

Nicholas backed up to a marble bench and sat. He ran a hand though his hair in frustration and disbelief. "How did she think she could get away with it? How long did she think she could pull it off?"

Leda had read the letter in sections while listening to their exchange. "*She* was not Claire?"

Celia shook her head.

His mother looked as stunned as Nicholas felt. "Then—then the baby...?" she voiced tentatively.

"Is not your grandson," he finished for her. "She was

never married to Stephen, never met him until that night on the train.''

"Then who fathered her baby?" Leda asked incredulously.

Celia shook her head. "Some young fellow who ran off on her. She waited as long as she could to tell her father and he kicked her out. She was making her way west when she met Claire and Stephen.''

"This is too preposterous," Leda declared. "I can't believe she lied to us all that time.''

"And you," Nicholas said to Claire's mother. "What did you have to gain by lying? You are Claire's mother. We would have provided for you regardless.''

She shook her head. "She begged me. She seemed—I don't know. I just went along with her.''

Nicholas knew precisely how impossible it had been to resist her. He'd been enamored with her from the first, and she'd used that advantage to steal from them and denigrate him.

Leda wept softly into her handkerchief. The sound angered Nicholas.

It was true. She wasn't Claire. That was why she'd never fit into the expected role. She'd managed the servants, planned dinners and entertained guests, and handled it all with practiced ease. He'd known all along that her skills hadn't reflected the upbringing of the woman he'd had investigated.

"Do you think she's gone back to her father?" Leda asked.

Celia shook her head. "He disowned her. And he made it impossible for her to work in Boston.''

That phony Boston accent hadn't been phony at all. She'd been raised well, brought up in society. Her father couldn't have been all that bad. No doubt she'd been spoiled, and this time he hadn't given in to her demands.

Maybe she'd planned to scare him into giving her her way, and had now run back home.

"What kind of father turns out his own child?" Leda asked.

Nicholas raised his head and gaped at his mother. "Are you *sympathizing* with her?"

"What choices did she have? Especially after she'd been in the accident and her leg was broken. Where could she have gone? How could she have cared for—for..." Tears filled her gray eyes. "Do you think she'll still call him William?"

Her misery carved a hole in Nicholas's chest. She'd been through enough, and now this! Anger quickly replaced the pain. "While you're feeling sorry for her, don't forget to mention how *poor Sarah* couldn't have gotten by without your rings and necklace and my stickpin and watch."

Celia looked at him in shock. "What?"

"Yes, the *poor girl* stole our jewelry before she left."

"Are you sure it was her?" Celia asked.

"Was it you?"

"Nicholas!" his mother admonished.

Celia unconcernedly raised her hands. "Search my room if it makes you feel better."

"It will."

"I wouldn't have believed it," Leda said, folding the letter and replacing it in the envelope. "If anyone else had told me I wouldn't have believed it. But this letter from her leads me to no other conclusion."

She stood slowly and looked at Nicholas with such pain in her eyes that he wanted to find the woman and strangle her. "Do you know?" she said. "If I had it to do all over again, even knowing what I know now, I wonder what I'd do differently."

Nicholas knew what he'd do differently. He wouldn't spare his conscience a second thought.

"I'm going to rest," she said.

Nicholas watched her enter the house with faltering steps. His eyes were so dry they burned.

"I wouldn'ta thought she'd steal from you," Celia said with a sad shake of her head.

He sat, thinking back over each incident that should have tipped him off. He should have put it all together. She'd wanted the file on Claire because she hadn't known anything about her and needed to play the part convincingly. She'd taken Stephen's letters to learn something of him. She'd never volunteered any information about her life or her relationship with Stephen. Any time they'd inquired, she hedged or lied.

She was everything he'd suspected her of being.

Wasn't she?

She'd tricked him, and that had him angry. But she'd hurt his mother, and for that he wanted retribution. Leda needed closure on this. He would find William for her, so she'd know the child was safe.

He would find Sarah Thornton.

Nicholas started over. The following morning, he was waiting for Howard Gramb when he opened his store. He grilled the man about the young woman who'd sold the bracelet, but turned up nothing new.

He checked the train station and found no record of either Sarah Thornton or Claire Halliday purchasing a ticket. The man at the counter vaguely recalled seeing a woman carrying a baby who fit Sarah's description, but he claimed to have sold too many tickets to remember where one particular woman was going. West, he thought.

Doggedly, Nicholas once again made the rounds of the jewelry stores. This time, he encountered a woman at one of them whom he hadn't spoken to before.

"I'm Nicholas Halliday," he introduced himself.

"How do you do? How can I help you today?"

"I haven't seen you here before."

"I fill in when my husband has business to attend to."

"I see. I left my card with him, and asked to be notified if anyone came in with these pieces." He showed her the list he'd compiled.

"I didn't know about your request, but those items came day before yesterday."

At last! Something more to go on. "Did you buy them?"

"Yes."

"Who sold them to you?"

"A woman."

"Can you describe her, please?"

"Well, she was dressed in mourning. I didn't get a good look at her face because she wore a veil."

"Anything else?"

"She had a perambulator. The baby was sleeping."

"I see." His last hope had been doused. She had stolen the jewelry and now she was gone. "I'd like to purchase the jewelry, please."

"All of it?"

"Unless you'd like to simply return it to me since it's mine."

His words took her aback. "Uh—no. I'll get the pieces from the safe."

Nicholas made the purchase. Everything was there except one ring. "Did you sell a ring already?"

"No. This is everything."

He closed the satin-lined box containing the valuables and placed it in his coat pocket.

His mother accepted the items without any show of emotion. Her lack of animation frightened Nicholas. She'd dealt with his father's death and Stephen's death, and now this seemed like the last thing she could bear. Her suffering tore at Nicholas.

Sarah had sold the gems only two days ago. That meant she'd still been in Youngstown. He checked the hotels without success. Perhaps she'd gone back to her father. He couldn't bring himself to locate and wire the man.

He found it impossible to concentrate on his work. He had dressed and gone to the foundry, had gone through the motions of walking through the buildings, checking with each foreman, sitting at his desk...but his mind wasn't on steel production and his heart wasn't in the effort it took to be there.

He sat at his desk, his hands folded beneath his chin, when Milos rapped on the edge of the desk.

Nicholas glanced up.

"You all right?"

"Yeah." He made a semblance of straightening the papers before him even though he had already confided in Milos, and knew he didn't have to put up appearances.

Milos tossed a stack of mail into a wire basket and held out an envelope. "You might want to see this."

"What is it?"

"I just came from Western Union. Sam Pierce's been holding this for..." He paused. "For Claire. Sarah."

"What is it?" Nicholas asked again.

"Seems she told him not to send it with anyone else, to hang on to it for her. But when I told him she wouldn't be back, he had me sign for it."

Nicholas took the envelope and slit it open. He unfolded the telegram. "It's from the Pinkerton agent who investigated Claire for me." He read further. "He's located a body he believes is Claire Halliday. She was buried in a Boston cemetery." He cut Milos a sharp glance. "As Sarah Thornton."

Eighteen

Boston, Massachusetts

Nicholas stood before a three-story brownstone and rapped the brass knocker gracing one of the black lacquered double doors.

A male servant opened it and greeted him. "Mr. Halliday?"

"Yes."

"Mr. Thornton is expecting you. This way."

Nicholas followed the man across a foyer and into a masculinely furnished library. A stout man with steel-gray hair stood and shook his hand. His eyes were as blue as Sarah's, but lacked the warmth. "You didn't state your business in your message," he said, immediately coming to the point.

"No. It's a delicate matter, and I thought it best to speak in person."

"And you've come all the way from Ohio to speak to me in person?"

"Yes."

"Must be important. Have anything to do with your foundry?"

Nicholas wasn't surprised the man had checked him out.

He'd have done the same. "No. It has to do with your daughter."

The man stiffened. "I have no daughter."

"Yes," he corrected. "You do."

Morris Thornton's expression hardened and he cocked his head. "If you're not here about investments, I have no wish to speak with you."

"I'm here about Sarah."

"If you've come to claim responsibility for her indiscretion, I'm afraid it's too late."

His words took Nicholas aback. Was he accusing Nicholas of seducing and then abandoning her? Nicholas's ire had been awakened, but he spoke with practiced composure. "I've come with some shocking news," he said without preamble.

"Oh, what? You weren't the first?"

Nicholas held himself in check. "Sarah is still alive."

The man seated himself without offering Nicholas a chair, opened a humidor and selected a cigar. "Sarah and her bastard are dead."

His cruelty shocked Nicholas. "No. You buried my sister-in-law and my brother's child in that grave. You didn't identify the body, did you?"

Sarah's father stared about the room before turning his gaze to Nicholas. "No."

"Did anyone identify the body?"

"It had been weeks since the train accident. I was notified, sent the body and her trunk. I knew it was the stupid girl. I had her buried next to her mother."

"I can understand why you wouldn't have been able to identify her. And I know you had Sarah's trunk as evidence that the body belonged to your daughter. But that young woman was not Sarah."

He gave Morris the details, sparing any mention of his feelings for her. "So you see, she's very much alive."

The man leaned back in his chair for a long minute, then

heaved himself forward and stood. "No. My daughter is dead. She will not destroy my reputation in this business community. I have important clients—clients who have invested with me since I began my business more than thirty years ago, and I will not allow her poor choices to harm my associations with them. My daughter died the day she defied me and defiled my good name."

Nicholas studied the hard-eyed, hard-hearted man. "You would choose appearances—money—over your daughter?"

Morris Thornton met his stare without flinching. "I have no daughter. As far as I am concerned—as far as this city is concerned, Sarah Thornton is dead."

In that split second, though he'd never seen it before, Nicholas recognized her father's face. He recognized the drive and the power and the all-consuming ambition.

He recognized the man he had almost become.

And he saw something else, too. He saw the reason a young woman who'd made a mistake had been forced out of her home and onto a train bound for catastrophe. And he understood why Stephen's kindness had been something she clung to like a last hope. For someone who'd received so little kindness from her own father, a stranger's benevolence must have seemed a godsend.

And perhaps it had been.

"You're right," he said, his tone low and controlled. "You don't have a daughter. A man like you doesn't deserve a daughter. And especially not one like Sarah."

The man's hard expression did not change. "Get your body," he said. "But do it quietly."

"I will see to it before I leave town. And I'll arrange to have the rest of Sarah's things picked up, too."

"There is nothing of hers left here."

Nicholas stepped to the door. "I believe that's where you're wrong. Her spirit is here. Her memory. Live with that."

He let himself out of the house.

* * *

A few nights later, Milos joined him in his study after dinner. "I spoke with Morris Thornton," Nicholas said, leaning back and lighting a cigar.

Milos clipped the tip from his and accepted the burning match from Nicholas. He puffed and tossed the match into the empty fireplace. "What did you learn?"

In deference to the sultry evening, both had abandoned their jackets and rolled back their sleeves.

"Why Sarah left," he replied dryly. "He had the coldest eyes I've ever seen. The man isn't human."

"And now you're joining your mother in sympathizing with her?"

"I simply understand her a little better."

"What is it you understand?"

"She felt guilty. That's why she had Pinkerton's find Claire's body."

"You've had Claire's body brought here?"

Nicholas nodded. "All these months the man believed his daughter was killed in a train accident. I went to him, revealed that she wasn't dead after all, and—it was as though the truth would have inconvenienced him. He preferred his daughter to be dead."

Nicholas still couldn't comprehend the man's denial and hostility.

"But Sarah found the real Claire for you and your mother."

"And for Stephen."

"She's not the woman you wanted to believe she was, is she?"

"What do you mean?"

"It was easier to have her run away when you believed she was only out for your money. Now that you know differently, it's more difficult to accept."

"But she stole from us."

"She said she'd pay it all back, didn't she?"

"The jewelry wasn't on the list she intended to pay back," Nicholas scoffed.

Milos seemed to mull that fact over at length. "She detailed her hospital debt, her clothing, everything down to the last flannel, promising to pay you back, and yet she never mentioned a fortune in gemstones. Don't you find that odd?"

He did. He blew a smoke ring and watched it dissipate into the humid air. She wasn't the person he'd first thought. She'd taken care of the Crane family without being asked, without expecting anything, without even letting him know. She'd seen that all of Claire's clothing had been put to good use.

She hadn't asked for clothing for herself, in fact Leda had insisted and forced her to accept the dresses and underclothing.

"I find it even more odd that she sold her mother's bracelet first," Nicholas said. "It meant a great deal to her, but she sold it before she sold our pieces."

Milos agreed. "That does seem illogical. You're sure the old woman didn't take it?"

"Positive," Nicholas said. "Besides, the jeweler's wife described Sarah."

"How did she describe her?"

Nicholas repeated her recounting.

"Had you ever seen her wear a veil besides the day of the funeral?" Milos asked.

"No."

They smoked. And thought.

"And the perambulator. Is something like that missing?"

Nicholas shook his head. "She never had one. Of course she could have bought it after selling the bracelet."

"Seems a bit odd to buy a baby buggy when one is planning to catch a train, don't you think?"

Nicholas agreed.

They observed each other.

"Perhaps it was a disguise," Nicholas said first.

"Someone else with your baubles who wanted it to look like Sarah took them."

"Who?" Nicholas asked, wondering aloud. He sat forward abruptly.

"What is it?"

"Judith!" Nicholas shouted, jumping out of the chair and gesturing with the cigar. "Why that—"

"The actress? When would she have had the opportunity to steal them?"

"That day she waited here at the house for Sarah. One of the servants probably brought her tea, and after that she had time to go upstairs before they checked on her again."

"This means you don't think Sarah took it."

"This means I don't want to believe Sarah took it."

"Now what are you going to do?"

"I'm still going to find her. And William. For Mother."

Milos gave him a skeptical glance. "Of course," he said knowingly. "For your mother."

"Did I get any messages while I was out?" Hot and cranky, Nicholas waited for a reply.

The desk clerk at the Hotel Gold gave Nicholas a patient once-over. "No, sir."

"If a telegram comes for me, I don't care what time it is, come wake me."

"Yes, sir."

Nicholas crossed the elegant lobby and climbed the curved stairs without noting any of the hotel's ornate appointments.

All day he'd walked the streets of Fort Wayne, looking for a woman with a baby, too impatient to wait in his room, and eager to find a lead to Sarah's whereabouts.

His Pinkerton contact had traced her this far, and prom-

ised that if she hadn't gone on west, they would locate her
within a day or two.

Letting himself into his room, he removed his jacket and
tie and opened both windows wide. He glanced around. The
bed had already been turned down, and fresh towels were
stacked near the bowl and pitcher set.

He removed his clothing and washed with the tepid water
in the basin, immediately feeling cooler and his temperament somewhat improved.

From his leather satchel, he withdrew a few papers, the
letter from Sarah among them. He unfolded it as though it
were a love letter, and read again the words he'd already
become familiar with.

She might have left her father a letter when she left him,
too. She might have written him since she'd been gone.
Nicholas envisioned the man throwing her letters away un-
opened. He was a cold, unfeeling man who probably had
no trouble sleeping at night even though he'd tossed his
daughter out into a dangerous world.

The image of Sarah, her lovely hair and lush body, never
left his mind. He could picture her now, as clearly as
though she were there with him. Any man would be drawn
to her. And obviously at least one man had been.

How would she protect herself? How would she take care
of William on her own? The thought of something happening to either of them was enough to tie his stomach in
knots. He hadn't eaten a meal without thinking of her, without wondering if she'd eaten that day.

He hadn't lain down to rest without wondering where
she slept at night.

She would be forced to do anything she could to survive.
And if he knew little else about Sarah, he knew she was a
survivor.

He refolded the letter and laid it on the bedside table.
Turning down the brass-based parlor lamp until the flame
went out, he lay down and stared into the blackness.

Where was she tonight? What thoughts crept through her head and kept her from sleep? Regrets. Shame. Fear.

She had intended to tell him, her letter said. It had been a misunderstanding, and she'd meant to straighten it out. Why hadn't she?

He'd gone to the hospital after making arrangements for his brother's body and their trunks. He'd first seen her sleeping in the hospital, so small and alone, with fading bruises on skin as pale and delicate as the petals of a white rose.

She'd had a bandage on her head, and her leg in a cast, and he'd known then that he would take her home and protect her from further harm.

And when he'd come back the next time, she'd been anticipating his arrival. Perhaps she'd been prepared to tell him then. She'd been sitting in the wheelchair he'd purchased for her, one hand holding a hat on her blond mane, the other struggling to secure it with a pin.

Had he given her the opportunity to tell him?

Her eyes, as wide and as blue as the Ohio summer sky, had followed him as he approached and beheld the tiny squirming infant he'd believed to be his brother's.

And then what had he said to her? He'd told her his mother was waiting for them. He'd assured her that she had a place to live, and reported that he'd paid the hospital and doctor.

She'd asked how much that had been.

She'd only met him, and already she was indebted to him for the chair, the clothing, the medical fees. And he'd been his usual brisk self and impatient to get going.

No, he hadn't given her much of a chance to tell him. And admittedly he wasn't the most open and understanding man she could have been indebted to. He'd been critical and suspicious of her as Claire, and she no doubt dreaded what he would have done if he'd known she wasn't Claire.

So then she'd planned to tell Mother upon their arrival.

And what had his mother done after setting eyes on the two of them? Immediately cried and professed her need to have them there. William had been her solace, a healing balm for her pain and anguish. And Sarah had recognized that. And been unable to hurt her any more than she'd already been hurt.

When he thought back over the time she'd been with them, Nicholas understood her confusion and her reticence. In her own strange way, not telling them had been a kindness.

He didn't know what he'd have done if she'd told him the first day...or the first week...or the first month. Each day she hadn't revealed her identity, doing so must have grown more and more impossible. He didn't want to think he would have tossed out a frightened young woman with a broken leg and an infant to care for. He hated thinking of himself as being of the same caliber as her father.

He wasn't.

But he'd been opposed to Stephen marrying someone from Claire's background, hadn't he? He had never approved of Stephen's acquaintances or his pursuit of the theater. He'd seen all those energies as directed wrongly, and constantly urged him to come back where he belonged.

Nicholas rose, wrapping the sheet around his waist, and stood before the window, the humid breeze cooling his damp skin. He'd been so damned hard on Stephen. He'd never given him credit for accomplishments he hadn't approved of or even allowed him to enjoy his time at home without criticizing and running him off again.

Maybe if he'd been more understanding, less critical, Stephen wouldn't have rebelled as fiercely.

It had been important to their father that Halliday Iron prosper, and that his sons pass it down to their sons. Nicholas had never wanted to let down his mother or his father's memory, so he'd done the work of two men.

And resented Stephen.

He understood the weight of guilt.

Tears blurred his vision. Several young women dressed in hotel uniforms passed through the golden halo of a street lamp below. Distractedly, he noted the late hour for them to be leaving their shifts, and went back to the bed.

Surely tomorrow he would hear.

Why had finding Sarah become an obsession for him?

He was concerned for her welfare.

Why? Because he wasn't like her father.

He needed to clear the air between them and assure her he didn't hate her as she feared.

Why? Because her guilt and shame weighed on his heart.

He had to see her again. Had to show her she belonged with them...with him.

Why? Because—Nicholas squeezed his eyes shut and looked deep inside himself—he loved her.

Chapter Nineteen

Sarah prepared William for the day and nursed him, noticing her breasts weren't as full as they had been. William had been unusually fussy for two days, which worried her. He could be coming down with something.

She didn't want to spend the price of doctor's fees, because after paying for her board and a few supplies each week, she didn't have much left to save. But William was more important than anything, so she left early, hoping she could see the doctor before she had to be at the hotel.

The office was located above a building a few blocks from the hotel. Climbing the flight of stairs in the side alley, she turned the crank doorbell.

A middle-aged man opened the door and stepped back. He opened another door and ushered her into a small room with an examining table and a row of cabinets. "What seems to be the problem?"

"It's William," she said, laying him on the table and holding him in place. "He has fussed the last couple of days. He's never cranky, even in the heat, but he cried last night."

"All babies cry, you know." The doctor looked him over, listened to his heart, looked into his eyes. "He looks perfectly healthy. I don't see anything wrong with him. He may be getting a tooth.''

"He has two teeth already, and he didn't behave like this.''

"Most of us get a little cranky in this heat.''

"I don't think so....''

"Is he hungry?''

She blinked up at him. "Well, he nurses regularly.''

"And your milk supply is sufficient?''

She blushed profusely, but considered his question. "I—I don't seem to have as much fullness as I did before. Is there something wrong with me?''

"Let's have a look.''

Sarah overcame her embarrassment to allow the doctor to examine her. "You're not feverish, and there's no infection. Your breasts don't hurt?''

She buttoned up her black dress. "No.''

"What about your diet? Have you been eating properly? Drinking milk? Plenty of water?''

Reluctant to admit she'd been scrimping on food, she hesitated, but confessed, "I eat supper each day. That's about it.''

"Well, that's the problem. If you want to produce milk for your baby, you have to eat regular meals and drink plenty of liquids. You young mothers are so concerned over your hourglass figures that you hinder nature's way of providing.''

Tears formed in Sarah's eyes and she blinked them away. She'd been making her own baby go hungry!

"If you insist on starving yourself, you will have to give him canned milk or find a wet nurse.''

Sarah picked up William. "I didn't realize,'' she said shamefacedly. "Of course I'll eat better.''

The tantalizing smell of brewing coffee wafted from the other room. Her stomach growled. "How much do I owe you?''

He told her and she dropped the coin into his hand, feeling more foolish and incompetent than ever.

"Help yourself to a cup of coffee," he offered.

"Thank you, but I saw a small restaurant on my way here, and I think I'll have something there."

"Excellent plan," he said. "Your William will stop being cranky in a day or so."

Sarah kissed her son's head and whispered apologies against his temple all the way along the street. She would not let William down. She would not. She swiped at the tears of mortification that streamed down her cheeks when she thought of his hunger.

With only seconds to spare, she gulped a bowl of oatmeal and a glass of milk. Trying not to begrudge the additional cost, she purchased a sandwich for her noon meal, and ran most of the way to the Hotel Gold.

Hannah, Mattie and a few other girls stood in the laundry room. "You look like you've already worked a full day."

"I feel like it, too." Sarah slipped William into the sling Hannah had helped her make and adjusted him on her back.

Hannah tapped William's nose, and he gurgled happily at her. "Sarah, why don't you let me carry him this morning?"

"Oh, I couldn't do that," Sarah objected.

"Just for a few hours. I would really like to. I carried my baby until he was over a year old, so it won't be a burden for me. Please let me."

William was not a burden to her, either, but a morning without his weight would be welcome. "All right," she agreed.

They transferred the sling from Sarah's shoulders to Hannah's. She kissed William's cheek and touched her nose to his.

"Whoever gets fourteen today, let me have the room," Hannah said.

"A handsome guest?" Mattie asked.

"As sin," Hannah replied.

"And we know he's rich as sin if he's staying here," one of the others said.

They all laughingly agreed.

"Maybe I'll catch a glimpse of him," Mattie said hopefully. "Do you suppose he's married?"

"Most of the good ones are," Hannah replied.

Sarah listened to their lighthearted banter until Mrs. Hargrove came with the day's assignments.

"You're looking a little peaked, Sarah," the woman said as the girls scattered to their chores. "Is there a problem?"

"No, ma'am. No problem."

"That baby getting too heavy for you?"

"No. He's not heavy at all. Hannah wanted to carry him for a while."

"I miss my baby," Hannah said in support.

The woman surveyed Sarah's appearance at length. Sarah had taken care with her dress and hair and cap that morning, but she'd been outdoors in the breeze. She resisted feeling her hair for errant curls. She took no chances with Mrs. Hargrove finding fault.

Finally the woman moved aside so she could pass.

Relieved, Sarah hurried to the linen racks.

The heat and the wait had done nothing to improve Nicholas's disposition. He rang for water, and answered the door at the light tap.

"Your water, sir."

"Thank you."

A slender young girl carried a pail to the gold-trimmed pitcher and bowl on the washstand and poured the water into the pitcher. She carried a baby on her back. "Will there be anything else?" she asked.

He still had towels. "I don't believe so."

He handed her a coin. She accepted it with a blush, and

gave him a wide smile that revealed a tooth that overlapped charmingly. "Enjoy your visit in Fort Wayne, sir."

He nodded, his head clouded with thoughts of Sarah.

She turned to leave and reached for the doorknob, placing the baby plainly in front of Nicholas.

The fair-haired child blinked at him with wide blue eyes. *Sarah's eyes.* William's eyes. Nicholas stared at the baby for several startled seconds. This baby was slightly bigger than William. But it had been weeks since he'd seen him.

He had the same wide blue eyes. The same chin. And though this baby's hair seemed longer than he remembered William's being, it curled on his forehead and over his ears.

The infant grinned at him, whisking the air from his lungs. *Sarah's smile.*

Nicholas forced himself to breathe. What did he know about babies? They'd all looked the same to him until William. He'd thought of nothing else for weeks; had he begun to see what he wanted to see?

She reached the hall, getting away from him.

"Miss," he said, stopping her with the word.

She turned back. "Yes, sir?"

"Your baby...your baby has the prettiest blue eyes."

She grinned. "He does, doesn't he? But he's not my baby."

Nicholas's heart stopped. "Oh?"

"No. He belongs to one of the other girls."

It started again with a violent chug. "Well, he's a handsome one. What's his name?"

She turned so that he could see the baby. "William," she replied.

At noon, Sarah joined the others at the back entrance where they sat on the stairs and ate. She had thirty minutes to allow William some freedom, rest her back and leg, and feed both of them.

"I saw him again," Hannah reported.

"Fourteen?" Mattie asked.

"Yup. William came in real handy."

"How's that?"

"Seems he likes children."

Mattie pumped water from the kitchen's indoor pump and carried metal pitchers out to them. Sarah drank as much as she could hold.

Hannah played with William, and when their dinnertime was over, helped Sarah slip his sling on.

The afternoon grew stifling hot, and before dinner all the guests asked for water to bathe. Sarah adjusted William's weight. He was napping and seemed to weigh so much more when he wasn't holding his head up.

She hadn't been able to find Hannah after the desk clerk gave her the instructions to carry water to room fourteen. Hannah would have her hide if Sarah actually got to see the fellow. She paused on the stairs, shifted the buckets and hurried on. She tapped on the door.

"Enter," a muffled voice called.

"Your water." She carried the buckets through the suite and poured the water into the copper tub behind a screen in the dressing room. She went back to the linen closet in the hall and returned with towels. Squatting to keep William balanced, she picked up the empty pails.

"His hair is getting as curly as yours."

That soul-stirring voice sent a tremor through her body. Sarah spun on her heel and faced him.

The buckets dropped from her fingers with a clang.

Nicholas!

Her heart hammered, and her breath caught in her chest. She tried to run past him, but he was too fast and too strong.

He halted her with a hand on her arm. "Sarah."

Her gaze flew to his, but she couldn't read his expression. She turned her face away in shame.

"Please, Sarah," he said. Her name on his lips alarmed and thrilled her at the same time. His touch warmed her skin through her sleeve. She hadn't wanted to face him once he knew the truth. She'd never planned on seeing his reaction to what she'd done. She was a coward.

"I don't know how to say the things I need to say to you," he said, his voice too gentle for someone who'd been betrayed.

She shook her head, swallowing fear and apprehension. "You hate me for lying to you. I don't blame you." She gathered her composure. "You don't have to hold me. I won't run."

He released her arm.

"How did you find me?"

"The Pinkerton agent traced you here to Fort Wayne. I came as soon as I heard. And then I saw William this morning."

She remained standing where he'd stopped her.

"Let's sit," he offered.

Hesitantly, she followed him into the other room. The offer to rest for a few minutes appealed, but she couldn't afford the luxury. "I'm expected back at the laundry room."

"No," he said. "You're not."

She looked at him then, tried to read his purpose in his dark, dark eyes. "What do you mean?"

"I spoke with Mrs. Hargrove. I asked her to send you up here, and I told her you would no longer be in her employ."

Panic stole over her entire being. She'd guarded her position so carefully. She'd never made a mistake to earn her a chance of losing this work. She'd put up with the woman's tyrannical orders and worked endless arduous days. And now, in a matter of minutes, he'd lost it for her? "You what? You can't do that! This is the only job that I can bring William to."

"This is no life for William. This is no life for you."

Tears blurred her vision. After her morning, this news

was almost too much tribulation to bear. "But it's our life, and you have no right to ruin it."

"I have every right."

He did. He had every right to do anything he could to make her life miserable. Listlessly, she sank to the edge of the bed, wondering where she could go from here. "Yes. You do," she whispered, tired of being vulnerable.

"Lay him down and rest your back," he said gently. He eased the sling from her shoulders and rested William on the coverlet. With long strong fingers he brushed William's damp hair away from his temples. Seeing him touching her baby so tenderly did something painful to her heart. "He's grown."

Her gaze traveled from his capable hands to his shirt-sleeves, and up to his face. He studied her child with a softhearted expression. He truly cared for him.

A terrifying thought crept into her mind. "Why have you come?" she asked, surprised at her flat tone.

He looked up.

"I won't let you take him from me." Her voice sounded a little hysterical now. Sure she'd made mistakes and she'd grown discouraged, but she still had some fight left. "He's not Stephen's baby, you know that now."

"Sarah, no." He covered her hand with his. "No. I didn't come to take William from you."

She took even breaths and tried to calm herself. "Swear it."

"I swear it. I thought you would want to know that Claire has been buried beside Stephen."

Relief flooded her heart. "You found her body?"

He nodded. "The Pinkerton agent you hired found her. She had been identified as Sarah Thornton."

That possibility had crossed her thoughts. Her father had been contacted. "So…"

"Your father buried her beside your mother."

She nodded, blinking back tears. "He thought I was dead."

Nicholas affirmed that with a nod.

"And now?"

"He allowed me to move her body."

The words he didn't say were as clear as the ones he did. "You wrote him?"

"I met him."

She closed her eyes against the vision. He'd met Morris Thornton. And now he knew just how disposable she'd been to her own father. "I'm sure that was enlightening."

"Yes. I saw something important while I was there."

"What did you see?" she asked, afraid to hear the answer, but more afraid not to ask.

"I saw the man I was turning into."

She opened her eyes and studied him curiously. "What do you mean?"

"Your father. I've been just like him. I just pray it's not too late to change."

The comparison was ridiculous. "You're nothing like my father. He's mean and self-serving and bitter."

"And I'm not?"

"No, you're not."

"All I cared about was Halliday Iron. It took over everything in my life until I had nothing and no one else."

"You had a responsibility to your father. And to your mother. You took that seriously."

"I took it seriously, all right. I took it so seriously, I couldn't see past it to what my preoccupation was doing to Stephen. I wanted him to be just like me. I drove him away."

Seeing the earnestness in his eyes, hearing his tone of voice, she recognized that they were discussing him—discussing his mistakes. Not once had he mentioned what she had done. No, he was not like her father.

"You were young, Nicholas," she said, hoping to relieve

his burden. "You weren't his father. You were a young man trying to fill a father's shoes. You did what you thought was best for him—for your entire family."

"But it wasn't best. If I'd done things differently—"

"We all find out the hard way that what we thought was for the best at the time, really wasn't," she interrupted. "You could have done things differently, and he still would have gone his own way. He was Stephen. You're not responsible for his death. What is it you're blaming yourself for? For being young when your father died? For taking over the foundry and making investments and treating employees decently?"

"No. I know it wasn't my fault that my father died." Nicholas stood and paced a few steps away and back. "I did what I had to do. I made wise decisions." He ran a hand through his hair.

"But?"

"But I resented Stephen for not helping me do all that," he admitted. "I carried all of it—the burden of the foundry, all the details, for years so that he could finish his education. And I expected him to appreciate that and repay some of the sacrifice. When he didn't, I got angry with him. The anger just grew and grew."

"Well, just forgive him now," she said simply.

He studied her. Beside them William made a soft sound in his sleep. "Just forgive him now," he repeated after her. She nodded.

It seemed then as though all the starch went out of his spine. He lowered himself to sit on the bed's edge again. "All right." He drew a shaky breath. "I forgive him."

In all the months she'd known him, she'd never seen this vulnerable side. He'd never permitted it. And she loved him more for letting down his guard. "Now forgive yourself for being human," she said.

"Nicholas, you're nothing like my father. You could never be. I've been in this room with you all this time and you have yet to mention my character flaws. You haven't even mentioned what I did to you.''

"Somehow it doesn't seem too important right now."

"How can you say that? Aren't you angry with me? Disappointed?''

"Not anymore. Not after I had a chance to think about it, to remember exactly what happened and how it happened and why you might have had trouble telling me the truth.''

"I wanted to tell you," she said. "I planned to tell you the truth from the first. But I couldn't. And the longer I waited, the more difficult it became.''

"I remember looking at you that first day in the carriage,'' he said as if not listening to her explanation. "From that minute forward I wanted to touch your hair. The feelings I had for you evoked so much guilt. I thought you were Stephen's wife. And I wanted you.''

Her cheeks warmed.

"You had on a pair of dangling pearl earrings. Where are they?''

"I sold them.''

A sorrowful look crossed his features before he got up and moved into the dressing room, returning and taking her hand.

The object he placed in her palm felt cool and hard. She opened her fingers and saw her mother's emerald bracelet. She stared at the glittering green gems. "Why did you do this?''

"I knew how much it meant to you.''

"But I can't pay you back.''

He closed her fingers over the bracelet and held her hand within his. "The only thing I would like from you is the truth...about why you left. Why that day? Why like that?''

Even the woman's name sickened her. "Judith,'' she admitted.

Anger flickered in the depths of his brown eyes.

"She wanted me to give her this bracelet or get money from you to keep her from telling that she knew the real Claire."

"That's why you left?"

"No. I left because I didn't belong there. I never should have been there in the first place. I promise to pay back every penny for the food and clothing."

"Didn't you hear what I said? I don't want anything."

"But I owe you."

"Sarah?"

"Yes?"

"We're starting over with a clean slate here. You owe me nothing."

She opened her hand to reveal the bracelet. "But—"

He silenced her with a fingertip against her lips. "It's a gift."

She drew his hand from her mouth and held it. "I don't understand."

"I want you to have it. And I don't want you to feel obligated to me."

"That's rather difficult."

"But not impossible," he said. "You already said it. It's about forgiveness, remember?"

He turned his hand within her grip and placed his other one over the back. With her hand between his palms, he brought her fingers to his lips and kissed them.

"Come back, Sarah. Please. Come home with me."

The way he asked her made it seem for just a few seconds that perhaps anything was possible. If she was a dreamer, she'd have placed plenty of meaning in his words. But she was a realist, and questions assailed her. Perhaps he felt sorry for her. Perhaps he intended to satisfy his physical craving at her expense. Perhaps he had a worse punishment in store than even she could imagine.

"Start over, you say." She drew her hand from his. "Come back home with you." She stood and placed a few prudent feet between them. And then she asked the question she didn't know if she was prepared to know the answer to. And didn't know if his reply would be truthful. But she had to hear his explanation.

"Why?" she asked. "Why should I? And why have you asked me?"

Chapter Twenty

Her earnest expression and the hope in those somber blue eyes tore at Nicholas's heart. *Because I don't want you to lack for anything. Because I can't bear to see you sad or alone. Because I need you.* "Because Mother needs you."

She couldn't disguise the disappointment that shimmered in the depths of her eyes. "I see."

She was wise to keep her distance. He wanted nothing more than to touch her, to pull her against him and never let her go. The change in her appearance broke his heart. She'd lost weight. A bluish smudge had appeared beneath each eye. The palm he'd held a minute ago bore blisters at the base of each finger.

The differences weren't only physical. He sensed her feelings of inadequacy and her resignation. He wanted to reassure her. Restore her optimism.

But how could he do that? She'd never been able to count on or trust the men in her life. No matter what she'd done it hadn't been enough to earn their favor. And Nicholas's own hot-and-cold disposition had given her no stability or ease.

She had no idea how he felt about her. Even though he'd shown her his most unpleasant side, she had hastened to assure him of his redeeming qualities, endorsement he didn't feel he deserved at this moment. He'd never told her his feelings.

"Sarah."

She turned that devastating somber blue gaze on him.

"*I* want you to come back." He stood and moved before her. "*I* need you."

A single tear trailed down her ivory cheek. He caught it with his thumb. Her skin was as soft and delicate as he remembered. Her pale lashes fluttered down and swept across her cheeks.

Ringlets escaped the white dust cap she wore. He reached for one, as he'd wanted to that long-ago day in the carriage, and stretched it to his nose.

Her lips parted. Her pulse fluttered in her throat.

Another tear followed the path of the first.

Nicholas leaned forward and touched his tongue to it. The drop tasted salty. This near, he could smell her hair, her skin, warm from the day and her tasks.

"Why are you crying?"

"Because I didn't think I'd see you again. Because you don't have it in your heart to hate me or hold what I did against me. Do you?"

He could never hate her. He couldn't blame her for the secret she'd kept. "No."

"Because you think you're like my father when you're the finest man I've ever known."

She'd obviously not known many fine men. "You thought highly of Stephen."

"Stephen was kind and generous. You are, too. But you're also solid and trustworthy and industrious. You did all the things you were supposed to when your father died. And you kept on doing them. You gave up your own dreams to fulfill his."

"I couldn't understand why Stephen didn't do the same," he said. "But he was the smart one," he added. "I always thought he'd made such poor choices, but now that

I look at it differently—him leaving the running of Halliday Iron to me made us a fortune. And he saw his plays produced and married the woman he loved.''

"Only because you made it possible for him," she replied. "What about you? Do you have any dreams left to fulfill?''

"I think maybe I do." He cupped her delicate cheek in his palm and brought her face up to his. She didn't resist; she met his kiss full on.

He kissed her as gently as he knew how, with as much tenderness as he could show her, hoping to express how he felt when he didn't understand it himself.

Sarah's hands clasped his upper arms and moved to his shoulders, their warmth burning through his shirt. She curled her fingers into his hair and pressed her mouth more solidly to his, gentleness obviously not what she desired.

When he was with her, he could think of nothing but her nearness. He saw only the delicacy of her skin and the softly formed curves of her body. Her scent drove his other senses away. He didn't care that she'd deceived him. He cared only that she desired to be in his arms as much as he wanted her there.

Nicholas held her close and rejoiced in the feelings she created in him.

"Sarah," he said against her lips. Sarah had never loved Stephen. She had not been his wife. She had not been anyone's wife.

Gently she eased away from his hold.

"Do you love someone else?" he asked, voicing his fear. Perhaps she was still in love with William's father.

"No," she said softly. "There is no one. No one except William in my life." Sarah smiled, a sad sweet smile, and the sight caught in his chest. She lifted the hair from her neck and plucked the fabric of her bodice away from her chest.

He pictured her removing this dress—another damned

black dress, the only thing about her that hadn't changed. He imagined her ivory limbs and her lush breasts. The breeze from the window didn't cool his fevered reaction. His heart slammed against his ribs.

"I really won't be working here again?" she asked.

He shook his head. "Come back with me. Please."

"Why do you want me to go back with you?"

"I've told you all the reasons."

"You have?"

"I thought I did."

She slanted an uncertain glance up at him. "What were they?"

The ringlets along her neck clung to her damp skin. " want you with me, that's why. I need you."

She placed her hands against his shirtfront. "How do you know I wouldn't just be pretending so you'd take care o me?"

He covered her hands with his. "I'd know."

"How?"

"Do you have to pretend to like it when I kiss you?"

"No."

"Were you pretending that night in my study?"

Her cheeks flushed prettily. "No."

"Some things you just can't fake," he said.

"I'm tired of pretending," she said. "I'm tired of lies."

"No more pretending between us," he promised.

She smoothed the fabric of his shirt across his ches leaned into him and pressed her cheek where her hands ha been. "Well, then, what's the truth?" she asked.

"About what?"

"About why you want me to come back with you."

"What do you think?"

"You've told me a dozen times how much you wa me," she said, leaning back in his arms to see his fac "That's being honest."

He knew she could feel the wild beating of his heart beneath her palms.

"But the truth for me is that—well, wanting me and needing me is not enough. I was foolish once, Nicholas. And I love William with all my heart, but I'll not repeat my mistakes. I won't do that to my son or myself."

He stared at her for seconds, absorbing the words as well as the heat of her body. He'd told her he wanted her. He'd shown her he wanted her. He'd admitted the need to himself long ago. But until this moment he hadn't realized why he needed her. Why everything about her drove him crazy and why he hadn't been able to eat or sleep or work until he'd tracked her down.

"It's not enough for me, either," he realized aloud.

Her pale brows rose in that inquisitive arch he knew so well.

"I'm a rude, insensitive fool," he said. "I press my ideas and opinions on others. I don't take no for an answer. I like having things my own way, and I have to be hit over the head to see another side of a situation. Up until I met you I thought I knew everything I wanted, and I didn't think I needed anyone else in my life.

"Needing you went against my highly inflated opinion of myself. It was…like a weakness. And I don't like being weak."

She raised a hand to his face. Nicholas placed his fingers over hers and pressed her palm to his cheek.

"I need you, Sarah. Because I love you."

Tears welled in her eyes again. "You don't even know me," she said, a shaky catch in her voice. "You don't know the real Sarah."

"Yes, I do," he assured her. "I know the Sarah who loves her son above all else. I know the Sarah who cared enough about total strangers to see their needs and meet them herself. The Sarah who is a capable hardworking person who can deal with people and situations and run a house effortlessly.

"And I know the Sarah who regretted her mistakes and wanted to bring closure to the Halliday family by finding Claire's body."

He drew her close against his chest. "And I know the Sarah who is passionate and responsive and has a lot of love to give a man who'd never take it for granted."

"Nicholas," she whispered. "Are you sure?"

"Oh, I'm sure," he replied with conviction. "And once I make up my mind, nobody changes it for me."

Sarah smiled. A smile just for him. A smile he'd craved.

"Marry me, Sarah. I'll spend the rest of my life making you happy."

"That won't be too hard," she said. "Having you love me is all the happiness I can hold."

"Oh, no," he said and kissed her neck. "There's much, much more happiness where that came from."

She brought her arms between their bodies and framed his face in her palms. "I love you, Nicholas."

Leda enveloped Sarah in one of her soft violet-scented hugs. After Leda released her, she dabbed at her eyes with her hankie. "You looked so beautiful in this dress," she said, referring to the pale green confection Sarah had worn as she and Nicholas said their vows that afternoon. "I knew it was perfect for you."

"Thank you for having it made for me," Sarah said. "And thank you for loaning me your necklace. I'm so glad you got all of your jewelry back."

"I'm just glad that dreadful girl didn't get away with stealing from us and making it look like you'd done it. She actually had the audacity to be wearing my ring when Nicholas's Pinkerton man led the sheriff to her!"

"I'll bet she did some fancy talking."

"It did her no good. You know the jewels weren't even important to me. It was just the principle of the crime."

Sarah touched the emerald on her chest.

"I love to see you in pretty things," the older woman said. "I'd like you to keep it."

"Oh, but I couldn't—"

"It matches the bracelet that was your mother's. This way you have something from both of your mothers."

Sarah clasped Leda hands. "I'll treasure it."

Nicholas, in his ruffled white shirt and black coat and tie, came up beside Sarah and slid his arm around her waist.

"Are the women in my life happy?"

"Very," Sarah assured him with a smile.

"You two are striking together," his mother said. "Nicholas so dark and you so fair. And I love you like my very own." She dabbed her eyes again. "I couldn't have made a better choice for you myself," Leda told her son.

He chuckled. "Most of the guests are gone," he said, then added, "A few of them seemed a little surprised that I was marrying my brother's wife so quickly, but no one seemed to care that you preferred to be called Sarah."

"In some cultures it's a man's duty to marry his brother's widow," Leda said. "And even now marriages of convenience are arranged all the time."

"Well, this marriage is convenient," Nicholas said. "Since Sarah loves me, and I'm mad about her."

As he hugged her, she caught sight of Claire's mother.

"Celia did just fine, didn't she?" Sarah said, pulling away.

"Not even a drop of champagne," he replied.

"I'm concerned about her, though," Sarah said. "She's not like you, Leda. She has no friends and few interests."

Gruver interrupted them just then. "Mrs. Rose is here, sir."

Nicholas turned. "Good, show her in." After Gruver had

left, he said, "Celia concerned me, too. And I believe I've come up with something."

"What's that?" Sarah asked, and both women looked at him curiously.

"I've hired a companion for her. Someone to keep her company." He gave her a sidelong smile. "Keep her out of trouble."

Sarah and Leda exchanged a surprised glance. "Well, that's generous," Sarah said.

"And William will have a companion, too."

"But William has Mrs. Trent," Leda pointed out.

"This is a playmate, not a nursemaid," he explained.

Leda stared at Sarah, and Sarah shook her head. "I have no idea what he's talking about. Who is Mrs. Rose?"

Nicholas moved to the doorway, where he waited only a minute. "I had hoped you would be here in time for the wedding."

His broad-shouldered form blocked her view of the person he spoke to.

"I wanted to, Mr. Halliday, but the train made a stopover and arrived late." The voice sounded familiar.

Nicholas stepped aside and led the girl carrying a toddler forward. Sarah recognized her at once. "Hannah!"

"Sarah!" Hannah hurried to Sarah and hugged her. "This is Amanda."

"Hello, Amanda," Sarah said, smiling at the chubby little girl.

"Nicholas, *this* is who you hired to be Celia's companion?" Sarah asked, incredulous.

He nodded.

She'd told him about Hannah losing her husband, and about the child she had to leave at her sister's. Sarah had also shared the desperation a young woman in that position experienced, and had prayed Hannah wouldn't have to marry someone horrible just to care for her daughter. The fact that he'd shared her concern and snatched Hannah out of that situation touched Sarah's full-to-bursting heart.

"Oh, Nicholas," she said, embracing and hugging him tightly. "You are the most wonderful man."

He cupped her face and smiled into her eyes. "Mother," he said, without turning his head. "Will you see that Mrs. Rose is settled? Give her a room upstairs."

"Call me Hannah, please," the girl suggested.

"Come on, dear," Leda said.

"I'm going to see to it that you always believe that," he said and kissed Sarah.

His warm lips kindled a barely banked fire, and embarrassed, Sarah stepped back and glanced around. There were still a few lingering guests.

Nicholas took her hand. "We're newlyweds. We're expected to leave." He led her up the back stairs, which bypassed the foyer and led directly to his wing. "Do you need to see to William?" he asked.

"He'll probably sleep until early morning. He's been doing that. He's very contented back in his lovely crib." And well nourished and well cared for, she thought gratefully.

"I have you all to myself, then," he said and whisked her into his suite—the suite they'd be sharing now. "And now that you're my wife, I can tell you how much I want you and not suffer the angst of waiting."

Sarah's heart beat wildly at their newfound liberty.

"I can *show* you how much I want you." He pulled her flush against him, and the length and strength of his hard body pressed along her curves. "How much I love you."

Sarah looked deeply into his eyes and needed no further proof. Rising on tiptoe, she took his jaw and guided his mouth to hers. Their kiss held joy and reverence and promise.

She wrapped her arms around his back and clung to him. He spanned her waist, but her corset prevented her from feeling his touch. Much to her satisfaction he moved to cup her breasts. She leaned into him hard, but he supported her weight easily.

She pulled back and spanned her fingers across the front of his shirt. Beneath her palms his heart beat furiously. She wanted to touch his skin.

He covered her hands with his for only the briefest moment, then led them to his tie as though he were a mind reader. She tugged on the bow and let the black silk fall to the floor. She worked on the pearl buttons until he had to help her tug the tail from his waist. He shrugged from the shirt, but she didn't allow him to drop it.

She carried the cotton garment to her nose, closed her eyes and inhaled his scent: starch, tobacco, man. The smell loosed an all-consuming craving as strong as that which his kisses created. When she opened her eyes again, he was looking at her, his dark gaze smoldering, and the look made her knees weak.

She dropped his shirt and caressed his chest, the dark hair springy, his skin hot and smooth. A tremor ran through him, telling her she had the same effect on him.

Gently, he turned her away and unbuttoned the row of buttons that ran down her entire back. "I imagined you in a color like this," he said. "Thank you for choosing it."

With a swish of satin, Sarah stepped out of her dress. Nicholas untied a petticoat, and she discarded it. "How many of these do you have on?" he asked.

"Two more," she said, and he grinned as she removed them.

His fingers went to work in her hair, removing the cluster of white flowers, finding pins and plucking them out. At last he had them all, and the mass fell across her shoulders.

He turned her back to him, but dropped his hands to his sides. "This," his said, his voice a deep vibration, "is the way I've wanted to see you."

He didn't have to tell her she was beautiful. His eyes

said it for him. To her surprise, he sank to his knees. One at a time he unbuttoned her shoes and drew them off while she steadied herself with her hands on his broad shoulders.

He glided his palms up her calves and inside the legs of her drawers to untie the ribbons on her garters. He removed each stocking slowly, brushing behind her knees gently, skimming her ankles, and setting the path on fire.

He stood again, seducing her with a lazy smile. Anticipation tingled along her skin and up her spine. A new kind of longing spread a surge of warmth on the inside, a bold urgency she hadn't been prepared for.

Without unbuttoning it, she drew her satin corset cover up and off, tossing it aside. Nicholas reached for her corset hooks, a perceptible trembling in his fingers. The garment met the same fate as the last, and with incredible gentleness, he untied her chemise, leaving her standing in only her white silk drawers.

"I thought we'd never get all those clothes out of the way," he said. "How does poor William ever wait?"

The air touched her breasts and her ribs where they'd been confined, and Sarah's skin turned to gooseflesh. He caressed her breasts. "You're skin is like touching silk."

Self-conscious but eager, Sarah closed her eyes and concentrated on the exquisite sensation of his hands on her flesh. Too soon, his touch disappeared, and she opened her eyes.

He removed his boots and held his hand out to her. She took it and he led her to his massive bed, where he pulled back the counterpane. Sarah contemplated the white sheets, the mound of pillows, and the ornately carved headboard, and a thread of apprehension squeezed her heart.

She was his wife now. He'd married her for better or for worse. He'd pledged his love and his fidelity. And she was so undeserving.

As though sensing her hesitation, he pulled her to sit

beside him and held her face in one palm, his mahogany eyes asking the question for him.

"I'm afraid," she whispered.

"You know I won't hurt you," he said.

"No," she said. "I'm afraid you'll be disappointed with me. I'm afraid you—" She drew a shaky breath past the lump in her throat. She'd been a disappointment to her father from the day she was born. It seemed no matter what she'd done or how hard she'd tried, she'd never done anything to please him. Or make him love her.

Obviously, she hadn't pleased Gaylen, either, or he wouldn't have turned tail and run at the first mention of commitment.

"I'm afraid you'll be sorry."

"Sarah," he said, and pulled her head to rest against his bare shoulder. "I will not be disappointed or sorry. I love you."

Twisting at the waist, she clung to him, wrapping her arms around his wide shoulders, clenching a fist in his hair. Yes, he loved her. Nicholas loved her. She didn't have to do anything to make him love her. His love was hers already.

He loved her.

He wanted her.

He feathered his fingertips up her sides. She curved her upper body away from his without releasing him, so he could reach her breasts. He ran his thumbs back and forth across the tips.

Sarah bracketed his face and kissed him hard.

His tongue teased at her until she met it with her own. This kiss was wild and hot and daring, and she hadn't imagined the emancipation a husband would bring. Excitement rushed though her—she was going to love being this man's wife!

She never had to hide her feelings from him again. She never had to worry what anyone would think.

At once it seemed so natural to be here like this with him, to feel this incredible need to be closer, to have more, to have it all.

She followed his lead as he urged her to stretch out on the soft mattress, as he removed their last pieces of clothing and the entire length of his hard, hot male body molded against her side. Nothing lay between them now, not clothing, not miles, not lies. His mouth, hot and velvety on her breasts, created a rush of sensation deep inside her. His fingers touching her within fired a depth of want that had her quivering.

She strove to give him pleasure in return, eager to learn every column and plane of his body, to learn the sleek rough textures so delightfully different from her own. He rewarded her with seductive short-breathed sounds and reckless, passion-inflaming kisses.

Sarah's body and emotions were strung so tightly, a little sob escaped her throat.

"What's wrong?" he asked in a husky voice.

She gave a quick shake of her head, as confused as he. "Nothing. I don't know."

Beneath him, her body trembled.

"Tears aren't the release you need, love." He rose above her then, and joined their bodies with slow, measured ease.

Sarah closed her eyes, arched toward him and reveled in the heat, the wonder, the pleasure.

"Ah, you're beautiful," he praised, setting her heart to thrumming and their bodies to straining with sleek thrusts.

An unexpected wave of fulfillment spread from the point where their bodies were joined to each of Sarah's limbs. The sensation took her breath away and brought a cry to her lips.

Nicholas closed the space between them, gathering her close, kissing her neck, her eyelids, her lips, and finally shuddering against her with swift thrusts and a deep groan of release.

Sarah feathered the damp hair from his temples and held him close. Their hearts, pressed against each other, beat in a frantic rhythm, and gradually slowed.

He slid his hip to the mattress to spare her his weight, one arm and thigh resting on her, and stroked her ribs with his thumb.

He was too much of a gentleman to ask, but she wanted him to know, so she said, "It was never like this before."

Lazily, he kissed her neck and palmed her breast.

"With William's father, I mean. It was all quite embarrassing and…"

He tipped his face up to look at her. "You can say it."

He didn't need her to stoke his ego. But she never wanted him to wonder. "I think I was drawn to him because he was forbidden. My father had given me choices. He wasn't one of them. I learned why the hard way."

Nicholas kissed the swell of her breast.

"I can't say I'm sorry, Nicholas. Because I love William so very much."

"I know."

"I just want you to know that it wasn't like this."

"I know that, too."

She moved her hand to his, and he entwined their fingers.

"I vowed to love and honor and cherish you today," he said. "But I also vow to love and cherish William. He is my son, Sarah. From this day on."

A rush of tears blurred her vision. She wrapped her arms around his neck, and he rolled them to their sides to hold her tightly.

"You taught me how to love, Sarah," he said into her hair. "You showed me that everyone has a right to his own choices. I promise you that William—and any other children we have together—will be allowed to make their own choices, fulfill their own dreams. I won't try to mold them into the people I want them to be. I made that mistake with Stephen."

She pulled away enough to look into his eyes. "Everyone makes mistakes. You haven't held mine against me. You haven't blamed me for Stephen's death."

"Because you're not responsible for Stephen's death," he said insistently. "You told me Stephen would have done exactly what he wanted to, no matter what I'd done or said."

"That's right."

"Well, the fact that he wasn't in his compartment that night doesn't mean he would have lived if you hadn't been there. No one can know that. You can't hold yourself responsible any more than I can."

She sighed. "You already knew how to love, Nicholas," she said. "You loved Stephen, and I've seen how much you love Leda."

"I'll probably make more mistakes before we're old and gray," he said with a wry smile. "But you'll help me keep my focus," he predicted. "Won't you, Mrs. Halliday?"

Sarah's smile came from her heart, a heart so full, she didn't know how she could contain it all. "I certainly will, Mr. Halliday. I certainly will."

Epilogue

Mahoning Valley, Ohio
July 1870

Sarah tucked eight-week-old Harris Templeton Halliday into the buggy that sat in the shade and turned just in time to see William toddling away down the grassy slope toward the picnic festivities.

Nicholas captured him and, planting him securely on his shoulders, carried him back to where Sarah had spread a quilt. "I think your mama wants you to take a nap," he said, running up the hill and bouncing William until he laughed.

"He'll never sleep if you shake up his lunch." Hannah laughed from her spot on the next blanket where she had convinced Amanda to lie down.

"Lie down there with Amanda," Nicholas told him gently, but firmly, handing him to Hannah.

"A kiss, Papa!" William said with his chubby arms open wide.

Nicholas kissed him soundly and tousled his wheat-toned head of hair.

"You need to rest, too," he said to his wife, wrapping his arms around her and gazing into the buggy at their son.

"I'm just fine," she said, and leaned back into his strong embrace.

"I know you are, but sit and rest anyway."

She did as he requested, and he brought her lemonade. "You didn't spend this much time with me at last year's picnic," she said with a smile.

"You weren't my wife last year."

"But aren't you missing out on the fun?"

He shook his head slowly. "I don't miss out on anything anymore."

She sipped her lemonade.

Mary and Elissa dropped by with slices of pie and admired Harris. Elissa wanted to hold him, and Mary finally had to carry her off, promising her a game.

A little while later Milos strode toward them, his shirtsleeves rolled back, his face colored by the afternoon sun.

"How's the new one?" he asked.

"As sweet and even-tempered as his father," Sarah replied with a grin.

"Looks like him, too," Milos said.

"Yes, he's a handsome one," she agreed.

"Is Amanda sleeping?" he asked.

Both William and Amanda had fallen asleep, his curly blond head contrasting with her straight dark-haired one, and the summer breeze entwined a few strands. Hannah looked up at Milos, and then over at her employers, a blush tingeing her cheeks.

"We'll sit with Amanda while she naps," Nicholas assured her. "Go have some fun."

Hannah gave him an appreciative smile and stood.

"I'll see you for the tug-of-war," Milos said to Nicholas.

"You'll see me win this year," he replied.

Milos grinned, and he and Hannah wandered toward the games.

Sarah remembered how new everything had been to her and how much fun she'd found the activities last year. Today Hannah was no doubt learning new things about the community, her employer and Milos.

"Have you seen Mother?" Nicholas asked.

"Oh, yes. She and her quilting troop have an adviser this year."

"An adviser? What's that?"

"Well, it seems many of the women weren't coordinating with their stitches, and they needed someone to—"

"Don't tell me. Celia is down there telling them all how their quilts should be sewn."

"Precisely. But no one seems to mind. She won them all over with that wedding dress she made for one of the workers' daughters last spring."

Nicholas lay back and tucked his hands beneath his head. "I have a surprise for you."

"You always have a surprise for me." She threaded his hair back from his temples with her fingers. "What have you bought me now?"

"I haven't bought you anything."

"Really? What is it, then?"

"I think I need a kiss to remember."

She lowered her lips to his and kissed him gently. When she pulled back, his dark eyes were filled with the bountiful love she always saw there. "Did that help?"

"I might need another one."

She kissed him again.

He smiled.

"What is it?" she asked.

"We're going to Virginia to visit the Kleymanns this fall."

"We are?"

He nodded.

"Oh, Nicholas, that will be wonderful! Is this a business trip?"

"Partially. But I will have plenty of time to sightsee with you and the boys. We can take Mrs. Trent, and that way you can do a few things with Kathryn, too."

"I'll look forward to it."

He gazed up at her, ran his fingers over her cheek and tugged on a curl that lay against her neck. "I look forward to every day now that you're part of my life," he said. "Not a minute goes by that I'm not grateful to Stephen for bringing us together."

"And Claire," she added.

"And Claire."

Something in his heart warmed and blossomed...as it did each time Sarah smiled.

* * * * *

All work and no play?
Not these men!

July 1998
MACKENZIE'S LADY by Dallas Schulze

Undercover agent Mackenzie Donahue's
lazy smile and deep blue eyes were his best
weapons. But after rescuing—and kissing!—
damsel in distress Holly Reynolds, how could
he betray her by spying on her brother?

August 1998
MISS LIZ'S PASSION by Sherryl Woods

Todd Lewis could put up a building with ease,
but quailed at the sight of a classroom! Still,
Liz Gentry, his son's teacher, was no battle-ax,
and soon Todd started planning some
extracurricular activities of his own....

September 1998
A CLASSIC ENCOUNTER
by Emilie Richards

Doctor Chris Matthews was intelligent, sexy
and *very* good with his hands—which made
him all the more dangerous to single mom
Lizette St. Hilaire. So how long could she
resist Chris's special brand of TLC?

Available at your favorite retail outlet!

MEN AT WORK™

 Silhouette®

Look us up on-line at: http://www.romance.net   PMAW2

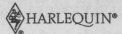

AWARD-WINNING
AUTHOR
TORI PHILLIPS

INTRODUCES...

An illegitimate noblewoman
and a shy earl to a most delicious
marriage of convenience in

THREE DOG KNIGHT

Available in October 1998
wherever Harlequin Historicals are sold.